ABSINTHE

WINTER RENSHAW

Books By Winter Renshaw

The Never Series
Never Kiss a Stranger
Never Is a Promise
Never Say Never
Bitter Rivals: a novella

The Arrogant Series
Arrogant Bastard
Arrogant Master
Arrogant Playboy

The Rixton Falls Series
Royal
Bachelor
Filthy
The Amato Brothers Series
Heartless
Reckless
Priceless (a Rixton Falls crossover)

Standalones
Dark Paradise
Vegas Baby

Cold Hearted

The Perfect Illusion

Country Nights

```
┌─────────────────────────────────────┐
│                                     │
│            Description              │
│                                     │
└─────────────────────────────────────┘
```

The name on the screen was "Absinthe."

But I knew her as the sultry voice blowing up my phone for late night chats about Proust and Hemingway interspersed between the filthiest little ... *conversations*.

We'd never met.

Until the day she walked into my office, her cherry lips wrapped around a candy apple sucker and an all too familiar voice that said, "You wanted to see me, Principal Hawthorne?"

AUTHOR'S NOTE: This full-length romance is steamy, scandalous, twisted, and, at times, divisive. It is a complete standalone and contains subject matter that may trigger sensitive readers. All characters are adults and all interactions are consensual. Please enjoy with an open mind. ;-)

First you take a drink, then the drink takes a drink, then the drink takes you.
—F. Scott Fitzgerald

Prologue

FORD

"YOU WANTED TO SEE ME, Principal Hawthorne?"

I know that voice. I'd know it anywhere.

Glancing up from my desk, I find a girl in skintight athletic leggings and a low-cut tank top standing in my office doorway, her full lips wrapped around a shiny sucker and a familiar electric jade gaze trained on me.

It's *her*.

The woman I spent most of all summer chatting with under the anonymous veil of a dating app—one specifically meant for adults seeking connections but not commitment. I purchased a stock photo for seven dollars, chose a pseudonym, *Kerouac*, and messaged a woman by the name of *Absinthe* who quoted Hemingway in her bio when everyone else quoted Nickelback and John Legend.

Fuck.

Me.

"You must be Halston." My skin is on fire. I stand,

smooth my tie, and point to the seat across from me. I never knew her name, but I'd know that voice anywhere. I can't even count how many times I came to the sound of her breathy rasp describing all the wicked things she'd do to me if we ever met, reading me excerpts from *Rebecca* and Proust. "Take a seat."

She takes her time pulling the sucker from her mouth before strutting to my guest chair, lowering herself, cleavage first, and crossing her long legs. The tiniest hint of a smirk claims her mouth, but if she knows it's me, she's sure as hell not acting like it.

"You want to tell me what happened with Mrs. Rossi?" I ask, returning to my seat and folding my hands on my desk.

I may be a lot of things; overconfident prick, allergic to commitment, red-blooded American man …

But I'm a professional first.

"Mrs. Rossi and I had an argument," Halston says. "We were discussing the theme of *The Great Gatsby*, and she was trying to say that it was about chasing the elusive American dream. I told her she missed the entire fucking point of one of the greatest pieces of literature in existence." She takes another suck of her candy before continuing, then points it in my direction. "The real theme has to do with manipulation and dishonesty, Principal Hawthorne. Everyone in that book was a fucking liar, most of all Jay, and in the end, he got what he deserved. They all did."

My cock strains against the fabric of my pants. It's her voice. It's her goddamned sex-on-fire voice that's doing this to me. That and her on point dissection of classic American literature. Sexy, intelligent, outspoken. Three elusive qualities I've yet to find in another human being. Until her. And knowing that now, I couldn't even have her if I wanted her, isn't doing me any favors. If I don't compose myself, I'm going to be hard as a fucking rock.

"Language," I say. The room is growing hotter now, but I keep a stern, undeterred presence.

She rolls her eyes. "I'm an adult, Principal Hawthorne. I can say words like *fuck*."

"Not in my office, you can't." I exhale. "And not in class either. That's why Mrs. Rossi sent you here."

"The jackass behind me was drawing swastikas on his notebook, but I get sent down here for saying 'fuck.'" Her head shakes.

"I'll discuss that with Mrs. Rossi privately." I scribble a note to myself and shove it aside.

"You're really young for a principal." Her charged gaze drags the length of me. "Did you just graduate from college or something?"

Six years of school and two years of teaching place me in the budding stages of a career shaping and educating the minds of tomorrow's leaders, but I refuse to dignify her question with a response.

"My age is irrelevant," I say.

"Age is everything." She twirls a strand of pale hair around her finger, her lips curling up in the corners. The cute-and-coy shtick must work on everyone else, but it's not going to work on me. Not here anyway. And not anymore.

"I said *my* age is irrelevant."

"Am I the first student you've ever had to discipline?" She sits up, crossing and uncrossing her legs with the provocative charm of a 1940s pin up. "Wait, are you going to discipline me?"

I take mental notes for her file.

- *Challenges authority*
- *Difficulty conducting herself appropriately*

- *Possible boundary issues*

"I'm not going to punish you, Halston. Consider this a verbal warning." I release a hard breath through my nose as I study her, refusing to allow my eyes to drift to the soft swell of her breasts casually peeking out of her top. Knowing her so intimately over the phone, and being in her presence knowing she's completely off limits, makes it difficult to maintain my unshaken demeanor. "From now on, I'd like you to refrain from using curse words while on school grounds. It's disruptive to the other students who are here to actually glean something from their high school education."

"I don't know." Her lips bunch at the corner, and she fights a devilish grin. "I mean, I can try, but 'fuck' is one of my favorite words in the English language. What if I can't stop saying it? Then what?"

"Then we'll worry about that when the time comes," I say.

"You could always bend me over your knee and spank me." She rises, wrapping her lips around the sucker before plucking it out of her mouth with a wet pop. "Or maybe you could fuck my brains out and break my heart."

"*Excuse me?*" My skin heats as she feeds me my own lines, but I refuse to let her see that she's having any kind of effect on me.

"You're him," she says, as if it's some ace she's been keeping up her sleeve this entire time. "You're *Kerouac*."

I'm at an extraordinary loss for words, trying to wrap my head around all the ways this could go very fucking wrong for me.

Chapter 1

HALSTON

3 Months Ago

I'm perched in Emily Miller's pillow-covered window seat, striking my thumb against an almost-empty lighter, a strawberry mint cigarette pinched between my lips.

"Are ... are you sure we should be doing this?" Her eyes shift toward her door, like her parents are going to magically come home early from work and bust us.

"Relax." I hold the flame steady, lighting the tip. "It's herbal. There's no nicotine or any of that bad shit."

Scooting closer to the open window, I inhale and then exhale, aiming rings of smoke at the pin-sized holes in the screen. Honestly, I find the whole idea of smoking to be completely idiotic ... all these people enslaved to these little white sticks of chemicals that turn their fingernails yellow and make their clothes reek. But I was walking over here this afternoon and some fourteen-year-old jackass offered to give these to me if I showed him my tits.

I snatched them from his hand, watching the shock register on his face, and said, "Let that be a lesson to you."

He stood there, eyes wide and blinking as I walked away. "I'm worth more than a half-empty pack of cigarettes you stole from your mother's purse. You're lucky I don't kick you in the balls, snotface."

I almost tossed the pack in some family's garbage can, but I decided I should smoke one of them out of spite.

Fuck him.

Fuck fourteen-year-old pricks who are destined to grow up and become STD-spreading man whores.

"Here." I hand over the cig, which now bears my red lipstick, and watch as Emily squeezes it between her thumb and forefinger. I titter. "It's not a joint."

"I don't know how to smoke." She bites her lower lip, looking like she's somewhere between laughing and crying.

Good God, Emily. Live a little.

If she weren't my only fucking friend in this stupid fucking town …

This is painful.

She's still hesitating, her eyes darting here, there, and everywhere. I'm seconds from taking it back and keeping it all to myself when she takes a puff.

"Exhale …" I remind her when it's been several seconds too long.

As soon as she opens her mouth, she starts to choke on the smoke tickling her lungs, fanning her hands in front of her face like that's going to help. Bolting up, she circles her princess pink room before diving into her *en suite* and filling a cup with water from the faucet.

Rolling my eyes, I take another puff. Then another.

This is dumb.

I head to Emily's bathroom, stamp the cigarette out in her pristine porcelain sink, and wash out the ash before flushing the stupid thing down the toilet.

I don't apologize.

Pulling the remaining pack from my back pocket, I go to toss them in her trash, but she grabs them from my hands.

"Are you insane?!" Her brown eyes are round, shaking. "What if my *parents* find these?"

Exhaling, I bite my lip. She's right. Her parents are dying for an excuse to dissolve our friendship. I see it in their eyes; in their forced smiles and terse body language every time I'm around. But Emily is quiet, nerdy. She doesn't make friends easily, and she mostly keeps to herself. Doug and Mary Miller were thrilled when we started hanging out—at first.

But that's how it always goes.

If you place Emily and me side-by-side, it doesn't even look like we belong on the same planet. She's a mouse; timid, quiet, with brown hair and small eyes. I'm a lion; crazy blonde mane, opinionated, and fearless.

"Shit, what time is it?" I ask, checking my watch. "I gotta go. Aunt Tabitha's going to be pissed if I'm late for dinner again."

It's weird actually having to live by someone else's rules.

Emily sniffs her shirt not once, but twice.

"You're fine," I say. "If you're that worried, put something else on."

Amateur.

Emily walks me to the door, and I catch her peeking out the window to see if either of her parents' cars are in the driveway yet. Maybe smoking in her room was risky. I'd hate for them to ground her. I was planning on a summer of corruption and debauchery, all of which would be in her own best interest.

She goes to college in a year. I'd fail her as a friend if I sent her into the real world as is.

Skipping down the front steps of the Millers' grandiose brick colonial and petting the stone lions as I pass them, I head down the block to my aunt and uncle's house—my permanent residence until I graduate high school.

I should've finished this year, but when you have parents making meth in your basement and they forget to send you to school for a few critical years, you get a little behind. And when your uncle is the superintendent of Lennox Community School District, you get to take an aptitude test and skip some grades—but unfortunately passing twelfth grade and fast forwarding to a high school diploma wasn't an option. I might turn nineteen this fall, but at least I'll have a piece of paper that says I attended the ritziest high school in America—the only one, that I know of, with a full-service Starbucks in the commons.

When I reach Uncle Vic and Aunt Tabitha's Tudor-style abode, I'm distracted by the slow beeping of a yellow moving van backing into the driveway next door. There's a man standing on the front steps in low slung sweats and a t-shirt that shows off his tanned, toned biceps. A White Sox ball cap casts a shadow over his face.

I can't even see if he's hot.

He waves at the driver to keep backing in, and then he heads to the end of the driveway toward Melissa Gunderman, who's run-walking in his direction with a pan of what appears to be some type of baked good.

She didn't waste any time. Paint's not even dry with this one.

I'm sure she's inviting him to her church singles' meeting, every Thursday at seven o'clock, and I'm sure she's giving him her normal spiel. She's divorced. Has one child, Rachel, who's eight, about to go into second grade, and extremely smart for her age. She loves to cook and bake, but more than that she loves Jesus and coffee—in that order.

Insert flirtatious laugh and hair twirling.

She's wearing yoga pants and a gray t-shirt that says, "*Mommin' Aint Easy*," and her hair is piled in a perfectly messy topknot she probably copied off her teenage babysitter.

I've never seen such a hypocrite in all my life. In the last six months since I've lived here, I've witnessed a whole bevy of men coming in and out of her house at all hours of the night.

The men *come* …

And then they go.

Growing bored with the Melissa spectacle, I head inside, where the scent of my aunt's pot roast mingles with chilled AC air. From the foyer, I can see into the dining room, where my cousin Bree has her nose buried in a textbook and her pen pressed against a notepad.

Studying away some of the best years of her life, that one.

Sometimes I wonder which of us has it worse … the one with the parents who care too much or the one with the parents who didn't care at all?

"Halston, is that you?" My aunt calls.

"Nope. It's the Culligan Man," I call back, kicking off my dirty white Chucks. She doesn't respond, but that's probably because the Stepford Robot manufacturer forgot to install her sense of humor chip when they delivered her to Uncle Vic.

"Dinner's almost ready." Her voice trails from the kitchen.

"Be there in a sec."

I trample up the grand staircase toward the guestroom, which I guess is my room even though I've been told "not to put any holes in the wall or rearrange any furniture." The room looks like a Pottery Barn catalog threw up in it and then hung my clothes in the closet. Needless to say, it doesn't feel like it's mine, but the bed is soft and it sure as hell beats switching foster homes every three months. Or sleeping in a cardboard box, which was my only option once I aged out of the system last year.

I peel out of my clothes and stuff them in a hamper before changing into something that smells more like Tide detergent than strawberries and herbs, and then I dock my phone on the charger. Uncle Vic has a strict "no electronics at the dinner table" policy, and while I normally have no qualms about challenging authority, I don't dare challenge Victor Abbott.

For starters, he doesn't mess around. He means what he says. He's alpha as shit, smart as fuck, and rules his home—and the dozens of schools in his district—with an iron fist.

Secondly, he took me in when he didn't have to.

He's my mom's brother. The only good apple in a family of ones that are rotten to the core. He didn't have to take me in, put a roof over my head, and enroll me in one of the best high schools in the area, but he did…

Much to Bree and Tab's dismay.

I'm a blemish to their country club lifestyle with my bold lipstick, short shorts, and wild green eyes. I'm the reason they lock their jewelry in safes—despite the fact that I have never and will never steal. I'm the jarring piano note ruining their beautiful symphony.

They're counting down the days until I leave for college, I'm sure of it. And Vic, bless his heart, has offered to put me through four years at a local state university about three hours from here.

I arrive at the dining room table and take my place

across from Bree. We were born a month and a year apart, she and I, but we have nothing in common. She's flat-chested, thin-lipped, and a spoiled only child who's never known what it feels like to go to bed with an empty stomach or to have to scrape mold off bread or pour expired milk onto stale cereal.

"How was your afternoon, girls?" Aunt Tab directs her question to both of us, but her attention is focused on her daughter. She places a tureen of brown gravy between us then moves to the china cabinet to grab place settings.

Every dinner is a production.

I've lived here six months now and I've yet to see them order pizza.

"I'm almost done studying for English comp," Bree says, her gaze flicking to me like I should feel like a failure for not taking college prep courses in the summer. Forgive me for not being an overachiever. "First test is tonight."

"I have no doubt you'll pass with flying colors." Tabitha smiles, placing her hand on her daughter's shoulder as she passes and heads toward the kitchen. She returns with the roast, placing it between us before taking a seat and checking her watch. "Hopefully Vic's on his way. It's not like him to be late."

That's my aunt. Always worrying over nothing because she literally has nothing better to do. I've realized that rich people like to manufacture problems, but I can't, for the life of me, figure out why. They have all this good shit going for them, but they're not happy unless they're miserable.

"I should call him." The moment Aunt Tabitha rises, the door to the garage opens and the security system beeps twice. She smiles, placing her hand over her heart, and then takes her seat. "There he is."

Uncle Vic places his briefcase on the kitchen counter

before emptying his pockets, and then sits in his usual chair at the head of the table. Without saying a word, he folds his hands and bows his head, saying grace. The three Abbotts make the sign of the cross and Vic dishes his food first.

Watching the three of them is like watching one of those old black and white TV shows from the fifties. From the outside, they're sickeningly perfect. My aunt wears dresses, even on the days she stays home, and Bree is a cheerleader, straight A student, and class president.

The tinkle of flatware on china fills the silence, and after a few moments my uncle clears his throat and glances in my direction.

"Halston, how's summer treating you so far?" he asks.

I shrug. "All right, I guess."

"I was thinking," he says. "I'd like to teach you how to drive."

He has my full attention.

My parents were always too strung out to teach me how to drive, and most of my foster parents didn't trust me behind the wheel of their cars because they didn't know me well enough.

"That would be amazing, Uncle Vic," I say. "Just say when."

He dabs the corners of his mouth with a napkin, his forehead lined in wrinkles like he's deep in thought. "This weekend. I'll take you out this weekend. We can practice in Bree's car."

Bree shoots me a dirty look.

"Perfect," I say.

"In the meantime, I'd like you to start looking for a part-time job," he says, chewing his meat. "At the end of the summer, I'll match what you've saved dollar for dollar, and then we'll go out and look at cars."

For once I have something to look forward to. No more rolling into school riding shotgun in Bree's Prius. No more waiting outside her locker after school for a ride home, looking like some stranded loser.

For the first time in my life, I'll have freedom.

Freedom to go where I want, when I want, for whatever reason I want.

Freedom to do anything, see anyone.

Freedom.

About fucking time.

I finish my dinner and ask to be excused, taking my plate to the dishwasher before going upstairs. When I crack open my laptop—a gift from Victor which is supposed to be strictly for homework—I pull up a job search website and see what I can find.

A little red flashing ad on the side bar advertises some dating app called Karma. I try to click on the x in the corner to make it go away, but I miss, and another webpage opens up.

The headline reads, "*Tired of swiping? Tired of being ghosted and cat-fished? Try Karma for FREE today!*"

Intrigued, I click on "learn more."

Karma is an innovative dating app that forces users to earn "karma points" before certain information is revealed. For example, ten karma points allows you to see each other's photo. Twenty karma points allows you to exchange email addresses. Thirty karma points allows you to exchange phone numbers.

How do you earn karma points? By chatting anonymously via our app! Each user is allowed to chat with only one other user at a time, ensuring the person you're talking to is genuinely interested in forming a deep and meaningful relationship with you—should that be what they're seeking! Our users can select a myriad of options displaying their intentions. Some are seeking a long-term commitment while others are seeking a fun and flirtatious, no-strings-attached experience!

We welcome you to try Karma today! We're a free app—no catch! Download the desktop version to get started, and be sure to add the mobile app to take Karma with you wherever you go!

Biting my bottom lip, I lift an eyebrow. Staring down the barrel of a long, hot summer, I could use a little something to fill my time besides binge watching Full House on Netflix with Emily Miller.

Pressing the download button, the icon is installed on my desktop in a matter of seconds, and I double click to begin.

A small gray box flashes across my screen, asking me to agree to their terms and conditions and check a box saying I'm eighteen.

Done.

Next, the app asks me for a pseudonym.

That's easy.

Green Fairy—a childhood nickname I earned because of the intense color of my eyes.

Wait, no. That's dumb. They're going to think I'm into fairies and elves and dragons and shit, and fantasies have never been my thing. I'm a realist.

Deleting *Green Fairy*, I type in *Absinthe*.

Much better, and it still fits.

Next, it asks for a small bio. But I'm not going to be able to spill my life story in a thousand characters or less, nor would I want to. Sitting back on my bed, I stare at the ceiling. Despite what one might assume about me and the fact that my education history is a hot mess, I've never met a book I couldn't devour. I'm guessing my love affair with books stems from all those years our heat got shut off midwinter and I'd find myself staying at the library until close just to stay warm. On days when it was exceptionally cold, the librarian would let me stay a little past close while she finished up her work for the day.

Pulling a notebook from beneath my mattress of quotes and things I've loved and saved throughout the years, I flip to a page in the middle and drag my fingertip along the faded ink words, stopping on a quote from The Great Gatsby. *"You see I usually find myself among strangers because I drift here and there trying to forget the sad things that happened to me."*

I think about using that one before determining it's too depressing.

Flipping to the next page, my eyes land on another one from my beloved F. Scott Fitzgerald, taken from This Side of Paradise: *"They slipped briskly into an intimacy from which they never recovered."*

Boom. Perfect. It's short and sweet and the sexiness is implied, not cheap.

Next, the app asks for my sex and then my age.

With lips pressed to the side, I debate this one. If I say I'm eighteen, I'm going to attract the perverts and weirdos with teenage girl fetishes. Not to mention, I may be eighteen in calendar years, but my life experience has given me a perspective of someone who's lived beyond that.

Typing in 100, I decide to come back to that later, and I click on the "next" button.

Karma asks me what kind of relationship I'm looking for, listing a handful of options and telling me to choose only one.

Marriage? Nope.

Long-term commitment? Nope.

Casual dating? Hm, maybe.

Open relationship? Nah.

Friendship? No.

No-strings attached fun? Yeah, okay.

I check the last box before moving on. Karma is now requesting a photo of me, reminding me that the person I'm chatting with won't see it until they reach a certain number of karma points, and at that time, I'd be able to see their photo too.

Sliding off my bed, I slick a coat of red lipstick over my mouth and fluff my blonde waves before returning to my laptop and snapping a smirking selfie with the camera. A second later, it's uploaded.

When Karma tells me I'm all finished and I can start looking for potential matches by typing in my zip code, I check the clock.

I need to look for a job, not a man.

Mama needs some wheels.

Closing out of the app, I'm prompted with a reminder to download it on my phone, but I return to my search. I'll worry about that later.

With no job history or work experience, I'm not sure how this is going to go, but I'm not above washing dishes or cleaning grease traps.

Settling on a part-time waitress position offering "on the job training," I click apply and fill out the form.

Thank you for your interest! Someone from The Farmhouse Café will contact you shortly!

I find a few more server jobs and submit my information, refusing to hold my breath. And when I'm done, I grab my phone, install Karma, and start shopping for a little summer fun.

Chapter 2

FORD

"I SHOULD GET INSIDE." I point toward the movers the second I'm able to get a word in with this woman.

My new neighbor, Melissa, frowns, but I don't feel bad. She's been talking my ear off for the past half hour, inviting me to singles night at her church and telling me all about her kid. She hasn't asked a single question about me, nor has she stopped to take a breath.

"Thanks for the brownies." I hold up the warm tray that's been singeing my palms this entire time. "I'll be sure to return the pan."

She knew what she was doing.

Melissa smiles, coiling a strand of hair around her fingers. "Take your time. Like I said, I'm in the yellow house across the street if you need me."

If I need her …

I stifle a chuckle before turning back to the house. The movers have made a good dent in the load already, and I walk into a living room stacked high with cardboard boxes. How one single man can accumulate so much shit by his late twenties is beyond me, though in my defense, most of my belongings are books—mostly college texts and literature classics—and I refuse to throw them out.

Good words never expire.

Moving to the kitchen, I grab a box cutter from the counter and get to work. My new job as principal of Rosefield High doesn't officially start for another couple of months, and I've got all the time in the world, but the clutter and boxes are going to drive me insane. The sooner everything gets to its place, the better.

I can't live with chaos. It's nails on a chalkboard.

A couple of hours later, my kitchen is done and the movers are bringing the last of the furniture pieces in. I tip them each a hundred bucks and walk them to the door. The second they leave, I spread across my sofa, kick my feet up, and rest my eyes for a minute.

My stomach growls, a reminder that the purchase of this house didn't include a stocked pantry, so I slide my phone from my pocket and see if there are any places around here that deliver something other than lightning-fast submarine sandwiches or soggy pizza.

Within five minutes, I settle on Thai food, place my order, and pull up my Karma app to kill time.

Starting a job like this in a town where I don't know a soul means hook ups can be risky. I need to establish my reputation first, and the concerned residents of Rosefield, Illinois would be aghast if they found out their children's principal is a commitment-phobic man whore.

Karma is safer.

I can actually get to know someone before deciding if they're worth hooking up with, though at this point in time, I've opted to use a stock photo and stick to phone sex.

It's less risky, and my career isn't worth an hour of electric sex with a stranger.

Tapping the app, it asks if I want to "search singles in the area searching for no-strings attached experiences." I press "okay," and the screen displays a list of options in alphabetical order.

Woman number one is named Absinthe, and her bio is an F. Scott Fitzgerald quote, which tells me she's introspected and a fan of the literary arts. Sticking in a pin on her profile, I move on to the next options and make my assessments.

BlaireWS1989. Her bio is a list of her college degrees and various professional certifications.

Pass.

DaringBoldly_SoulfulAries. Addicted to self-help books. Probably consults psychics on a regular basis.

Nope.

FoxyMamaIL. Her bio says she's a mom to three and fur-mom to four. I can't do the single mom thing. They always want more, even if they say they don't.

Moving on.

HeavenlyHannah. Is that … is that a Nickelback song she's quoting?

Seriously, people.

I check out another dozen before going back to *Absinthe,* making absolutely certain I want to send her a message. Once I do, I won't be able to communicate with anyone else … though the last five minutes of my life have shown me that I'm probably not missing out on much anyway.

Tapping the "initiate contact" button, I type a message and press send.

Chapter 3

HALSTON

I BARELY HEAR the ding of my computer over the music piping through my earbuds, but sure enough, there's a push notification coming through from Karma.

Kerouac would like to introduce himself! Do you accept?

Kerouac? Ugh. Jack Kerouac is one of the most over-rated writers I've ever had the disservice of subjecting myself to. On the Road was boring and self-indulgent.

I check out his message next.

"Pretty tech savvy for being 100," he writes.

Laughing out loud, my head tilts to the side. He's got a sense of humor. I can work with that. And I can maybe forgive him for the screen name if he'll allow me to broaden his horizons with some hand-selected book recommendations.

Clicking on the "reply" icon, Karma tells me that by responding to this conversation, I won't be able to communicate with any other users. And if I decide to cease conversation with this person, I need to click on the black "x" in their profile, which will prevent them from being able to contact me again and vice versa.

Forever.

Absinthe: My grandkids got me one of those iPad things for Christmas.

Kerouac: How many grandkids do you have?

Absinthe: Way too many. I was a bit of a floozy in my younger days, popping out babies left and right. I couldn't help myself. They were so damn cute and so were the men. Sadly, I think I peaked in the 1940s. I never could resist a man in uniform! Those sailors with those little round hats got me every time. Never missed a Fleet Week!

Kerouac: No regrets?

Absinthe: No regrets.

Kerouac: Seriously though. How old are you?

Absinthe: Does it matter? Age is literally a number.

Kerouac: It matters to me.

Absinthe: How old are you?

Kerouac: Didn't you read my profile?

Absinthe: No. I was too distracted by your horrendous screen name. Kerouac? Seriously?????

Kerouac: On the Road is a classic.

Absinthe: On the Road is shoddy drivel at best. Anyone who thinks otherwise doesn't deserve the privilege of calling himself a reader.

Kerouac: That's the cool thing about being a reader though, YOU get to decide what you like and other people's opinions don't matter.

Absinthe: Doesn't make me judge you any less.

Kerouac: How old are you?

Absinthe: So you're going to change the subject, just like that?

Kerouac: Answer the fucking question.

Absinthe: Oh, man. You said "fucking." Are you pissed? Or trying to prove that you're some big, bad alpha male who needs to be in control at all times?

Kerouac: Not pissed. Just impatient.

Kerouac: But control is a good thing. I like to be in control.

Absinthe: Then that's going to be a problem, because I like to be in control too.

Kerouac: Your age, Absinthe.

Absinthe: Old enough to drink.

It's not a lie. I mean, I might not be old enough to drink *legally*, but I'm still old enough to drink in the literal sense.

Kerouac: That's the best you can do?

Absinthe: I need to keep a low profile.

Kerouac: Are you someone important?

Absinthe: You're being sarcastic. Ass. And no, I'm not anyone important. I'm just me. And I want to keep a low profile because for all I know, you're a creepy stalker.

Kerouac: Even if I was a creepy stalker, I'm pretty sure I wouldn't be able to locate you simply based on your age. I think you're safe.

Absinthe: Anyway, back to your horrible taste in literature …

Kerouac: My extensive library collection would beg to differ.

Absinthe: Oooh. You have a library. You must be fancy.

Kerouac: Not fancy. Just well read.

Absinthe: You know what would be really fucking hot?

Kerouac: What?

Absinthe: Sex in a library. A public library.

Kerouac: Way to get to the point. I was content discussing great American writers of the 20th century for another hour, but this works too.

Absinthe: If you could see me right now, I'm rolling my eyes at you. Don't be lame. Just go with it. Tell me how we'd do it. Tell me what you'd do to me.

Kerouac: What do you look like?

Absinthe: Why?

Kerouac: I need a visual. For my fantasy.

Absinthe: Blonde hair. Green eyes. Big tits. Long legs. That work?

Kerouac: Highly doubt that's what you really look like, but okay.

Absinthe: It's true. Maybe one of these days, you'll get to see for yourself.

Kerouac: Doubtful. I have no intentions of ever meeting you.

Absinthe: Why not??? Oh, shit. Are you married?!?

Kerouac: No. Not married. Just a professional starting a new job in a new town.

Absinthe: So, you just want phone sex …

Kerouac: Yes.

Absinthe: And no matter how hot and bothered I get you, you'll never change your mind?

Kerouac: Never.

Exhaling, I rest my chin on my hand and glance away. I suppose if we're never going to meet or know each other's real names, I can be as dirty as I want to be with him. I can tell him everything without giving two shits about whether or not he's going to judge me because it won't fucking matter.

Absinthe: Fine. Lay it on me. Tell me how you'd fuck me in a library.

Kerouac: I'd make you wear a skirt.

Absinthe: You'd MAKE me wear a skirt?

Kerouac: Yes. I'd make you.

Kerouac: By the way, you're not wearing panties.

Absinthe: Obviously.

Kerouac: I'd take you to the F-K aisle, turn your back toward me, and spread your thighs. My hands would pull at the hem of your skirt, revealing your ass. If anyone walked by, they'd see my fingers trailing up your inner thighs and plunging into your wet pussy. You'd moan, and I'd cover your mouth. We have to be quiet.

Absinthe: Damn, K. This is, um, good. Keep going.

Kerouac: Your hips would buck against me. You're so fucking hot you can't even stand it, and you're close, but I won't let you cum unless you're riding my cock. Pulling my fingers from your slit, I give you a taste before massaging your tits and pulling your body against mine. When you whimper and beg for me to fuck you, I'll have to tease you first … I'll have to remind you that I'm in control. Dragging the tip of my cock along your seam, I'll slide my length inside you at the height of your anticipation.

Absinthe: Go on…

Kerouac: With your hands gripping the bookshelf and your hair gathered in my fist, I'll fuck you like the dirty girl you are, demanding your silence and commanding your body in ways no other man has done before.

Absinthe: Wait. How do you know what other men have done to me before?

Kerouac: Seriously?

Absinthe: Just kidding. No man has ever fucked me in a library, that right there probably puts you at the top of my list. Forgive me for interrupting you. Continue.

Kerouac: Through the shelves, we see someone coming. The librarian. I press my thumb against your clit, circling it as I fuck you harder and faster, my cum jetting inside you as your body melts against mine, your pussy clenched in spasm. Pulling myself out of you, I zip my fly and you straighten your skirt. The librarian comes around the corner, giving us each an evil look. And then she carries on her way, none the wiser.

Absinthe: Not bad.

Kerouac: Not bad?

Absinthe: Yeah. It wasn't bad. I mean, I've been touching myself this whole time. And I came. Please tell me you're not one of those guys who needs constant reassurance.

Kerouac: I'm not.

Absinthe: Good, because you won't get it from me. If we ever fuck in real life, I'm not going to lie in your arms and cry because the experience moved my world. I'd probably climb off you, wipe your sticky semen out of my pristine vagina, and make myself a sandwich in your kitchen wearing your shirt.

Kerouac: We're never going to fuck in real life, so ...

Absinthe: Yes, K. You've made that clear. Thank you for the reminder though.

Kerouac: Same time tomorrow?

Absinthe: Oh, you got your rocks off and now you're done with me?

Kerouac: I ordered food. It just arrived.

Absinthe: Sure.

A picture fills our chat screen: white Styrofoam containers filled with pad thai noodles and spring rolls.

Absinthe: You didn't have to prove yourself. I was only fucking with you.

Kerouac: Tomorrow? Seven pm?

Absinthe: If you're lucky.

A knock at my door prompts me to shut the lid of my laptop, and before I get a chance to answer, Bree barges in.

"Where's my gold cross necklace?" she asks, her blue eyes wild and her tone accusatory.

I lift my palms. "No clue."

"It was in my bathroom next to my sink this morning and now it's gone. I need it. I have a test in fifteen minutes, and it's my good luck charm."

"You know good luck charms don't actually work, right? It's all in your head."

Her face is red, her lips shaky, and she begins rifling through my closet, through dresser drawers. Tossing throw pillows and dirty clothes off the floor, she turns my room upside down.

"You took it. I know you did." Bree points, wearing her mother's scowl.

"I can assure you, I didn't touch your stupid necklace. Thing's ugly anyway." I roll my eyes. "What would I even do with it?"

"I don't know … pawn it?"

I smirk. This girl has never even set foot in a pawnshop. She's never known the burden of having to pawn your brand-new shoes for lunch money, which happened to me on more than one occasion, I might add.

"A piece like that would get me eight, maybe nine dollars tops. Hardly worth the bus fare and the trip spent in the bad part of town," I say.

Her jaw falls. "That necklace is from Tiffany! It's worth way more than eight dollars."

"I didn't pawn it. I'm just saying, if I did, that's probably all they'd give me for it," I say.

She stands at the foot of my bed, staring, jaw clenched. She wants, so badly, to pin this on me. More than likely the cleaning lady moved it today or it fell down the drain.

"Don't you have a test or something to get to?" I wave my hand, shooing her.

Bree lets out a juvenile groan, her fists clenched, and then she spins to leave my room, her cheerleader ponytail bouncing with each stomp. She'd slam my door if she knew she wouldn't get in trouble for it.

Stupid twat.

Lifting the laptop lid, I return to the chat.

Kerouac has signed off.

Chapter 4

FORD

THE GARAGE IS FILLED with random paint cans and yard tools left by the previous owner. They were supposed to clear everything out before they signed the closing papers, but they must have conveniently forgotten a few things.

Sweeping the dusty floor with a push broom while Aerosmith plays from an old tape player—another forgotten possession—I take a break and head inside to grab a Heineken, only I'm stopped by a familiar voice on the way inside.

"Ford," the man says. I turn to face him. "Thought that was you."

Superintendent Abbott walks toward me, though he's nearly unrecognizable in khaki shorts and a golf polo.

"Victor," I say, extending my hand. "Not used to seeing you out of your three-piece suit."

This man put me through five rounds of interviews for this position, grilling me with impossible questions and hiding his shock when he realized it was going to take more than that to rattle me.

"So you're the new neighbor," he says, staring at my house, his hands on his hips. "The Smiths were good people. Really going to miss them. They don't make neighbors like that anymore." He pauses, his smile fading. "So, you getting all settled in?"

I nod, neglecting to tell him I haven't even been here a full twenty-four hours yet. "I am. Taking it one day at a time."

"Well, that's good to hear, Ford." He pats me on the back. "We'll have to have you over for dinner one of these nights. My wife, Tabitha, makes a mean *duck a l'orange*. And I'm sure my daughter would love to meet you. She's going to be a senior this year at Rosefield. So is my niece. She's staying with us while she finishes her senior year."

"Of course. I'd love to meet your family sometime," I lie.

Shoot me now.

"Anyway, I know the board's really excited to have you. Your interviews really blew us away, and that recommendation from U.S. Education Secretary Carl Broadbent really sealed the deal."

Carl is an old family friend who's never worked a day in his life with me, but he offered. And I couldn't say no to that.

"I won't keep you any longer," he says. "Looks like you're busy here." Abbott checks his phone. "Meeting the guys at the club for a round. You golf much, Ford?"

"Sometimes."

"You should join us next time."

"Yeah, why not?" I smile, like I'm excited about playing golf with Victor Abbott and his cronies, but like my father always said, if you want to win at life, you have to play the game.

Victor gives a little wave before climbing into the driver's side of his Infiniti and backing out of the driveway. Glancing toward his backyard, I spot an iron fence surrounding an in-ground pool.

A girl with blonde hair piled on top of her head and oversized sunglasses sits in one of the lounge chairs, paging through a thick book. Must be his daughter or his niece, both of which are seniors at Rosefield, so I don't give her a second look.

Maybe she's pretty. And maybe I haven't been laid in longer than I'd like to admit. But so much as thinking about messing around with a student is a line I refuse to cross. I don't even entertain those types of fantasies in my "alone time."

Far too many careers have been ruined all because a teacher or person of authority couldn't keep his dick in his pants.

But that's not me.

I have complete control.

Heading inside, I grab a beer from the fridge and take a seat at the kitchen table to cool off for a bit. Grabbing my phone, I pull up the Karma app, which promptly reminds me that I haven't spoken to Absinthe in almost twelve hours and that it will give me two karma points if I send her a message right now.

Kerouac: I never asked why your name is Absinthe.

Absinthe is online …

Absinthe: Good morning to you too.

Kerouac: You were waiting for my message, weren't you?

Absinthe: It's called a push notification. I was alerted the second you sent me that.

Kerouac: Most girls would play hard to get. They'd make

me wait several hours or maybe even several days before responding.

Absinthe: No point in playing hard to get when you have no intentions of getting me.

Kerouac: Fair point.

Absinthe: My eyes are green. Like the color of absinthe liquor. And I've been told that I have addictive qualities.

Kerouac: Addictive qualities?

Absinthe: One taste and men get hooked.

Kerouac: How many men have you been with, Absinthe?

Absinthe: Enough.

Kerouac: A number, please.

Absinthe: A handful. You?

Kerouac: More than a handful.

Absinthe: So basically, what you're saying is … you're experienced.

Kerouac: You could infer that, yes.

Absinthe: Some people get turned off by that. It's the opposite for me. A man with experience is a good thing.

Kerouac: How old were you when you lost your virginity?

Absinthe: Does it matter?

Kerouac: Fine. I'll go first. I was fifteen. She was the sixteen-year-old girl next door.

Absinthe: Who seduced whom?

Kerouac: She seduced me. And she had big tits. I couldn't have said no if I wanted to.

Absinthe: Weak.

Kerouac: Your turn, Absinthe. Tell me about your first time.

Absinthe has signed off.

Chapter 5

HALSTON

I'M NOT sure what I expected from a restaurant called Big Boulders, where the woman on the sign is standing in front of two giant rocks that, I guess, are supposed to represent her breasts? But after filling out a dozen job applications over the past week, this is the only place that called me back.

"How many in your party?" The hostess, wearing a low-cut top that barely covers her nipples and leaves her belly exposed, gives me a dazzling smile.

"I'm here to see Todd Chadwick," I say. "I have an interview."

"Oh, yes, right this way." She leads me to a back room before knocking on a door with a "manager" plaque taped to the outside. It smells like fried food and spilled drinks in here, and all of the girls are dressed in such a way that invites blatant ogling from the male patrons. "Todd, your one o'clock is here."

The door flings open a second later, and a generic-looking white guy stands before me. Before he extends his hand, his eyes drag the length of me, lingering on my breasts, and then he invites me in, telling me to take a seat on a blue chair with a questionable white stain on the fabric.

"So you're … Halston," he says, grabbing my application from a stack on his desk. "What kind of name is Halston? If you don't mind my asking?"

"I guess my parents named me after a perfume," I say, monotone and repeating the answer I give everyone else who's ever asked me the same stupid question. Supposedly it was the perfume my mother was wearing the night she met my father, when they were a couple of innocent high school kids with their whole lives ahead of them. But I don't share that story. It romanticizes them, and they're selfish assholes. "Anyway, your ad said you offered on-the-job training. Is that right?"

He nods, his hand partially covering his mouth as he rests his elbow on his desk. Todd can't keep his eyes off my breasts for more than a few seconds, and I'm just now realizing his shirt says, "Get Your Rocks Off at Big Boulders!"

"Do you understand what kind of restaurant this is?" he asks.

I nod. "Yeah. Like Knockers."

"We're better than Knockers." His voice rises. Must be a hot button topic for Todd. "Anyway, we're classier. Our women don't look like ex-strippers and our food is all hand-made, nothing frozen."

Because I'm sure *that's* what's bringing their customers here night after night.

"You'd be a server," he says. "But we have a strict dress code. We provide the uniforms. I'm sure you saw some of the girls. Just think of it as a bikini. It's no different. In fact, it hides a little more than a bikini would."

Way to justify it, Todd.

"If there's any doubt in your mind, any part of you that thinks you'd be uncomfortable in this kind of setting, I want you to get up right now and walk out of my office," he says.

"I can handle this," I assure him. "They can look, but they can't touch, right?"

His eyes widen. "Absolutely. If anyone so much as puts their hands on you, you let me or one of the guys at the bar know. They'll be shown the door immediately. We do *not* tolerate that."

"Then we should be fine."

"I will say, though. You're going to be hit on," he says. "Men of all ages, social classes, and backgrounds frequent this pub, and they come here because they want good food, pretty girls to look at, and someone to fantasize about when they're lying next to their old ball and chains that night. That said, show them a good time. It's okay to flirt back. It's okay to let them think that maybe they have a chance. But our girls aren't allowed to go home with the men or give out their numbers. We keep it professional." He leans back in his chair, studying me. "How does that sound? You think you might be interested in something like that?"

"Absolutely. When can I start?"

It's not like I have a choice. I need a job so I can get a car so I can get the hell out of here the second I graduate from Rosefield. There's not much I won't do at this point.

"Tomorrow?" he asks. "Can you start tomorrow? We'll have you shadow someone for a week, but then you'll be on your own. Shifts are eleven to five and five to eleven. You have a preference?"

"Eleven to five is fine," I say. Vic and Tab would freak if I came home after eleven every night.

"Perfect. Let me grab your paperwork here. We'll need a copy of your Social Security card and ... well ... everything's outlined here. Take it home, fill it out, bring it back tomorrow, and we'll get you suited up. Maybe get here about ten-thirty?"

I rise. He rises.

It's done.

I have a job.

"Thank you, Todd," I say.

I feel the weight of his stare on my ass as he walks me out.

<hr>

LYING IN BED, I double click on Karma and send Kerouac a message. I haven't talked to him since I ended the conversation several days ago. Sure, I could've made up a story about the way I lost my virginity ... saying it was some high school boyfriend and we were madly in love and it was sweet and romantic and perfect.

But my mind kept playing the real scenario, and my instinct was to shut down and walk away.

"You there?" I send him a message, biting my thumbnail as I wait.

Five minutes pass, then another five, then ten.

I watch some music videos on YouTube to pass the time.

Kerouac: I'm here. What's going on?

Absinthe: What's the most desperate thing you've ever done for money?

Kerouac: That's random.

Absinthe: Just answer it.

Kerouac: I'm not a desperate man and I'm good with my money, so … nothing?

Absinthe: Bullshit.

Kerouac: I'd need to think on this a while. Can I get back to you?

Absinthe: I guess.

Kerouac: What's wrong? Thought it was weird you went silent on me for a week.

Congratulations! You've reached ten Karma points! You may now view the photograph of the Karma user you're chatting with!

I have no idea how they dole out points, if it's based on how long you chat or how many messages are sent, but a flashing blue icon in the upper corner blinks at me, begging to be clicked.

So I click it.

And an image fills the screen.

It's a man, late twenties, with brown hair, hazel eyes, and a perfect smile. He's incredibly handsome and clean cut, and he wears a navy sweater over a gingham tie. He belongs on a Ralph Lauren billboard. Grabbing a screen-shot of the image, I pull up Google and do a reverse image search, which leads me to a stock photo website.

Kerouac's photo is stock. Not him.

Shaking my head, I'm imagining some beer-bellied pervert sitting in his mother's basement trying to hook up with people on Karma, lying about his good looks and making himself seem more charming and intelligent than he actually is.

Fucking jackass.

Closing out of Karma, I clap the laptop lid shut and shove it to the end of the bed.

Chapter 6

FORD

"THANK YOU ALL FOR COMING HERE," I say Monday morning, though I shouldn't have to thank my teachers for making it to a mandatory mid-summer meeting.

A row of women, all in their mid-forties and sporting suntans, shorts, and t-shirts, are talking amongst themselves, ignoring me. I'd expect this sort of behavior from students. Not seasoned teaching professionals.

"Let me know when you're finished, ladies," I say into the microphone.

They glance up, startled, and all eyes are on them. The woman on the far left mutters an apology.

"Yes. That's better." I stand before the podium in the Rosefield Performing Arts Auditorium, which is high tech and state of the art, having just been remodeled last year. The first several rows are filled with teachers, secretaries, guidance counselors, and maintenance staff. "I wanted to introduce myself." A group of young teachers to my left are whispering, giggling. One of them nods, another practically wipes the drool off her chin. I get that I'm young for a principal, that I'm educated, intelligent, and professional, and that I've won the genetic lottery in the looks department, but I can assure each and every one of those teachers that I have no intentions of so much as thinking of hooking up with them. "My name is Ford Hawthorne. I'm originally from Connecticut, though I attended college in New York City and subsequently taught there as well before coming to Rosefield."

The auditorium is finally quiet.

"A little about me, I'm a straight shooter. I don't sugarcoat. I have ridiculously high expectations for my students, teachers, and staff, and if there's anything I've learned in my career thus far, it's that in the education system, reputation is everything," I say. "The reputation of the school, the reputation of the students and staff, of the leadership ... it's all paramount. And everything we do, day in and day out, contributes to that reputation." I glance at one of the younger women, who instantly blushes. "The second your name or your school's name has been destroyed, it could take decades to be repaired."

Moving on.

"A little about me personally? I'm an avid runner. I enjoy classic literature, travel, and I hate small talk." I smirk. "Over the coming weeks leading up to August 1st, I plan to call you in for some one-on-one meetings, just so I can put your faces with your names. That said, I wanted to keep this short and sweet. I'm sure you're anxious to get back out there and enjoy your summer break. If you need to reach me, I've left a stack of business cards on the table in the back with my contact information."

The buzz of conversation fills the auditorium once more, and I step down from the stage, heading up one of the aisles. I linger at the back table for a bit, watching as one out of every five people passing by takes a business card, and I sigh.

These people are checked out, but I don't blame them.

Teaching is one of the toughest, most draining and challenging careers.

"Mr. Hawthorne?" A woman's voice fills my ear. I glance over the desk to see a petite little thing with a pale blonde pixie cut, a purple dress, and teal earrings. "I'm Sara Bliss, the art teacher at Rosefield."

She extends her hand.

"Lovely to meet you, Sara," I say.

"I just wanted to introduce myself." She fights a smile, her eyes lighting in my presence as she fidgets, and I wonder if everyone makes her fidget or if it's just me. Either way, it doesn't matter. I don't get involved with my teachers. "Rosefield is a good school. Our students are maybe a little more privileged than the average student. And most of them drive nicer cars than the teachers." She chuckles. "But they're good kids. At the end of the day, they do what they're told to do, and they're so focused on getting into the best colleges that they're all little over-achievers. Even in art class."

"I see."

"Anyway, I didn't know if anyone had told you much about our school ... you know, outside of the hiring committee. Thought you might want to hear this stuff from someone who sees it all firsthand."

"Of course. I appreciate that."

"Well, I guess I'll see you around?" She shrugs, flashing a sweet smile.

"Yes, enjoy the rest of your summer, Miss ..."

"Bliss," she reminds me. "Sara Bliss. If you ever need anything, please don't hesitate to ask."

A man with gray hair and a faded white t-shirt emblazoned with the school's mascot ambles toward my table.

"Bernie," he says. "School custodian. Been here over thirty years."

"Bernie, nice to meet you." I extend my hand.

"This is a good school," he says, his chin jutting forward as he answers a question I didn't ask. "Think you'll really like it here."

"That's what I hear. And I certainly hope so."

"If you ever need anything …" He points at himself before nodding and walking away.

When the last person has left the auditorium, I grab my cards and head to my new office. It's empty save for a couple of plants the last principal left behind. And a Mac computer sits dusty and untouched on the center of a desk.

Taking a seat in the chair, which is painfully uncomfortable and going to have to be replaced, I stare out the window that overlooks the commons, an open air, upscale food court type of place that wraps around a courtyard filled with picnic tables.

I envision the students filling the area, their little Louis Vuitton backpacks and MacBook Airs in tow as they ask the food service workers if the apples are organic or farm fresh. Students at a school like this are no doubt going to be spoiled and entitled.

My only hope is that I can make a difference, instill a little humility in them so they can grow up to be good people, not just smart people. I hope that long after they're gone, and even long after I'm gone, they'll still remember me.

If I can make a lasting impression, I'll have done my job.

Chapter 7

HALSTON

MY STOMACH IS in knots as I sit on the lid of the toilet in the staff restroom. Today's my first day at Big Boulders, and Courtney, my mentor, handed me a uniform and told me to get changed. At first, I figured it wouldn't be a big deal. I wear bikinis all the time at Uncle Vic's pool. But knowing that I'm wearing this skimpy outfit for the sole purpose of letting men stare at my tits and ass … almost makes me want to throw up.

Courtney knocks on the door. "Halston, you okay?"

"Yeah," I say. "Almost done. Just … touching up my makeup."

I need a distraction, something to soothe my nerves, so I retrieve my phone and pull up one of the many time-wasting websites I have bookmarked. I'm halfway through the front page of BuzzFeed when I get a notification from Karma.

Kerouac: What happened yesterday? Everything okay?

Kerouac: Also, can I just say, holy fucking shit, you're beautiful.

Shaking my head, I don't know whether to laugh or cry. No one's ever called me beautiful before. Pretty? Yeah. Sexy? All the time. But beautiful? Never.

I so badly wish Kerouac was real.

Absinthe: Wish I could say the same about you, but you decided to use a stock photo as your profile pic. That's cheating, Kerouac. Not fair.

Kerouac: In my defense, the stock photo guy looks a lot like me … if you squint. We share a lot of the same features.

Absinthe: You expect me to believe you now? After you pulled that stunt? I should block you.

Kerouac: Don't block me. I'm sorry. I wish I could show you my face, but I'm not in a position to risk that right now. I'm starting a new job soon. A public sector job. I can't be that guy hooking up with random women on dating apps.

Absinthe: But you *are* that guy. That's exactly what you're doing.

Kerouac: We're just chatting. I'm not going to hook up with you.

Absinthe: We had chat sex. Did you forget about the chat sex?

Kerouac: Again, that's not hooking up.

Absinthe: I have to go.

Kerouac: Chat later?

Absinthe: Maybe. Still mad at you.

I turn my phone off and give myself one last look in the mirror. My full lips are slicked in fuck-me red. My tits are pushed up to my chin thanks to the standard issue push-up bra Todd assigns to his wait staff, and the little skirt I'm wearing barely covers my ass cheeks, but I'm doing this.

Yanking the door open, I catch Courtney off guard.

"There you are," she says, her mouth pulling wide. "I was beginning to think you were having second thoughts. Happens all the time."

She loops her arm around mine and pulls me to the bar. It's barely eleven and the place is already beginning to fill. Climbing on a stool, she stands on the bar before motioning for me to join her, and the bartender hands her a megaphone.

Oh, god.

What have I gotten myself into?

I take my place at Courtney's side as she lifts the loud-speaker to her mouth. "Heyyyy, guys! We have a new server starting today! Let's give a warm Big Boulders welcome to Halston!"

All eyes land on me, men hooting and hollering and clapping and grinning.

It's a feeding frenzy, and I'm dessert.

We climb down a second later, and she pulls me to a little galley just off the kitchen, handing me a pen and notepad along with an apron.

"You won't need those today since you're shadowing me, but those are yours to keep. You can put them in your locker or you can wear them." She ties her apron around her tiny waist, her grin falling. "What's wrong? You look scared?"

I shake my head. "I'm fine."

"You're going to make so much fucking money here, Halston. I promise you. When you count your tips at the end of the night, you won't even remember the guy at table five that slapped your ass earlier."

"That happens?" I ask. "Todd said the customers aren't allowed to touch us."

Her eyes grow round. "They're not. But it doesn't stop them from trying."

"Do you get them thrown out?"

She waves her hand, pressing her lips flat. "If we did that to every customer who slapped our asses or brushed their arms against our boobs or whatever, we'd be out of business. None of them would come back."

I think I'm going to be sick.

"Oh, hey. First table's ready. Come on." She motions for me to follow her, and we head toward a half-moon shaped booth in the far corner where four men in business suits order beers, wings, and cheeseburgers.

They're nice.

And this isn't so bad.

They look at us, but they don't make it obvious. Three of them have wedding bands on.

The hostess tells Courtney we have two more tables, and she asks if I'd be comfortable taking drink orders from one of them.

"The longer they have to wait, the lower your tip will be," she tells me.

Nodding, I make my way toward a table with an older gentleman with lonely eyes and a Ron Jon t-shirt.

"Hi, sir," I say. "I'm Halston. I'll be taking care of you today. Can I get you started with something to drink?"

This reminds me of playing restaurant as a kid.

Piece of cake.

"Dr. Pepper, no ice," he says. "Then a stack of onion rings and a cowboy burger, no pickles."

Oh.

Scrambling to grab my pad and pen, I jot everything down before it leaves my memory, and then I repeat it back to him. When I glance up, his eyes are on my breasts.

"You're new here," he says, his gaze still below sea level.

"I am. It's my first day." I force a smile. "Go easy on me."

I'm teasing, but he doesn't laugh.

"Let me go put in your order and grab your drink," I say, trotting away from him.

I find Courtney in the galley where she's frantically scooping ice and filling cups.

"He gave me his order. What do I do now?" I ask.

"Put it on the line," she says, pointing back toward the kitchen. "Left is newest, right is oldest. Put it on the left. The cooks will take it from there."

"How do I know when the food is ready?"

"They'll slide your ticket down. Food will be under the warmers," she says. "Just check back here every so often. We don't like to keep customers waiting longer than ten minutes. If it's been longer than that, check with the kitchen to see what the holdup is."

She carries a tray of drinks to the second table before retrieving the beers from the bar for the first one, and I fill the lonely guy's Dr. Pepper. With ice.

Shit.

Dumping it out, I pour another one *without* ice, and take it to him.

"Here you go, sir." I place it on a napkin in front of him.

"Where's my straw?" he asks.

"Completely forgot. I'm so sorry." I begin to run back when he stops me, placing his hand around my wrist.

"It's a good thing you're pretty," he says.

"Excuse me?"

"You've got looks but not brains. I can tell. It's a good thing you're pretty."

I'm speechless, utterly speechless. And while I'd love nothing more than to rip this saggy-balled geezer a new one, it's probably not the best idea with this being my first day on the job and all.

He releases his hand from my wrist, letting it fall down the side of my hip, grazing the outside of my ass.

Completely intentional.

Returning to the galley for a straw, my body burns, my skin on fire. That sorry excuse for a man made me feel less than human all in the span of a handful of seconds, but I'm too pissed off to cry about it.

Glancing around, I wonder what the chances are that I could spit in his food and no one would notice?

I drop the straw off at his table in passing, not stopping. I just toss it toward him. When his appetizer comes out a few minutes later, I ask a food runner to handle it for me. When he leaves, he tips me two dollars on a twenty-five-dollar check.

Eight percent.

"You okay?" Courtney rubs my back when she sees me examining the man's signed receipt. "Did he stiff you?"

I don't want to talk about it.

"The good tippers will *more* than make up for the bad tippers, I promise," she says. "Stick with it. It's going to get better."

I give her a close-lipped smile.

"On a good note, you did your first table all by yourself, and you did wonderfully," she says. "You might not even need to shadow me!"

Not like this job is rocket science …

"You want to try another?" she asks. "There's a table

of young guys you can have. They just sat down. Three of them. The younger ones are the better tippers."

Glancing to the main floor, I watch them. Just a few college-aged buddies sitting down for lunch. One has his nose in his phone and the other two are laughing about something. They don't look like ass-grabbers.

"Yeah. I'll take it," I offer, sucking up my pride and making my way to the guys. "Hi, I'm Halston. I'll be taking care of you today."

Two of the guys nudge each other, exchanging looks. I almost wonder if I have something in my teeth when I glance down and see my left breast is almost completely out of my top—half of my nipple is showing.

"Sorry. I was going to say something," the guy on the left said.

Yeah, right.

"You're gorgeous by the way," the middle guy says. "I saw you when we walked in. Was hoping we'd get you. You're new, aren't you?"

I nod. "First day. Go easy on me."

The guys smile and keep their eyes on mine for the time being, though I'm sure they have every intention of checking out my ass when I walk away.

"What are we drinking?" I ask, lifting my pad and pen.

The guys order two beers and an iced tea, and they seem more focused on the TVs above the bar area than scoping out all the beautiful, scantily-clad servers. Maybe it's enough for them to be in the mere presence of half-naked women? Or they all have girlfriends, budding relationships, and this is the closest they're going to get to a strip club until their respective bachelor parties.

Either way, I'm content with this table, and when they leave, they each tip me five dollars.

"What'd you get?" Courtney asks. "*Damnnn*. Fifteen

bucks on a fifty-dollar table. That's amazing. Told you the young ones tip the best."

Courtney has bottle blonde hair with dark roots, rocks a spray tan, and smells like she showers in Sun Ripened Raspberry body spray, but she spends the rest of the afternoon encouraging me, distracting me from watching the clock.

When the next shift comes in, we head back to tally up our tips, and I walk away with almost a hundred dollars.

Courtney has two hundred and fifty.

"Will I see you back here tomorrow?" she asks.

Staring at her pile of cash, I nod.

I need to take my pride out of this equation and take a page from her book.

The hustle begins now.

Chapter 8

FORD

ABSINTHE: "Many years have passed since that night. The wall of the staircase up which I had watched the light of his candle gradually climb was long ago demolished. And in myself, too, many things have perished which I imagined would last forever, and new ones have arisen, giving birth to new sorrows and new joys which in those days I could not have foreseen, just as now the old are hard to understand."

Kerouac: Good evening to you, too.

Absinthe: Reading Proust. Swann's Way. That really spoke to me. Just wanted to share it.

Kerouac: Melancholy mood tonight?

Absinthe: Lost in thought kind of mood tonight.

Kerouac: Same difference. Either way, don't linger there too long. It's not good for you.

Absinthe: Tell me about your day. I need a distraction from mine.

Kerouac: Life isn't half as bad as you think it is, Absinthe.

Absinthe: Easy for you to say.

Kerouac: How about you tell me about yours first?

Absinthe: Started a new job. Hate it.

Kerouac: What kind of job?

Absinthe: Customer service.

Kerouac: Vague, but okay.

Absinthe: There are customers. And I serve them.

Kerouac: You can say you're a waitress. There's no shame in that.

Absinthe: Server, Kerouac. The politically correct term is server.

Kerouac: My mistake. So you hate it?

Absinthe: So much.

Kerouac: So find something else.

Absinthe: That's the plan. Just have to tough it out a little longer. The money's not bad.

Kerouac: Christ, Absinthe, don't do any job for the money. That's the worst thing you could do.

Absinthe: Not everyone has a choice. Unfortunately, I wasn't born with a silver spoon.

Kerouac: Silver spoons sometimes rust.

Absinthe: You speak from experience?

Kerouac: Perhaps.

Absinthe: You blow through Daddy's trust fund?

Kerouac: No.

Absinthe: Then what happened? You can't make a statement like that and leave me hanging.

Kerouac: It's a story for another time. Wounds are still fresh.

Absinthe: Whatever. You going to tell me about your day or what?

Kerouac: I went to work. Held a meeting. That's about it.

Absinthe: What do you do for a living?

Kerouac: That's private information.

Absinthe: Okay, fine. So you're the boss of wherever you work?

Kerouac: You could say that. I'm in charge, yes. I run the place.

Absinthe: You like being in control?

Kerouac: Very much.

Absinthe: What's your favorite sexual position? Since you like being in control so much?

Kerouac: Doggy style. Terrible name. Fucking amazing position.

Absinthe: Ugh.

Kerouac: What?

Absinthe: That's my least favorite. I don't like being fucked like a dog.

Kerouac: You speak from experience?

Absinthe: I do.

Kerouac: Then you've never experienced it with the right man.

Absinthe: Okay, so how would it be with you? Since you're apparently the authority on doggy-style sex.

Kerouac: I am. And I'd be glad to share that with you. First of all, I'd place you on your hands and knees, spreading your thighs before tonguing your pussy from behind to put you at ease. When you're soft and wet, I'd take my position behind you, gripping your hips with one hand and teasing your clit with the tip of my cock before gliding myself deep inside you, one teasing inch at a time. Once your pussy is clenched around my cock, I'd control your hips, making them meet my cock thrust for thrust as you rub your clit. I won't go fast, and I won't go slow. I'll take my time, ensuring you feel every inch of me filling you, rubbing against your g-spot. And when you get close to the most amazing orgasm you've ever had in your life, I'd gather your hair in my hand, guiding you closer to me, my body leaning over yours so you can taste yourself on my lips as you come all over my cock as your hips writhe against me.

Absinthe: Fuck. Um. Wow.

Kerouac: Deeper, hotter, harder.

Absinthe: Sold.

Kerouac: Your turn. What's your favorite position?

Absinthe: Missionary. And before you make fun of me, know that I'm not sorry. That's what I like. Not fucking apologizing for it.

Kerouac: You're not very experienced, are you?

Absinthe: I'm experienced enough.

Kerouac: You're a virgin.

Absinthe: Nope.

Kerouac: I think you are.

Absinthe: You can think that all you want. Doesn't make you correct.

Kerouac: So what do you like about the missionary position then?

Absinthe: It feels … safe, I guess? You get to look each other in the eyes and kiss and your whole bodies are touching everywhere. It's intimate. And sweet.

Kerouac: Typical woman. You just need to live a little. Erotic sex can be just as fulfilling as romantic sex.

Absinthe: I'd ask you to teach me some time, but …

Kerouac: Yeah. Not going to happen. Not anytime soon at least.

Congratulations! You've earned twenty Karma points! You may now access your Karma email addresses! Karma encourages its users to get to know one another on a deeper level, sending longer messages outside the chatroom setting. You may continue to use the chatroom, but utilizing the email feature will put you that much closer to the next step, which is accessing your Karma phone numbers!

Absinthe: Look at that. Now we can email each other.

Kerouac: I like chatting this way.

Absinthe: Me too. But I kind of want your phone number. What happens if you type it in?

Kerouac: Karma will block out the numbers. Like this: ***-***-****.

Absinthe: So we're going to have to email each other. Ugh. Who designed this? An AOL developer from 1995? Nobody fucking emails anymore.

Kerouac: For a girl who likes missionary sex, you have a bit of an edge to you. I like that.

Absinthe: Because I say fuck a lot?

Kerouac: Yes. I also have a weak spot for women with pretty mouths who say naughty things. Love a good contradiction. It goes against everything I stand for in real life. Makes me hard as a fucking rock.

Absinthe: You like it dirty?

Kerouac: I do.

Absinthe: And let me guess, you're a clean-cut, educated professional.

Kerouac: Close enough.

Absinthe: You're a complicated man, Kerouac. And I happen to have a weakness for complicated men.

Kerouac: Something tells me you're just as complicated as I am.

Absinthe: If not more so. Goodnight, K.

Chapter 9

THE PHONE NUMBERS of two men are scribbled across two crumpled receipts as I empty out my pockets. Being hit on at work is flattering, but the last person I'm going to date is some guy who prefers his BBQ wings with a side of tits and ass.

Definitely not boyfriend material.

Sliding my tip money from my other pocket, I count out one-hundred fifty-eight dollars and add it to my secret stash.

Almost five hundred dollars cash rests in an old makeup bag buried at the bottom of my sock drawer. Two weekends in a row waiting tables at Big Boulders has gotten me that much closer to getting a damn car. If I can save up three grand and Uncle Vic matches it, I should be able to get a used Honda or something that's going to last me for years to come.

I don't need anything fancy, just something that's not

going to fall apart when I'm cruising down the highway going seventy-five miles per hour leaving Rosefield, Illinois in the dust.

I flip to the calendar, adding up the remaining weekends for the summer. As long as I can keep this job on the down low another month or so, I'll be golden.

And one of these days, when I finally get my hands on my birth certificate, I'll head to the bank so I can finally open an account and keep this money someplace safer than hidden under a pile of neon, no-show Nike socks.

There's a bus stop two blocks down from here, just outside our gated neighborhood, and Vic and Tab think I'm working at the Waterfront Sea Food Restaurant downtown. Heaven help me if my cover is ever blown, but thank God I don't have to keep this up forever.

Covering my savings with a stack of pajama pants, I head downstairs to Aunt Tabitha's Sunday supper, though I'm not hungry. We munch on everything between tables, and we're always hungry because we're running around like animals. Courtney knows the caloric content of almost all of the entrees, and she's been happy to point out which ones to avoid.

"We have to maintain our girlish figures," she said. "That's how we make the big bucks!"

Taking a seat at my usual spot, Bree's nose crinkles. "It smells like fried food in here."

My uniform stays at work, in my locker, but maybe the stench of bar food has seeped into my hair and pores?

"We had a special on fried calamari," I lie, spreading my napkin over my lap and offering a smart-mouthed smirk.

Bitch.

I'd love to see Bree wait tables anywhere. She wouldn't last more than a minute.

"How can you just sit there, smelling like that? Don't you want to shower?" Bree won't let off.

"Bree." Uncle Vic says her name and clears his throat. "That's enough. I'm very proud of you, Halston. You've shown real initiative. You're a hard worker. That's going to get you far in life."

"I was thinking of getting a job too." Bree straightens her posture, staring across the table in my direction. "Maybe babysitting or nannying or something? Something with kids. And it makes sense since I want to go into education."

Uncle Vic smiles his proud, fatherly smile, reaching over and placing his hand over hers.

"That's my girl," he says.

Tabitha places a dish of herbed chicken resting on a bed of garlic couscous between us all before taking her seat.

"Vic, would you like to say grace?" Tabitha asks.

Bree folds her hands and nods her head, and when I peek up at her, I find her staring at me, so I give her a dirty look before kicking her under the table.

Vic and Tab are in their own little world, and by the time they make the sign of the cross, they're none the wiser.

I choke down Tabitha's dinner before excusing myself to my room and jumping in the shower—because I want to, not because Bitchface told me to.

When I'm done, I change into pajama shorts and a tank top and check my Karma app. I haven't heard from Kerouac in almost a week now, but I'm trying not to obsess over it. I'm assuming he's busy with work stuff, being an "educated professional" and all. Plus, he's complicated. I'm complicated. Nothing good—or real—is going to come of this anyway. It's nothing more than a time waster. A boredom crusher.

From: Absinthe@karma.com

To: Kerouac@karma.com

Subject: Where for art thou?

Time: 6:48 PM

Message: I feel like you dropped off the face of the earth this week, and I can't help but think it had to do with my missionary sex confession. I turned you off, didn't I? I should've said reverse cowgirl. Fuck. What was I thinking? Have I lost you forever, my sweet Kerouac? Will you ever give me a second chance? Obviously, I'm kidding. Kind of. I miss chatting with you. And I had a sex dream about you the other night. I mean, the guy had your stock model's face and sounded a lot like Ryan Gosling, but it was you. And before you ask, yes, it was "doggy style." Ugh. But I enjoyed it. Anyway, just thought you should know.

I push my laptop to the side and grab a book off my nightstand. I'm halfway through Daphne DuMaurier's Rebecca for the fourth time because for some reason I've yet to get sick of it. Fifty pages later, Karma dings.

You have an email from Kerouac! Click here to review!

From: Kerouac@Karma.com

To: Absinthe@Karma.com

Subject: Re: Where for art thou?

Time: 7:27 PM

Message: Dearest, you could never turn me off. Just the mere idea of fucking you like an animal until you collapse with satisfaction is enough to hold my interest. Okay, enough with the cheese. Not ignoring you. Family's in town. I hope to resume our virtual fuck sessions in the next week. Feel free to email me still. I'll respond when I can. In the meantime, I'd like a full detailed report of that dream you had for my records. Also, I thought about you this morning in the shower. Don't think I've ever come so much in my life. What are you doing to me? I've never wanted to fuck a complete stranger so badly in my life.

From: Absinthe@karma.com

To: Kerouac@karma.com

Subject: Re: re: Where for art thou?

Time: 7:33 PM

Message: I was going to make you wait until tomorrow for a response, but honestly, I've never been into playing games and it's getting late and I'm tired because I work a soul-sucking job (that's going to be my excuse for everything from now on, btw). I think I've earned it. Anyway, I don't have time to type up a detailed report of my dream because, quite frankly, I have better things to do with my time and based on previous conversations, your imagination seems to function just fine. Going to bed now. Enjoy family time. Hope you were blessed with a "normal" family and that you're not counting down the hours until they leave. Later.

Closing the lid, I stick my computer on the charger and climb back into bed. I don't realize it right away, but my lips are curled at the sides and there's a faint fluttering in my middle.

What the fuck is this shit?

No.

Just ... no.

I'm not falling for some Internet stranger—especially one using a stock photo for a profile picture.

Clasping my hand over my eyes, I exhale, silently telling myself to get a goddamned life.

Chapter 10

FORD

"HI, Ford! I hope it's okay that I stopped by." Melissa Gunderson stands under the stoop of my front porch, another tray of tin foil-covered food in her hand.

"Oh, hey." I don't hide my annoyance. "Give me two secs. I'll grab your brownie pan."

"No, no." She waves her manicured hand in front of my face, her hot pink nails a little too close to this chiseled mug of mine. "I brought you a casserole! Hope you don't think I'm being nosy, but I've been noticing you order a lot of takeout, and I thought you could use a home cooked meal. Made you a casserole. I hope you like chicken."

"Honey, who is that at the door?" My sister Nicolette calls from the living room.

I hide my laugh with my hand, glancing down, and Melissa's eyes dart over my shoulder, her face falling.

"Hi! I'm Nicolette Hawthorne," she says, pushing me out of the way. "You must be one of the new neighbors?"

That's my sister. Sharp as a tack and doesn't miss a beat.

Melissa's words must be caught in her throat, and she visually assesses Nicolette the way insecure, lonely women tend to do.

"I'm so sorry," Melissa manages to say a moment later, extending her free hand. "I didn't know …"

I can only hope Melissa's too in shock to notice our uncanny resemblance, right down to the dimples in our chins.

"Well, I should be on my way." Melissa hands over the hot dish and Nicolette thanks her before closing the door.

"Completely unnecessary," I say.

"Bullshit, Ford. That girl was a stage five clinger situation waiting to happen. You should be thanking me."

"Should I also thank you when she discovers I'm your brother and starts spreading rumors around the neighborhood?"

"She's not going to know. Women like that aren't bright enough to put those kinds of things together." Nicolette takes the casserole to the kitchen, where my five-year-old nephew, Arlo, is hard at work on a page in his Transformers coloring book. "Anyway."

Nicolette ruffles Arlo's curly blond hair before leaning to kiss his forehead.

"You going to miss me, buddy?" she asks.

"Yep." He doesn't look up.

"I'm going to miss you," she says.

"I know." He reaches for a blue crayon, inspecting the tip to ensure it's sharp enough.

We laugh.

"He'll be fine," I say. "It's just a week. We've got fun stuff planned."

"Like what?" she asks.

"Guy stuff. Super secret guys stuff that only guys can do," I say, smirking at my nephew, whose face is lit like Christmas.

"Thanks for doing this for me," she says, ruffling his silky curls again. "You're the only person I trust with my baby."

Nicolette hugs him one last time, tickling his ribcage until he giggles. Her annual girls' trip begins tonight with a flight from O'Hare International to Miami, where she'll meet up with some old friends from college. I don't even want to think about what they're going to do from there.

Being a single mom with zero help from Arlo's dad, she needs this time to herself, and I'm happy to help.

"You're cool with me getting a babysitter for a few hours a day?" I ask. "It'd only be in the morning."

"Let me guess. Gym?" She rolls her eyes.

"And work."

"Thought you had the summer off?" she asks.

"Prep work. Boring stuff. Just a couple hours a day."

"Whatever," she says. "That's fine. I trust you."

Nicolette grabs her suitcase from the bottom of the stairs as her cab pulls into the driveway, and I can only hope Melissa's not standing outside watching me walk my sister to the car and send her off with a friendly wave instead of a romantic embrace.

"Be right back, bud," I say to Arlo. "Don't move a muscle."

He freezes, his lips fighting a giggle.

"I want you just like that when I get back." I point my finger at him before heading out the front door and helping Nic into her car. And just as I'm turning to get back inside, I spot Victor Abbott in his driveway, waxing his car.

He waves. I wave. At this point it would be rude to

walk away, especially considering the fact that he's my new boss.

"Victor," I say, striding between our driveways.

"Ford," he says.

"Have a question for you."

"Shoot." He stands, his hand resting on his lower back. Why he doesn't just pay someone to wax his car is beyond me, but I suspect a man like Victor Abbott does things himself if he wants them done right.

"My nephew's in town for a week. Looking for a babysitter. Just a few hours a day, Monday through Friday. You know anyone in the neighborhood? Looking for someone reliable and responsible."

His face lights up, something I wasn't sure was possible. "Matter of fact, my daughter, Bree, was just saying she wanted to get into babysitting. You want to meet her?"

That was easy.

"Sure." I glance toward the house, waiting as Victor heads in and returns with a bobble-headed cheerleader type—of the studious variety, not the slutty—complete with a tied bow in her ponytail. Victor's daughter looks like she walked off the set of a Taylor Swift music video, but she comes from good stock, and I'm not exactly in a position to say no.

"Bree, this is Ford," her father says, clearing his throat. "Principal Hawthorne come August twenty-third."

"So you're the new principal!" Bree extends her hand, her blue eyes wide and smiling. "It's so wonderful to meet you. You're going to love Rosefield. We're one of the top high schools in the state."

"That's what I've been told," I say. She's still holding my hand, almost refusing to let go. I give a gentle tug and sever the tie. "Very honored to lead the charge this fall."

"Dad says you need a babysitter?" She bounces on her tennis shoe-covered toes.

I nod. "My five-year-old nephew's in town for a week. Are you available in the mornings? Eight to eleven or so?"

"I am." She smiles. "When would you like me to start?"

"Tomorrow?"

"See you then, Principal Hawthorne." Bree tugs on the hem of her scoop neck top once she's out of her father's periphery. If she's trying to give me a show, she's wasting her time.

There's nothing there.

And I don't fuck my students.

Chapter 11

FORD

"TELL ME ABOUT GRANDMA AND GRANDPA." Arlo shoves a spoonful of Lucky Charms into his mouth.

I do the same.

"What has your mom told you about them?" I ask.

He shrugs. "Just that they were nice. And they would've loved me."

"They would've adored you," I say. "They would've been obsessed with you."

"What does that mean? Obsessed?"

"It means they think about you all the time. They can't stop thinking about you." Eh, good enough. "It's a grown-up thing."

Arlo takes another bite. "What happened to them?"

I almost choke on my cereal. "What'd your mom say happened to them?"

"She won't tell me."

Sucking in a deep breath, I mull it over. "It's kind of a long story."

"I'm not going anywhere, Uncle Ford." His big blue eyes blink. "I want to know. Will you tell me?"

Checking my watch, I calculate that Bree's going to be here in about five minutes, so I'll give him the condensed, Grimm's fairy tale version.

"All right." I rise, taking my dish to the sink and rinsing it out. "Once upon a time, there was a king and queen who ruled a kingdom. The kingdom was known for pioneering wind energy, which I don't expect you to know anything about, but just know that it was a very wealthy and very successful kingdom. The king and queen had a prince and princess, and they were living happily ever after until the queen got sick. The king didn't want to lose his beloved queen, so he hired one of the best nurses in the kingdom to take care of her day in and day out so she would never be alone and never be in pain. Months and months passed, then years. The queen was still sick, unable to get out of bed most days. The king became lonely and sad. The nurse and the king began a friendship because the king was so lonely, and when the queen eventually passed away, the king married the nurse, making her his new queen and her son a new prince."

Arlo yawns. I think I'm losing him. I should've told the story in the context of Transformers using Autobots and Decepticons.

"Anyway, the new queen didn't like the first prince and princess. She sent them away to school while she ruled the kingdom with her son and her king by her side. Eventually, the king got very ill and passed away, and the evil queen and her evil son inherited the entire kingdom, banishing the prince and princess forever. The end."

My nephew's nose wrinkles. "That's it?"

"Pretty intense, right?"

"I guess."

"Were you even paying attention?" I ask.

"You lost me at 'princess.'"

The doorbell chimes. Bree. And I go to let her in.

"Good morning, Principal Hawthorne." Her hands clasp together in front of her hips, her arms pressing against her flat chest. She wears yet another low-cut top, and skintight shorts hug her non-existent curves. A hint of pink gloss covers her thin lips, and she can't stop grinning in my presence.

She's crushing. Hard.

Happened all the time back in New York. I guess I have that effect on young ladies. Good thing I couldn't care less.

"Thanks for coming, Bree." I point down the hall, toward the kitchen. "Arlo's finishing up his breakfast."

She follows me, walking too close for comfort, and when I stop in the kitchen, she nearly bumps into me.

"Sorry." She giggles, brushing hair out of her face. "Oh, my goodness. You must be Arlo. Look at you! You're the cutest little thing."

Her voice is whiny as she gushes, and I can tell Arlo's getting annoyed.

"I'll be back in a few hours, buddy," I say. "We'll go see that new Minions movie this afternoon, okay? Extra butter on the popcorn. I won't tell your mom if you won't?"

Arlo grins, marshmallows stuck in his teeth, and I grab my keys from the counter.

"Numbers are on the fridge," I say. "Feel free to play outside, just stick around here, okay?"

"Yes, Principal Hawthorne." She takes a seat next to Arlo, giving me a dainty wave. I almost tell her the formal addressment isn't necessary in my home, but I don't want to give her the wrong impression.

"Be good, bud." I tap Arlo on the shoulder as I pass, exiting through the back door and heading to my car.

A moment later, I'm backing out of the driveway, and I happen to catch Bree peeking out from behind a curtain in the living room window, watching me leave.

Shuddering, I shake my head.

I'm going to have to keep a close eye on that one.

Chapter 12

HALSTON

FROM: Absinthe@karma.com
    To: Kerouac@karma.com
    Subject: Re: re: re: Where for art thou?
    Time: 9:05 AM
    Message: Tell me it gets better than this.

FROM: Absinthe@karma.com
    To: Kerouac@karma.com
    Subject: Re: re: re: re: Where for art thou?
    Time: 9:08 AM
    Message: Oh. You probably need context. I'm feeling sorry for myself because I hate my job. And I miss having you at my instant disposal. Some guy hit on me at work yesterday, and then he tried to follow me to the bus station. I told him off. Now I'm worried I'm going to get fired. It happened outside of work, but he could still

complain to my boss. Going to be a long week for me, Kerouac.

FROM: Kerouac@karma.com
> **To**: Absinthe@karma.com
> **Subject**: Re: re: re: re: re: Where for art thou?
> **Time**: 9:16 AM
> **Message**: I wish I could tell you it gets better, but I don't think it ever does. Most men are assholes who will break your heart when they're not fucking your brains out (present company unfortunately not excluded). Most jobs will steal your soul if you're not careful. And love is only temporary, at least it has been in my experience. But you weren't asking about love, were you? I digress. Keep your chin up, Absinthe. Have yourself a glass of wine, a hot bath, and a good, old-fashioned orgasm when you get home tonight (make sure you're thinking about me). I promise you'll feel better.

FROM: Absinthe@karma.com
> **To**: Kerouac@karma.com
> **Subject**: Kerouac sucks. The author. Not you.
> **Time**: 9:20 AM
> **Message**: I changed the subject line. It was getting annoying. But thank you for enlightening me. And for not making me wait too long for another Kerouac fix. What are you doing today? What do normal families do together? I wouldn't know. Story for another time, as you would say.

FROM: Kerouac@karma.com

To: Absinthe@karma.com
Subject: Re: Kerouac sucks. The author. Not you.
Time: 9:24 AM
Message: I'm at the gym right now, running on the treadmill. If I fall off and bust my lip, I'm blaming you. Not sure what we're doing today. And not sure what your definition of a "normal" family consists of, but I doubt that entails having your sister pretend to be your wife to fend off stage five clingers. Yeah, that happened. I'm not proud. But it worked.

I SMIRK, laughing through my nose.

I like him.

Leaning against my headboard, I forget the fact that he might be some Quasimodo basement dweller who uses a stock photo and I imagine him at the gym, his shirtless runner's body, his shorts slung low on his hips. Women passing by, checking him out. Him smiling at them …

The fact that he's a real person living a real life outside of this weird little bubble we've created is something I haven't given much thought to, until now.

Kerouac is real. Kerouac exists. And we'll never have more than what we have right now.

I picture him with another woman for reasons I can't explain. Someone else will know what it feels like to touch him, to feel him. But it will never be me.

Heat blooms through me. My stomach turns.

Is this … is this what jealousy feels like?

━━━

"I NEVER SEE YOU ANYMORE." Emily lies on her bed

that night, her head in her hands as I flip through a stale issue of Seventeen on her floor.

"Trust me, I wish I didn't have to work, but I need a car." I turn the page to an article on clearing up acne using all natural remedies.

My feet hurt from working all day, and my hair smells like mozzarella sticks and fried pickles, but I didn't feel like hanging out at home after dinner tonight, so I came over here to bother Emily.

"You going to tell me where you're working?" Emily asks.

I wince. "It's not that exciting. Just a seedy bar and grill kind of place."

"What's it called?" Her eyes widen. "You can trust me. I'm not going to tell anyone."

And it's true. She wouldn't tell anyone because I'm her only friend and she doesn't want to jeopardize that.

"Big Boulders," I say, exhaling.

Her jaw falls. She says nothing. Doesn't even blink.

"Come on." I toss the magazine aside. It bores me. "You act like I just told you I became a stripper or something."

"Do you have to wear those little skimpy outfits?"

"How do you know about those little skimpy outfits?" I cock a brow.

"I might be a little sheltered, but I know what places like that are like." She seems offended by my question. "Do they know you're in high school?"

"What they won't know won't hurt them, right?" I chuckle. "They didn't ask. They just made me check a box saying I was over eighteen and then prove it with a copy of my social security carde."

It probably helped that I don't look like I'm in high school. Growing up, I've always been mature for my age, both physically and mentally. I got my period in third grade and by fourth grade I was filling out a full C-cup. By sixth grade I was the tallest girl in my class and by junior high, at least when I was attending, I'd catch teachers checking me out when they thought I wasn't looking.

I'd have reported them, but school lunch was my only hot meal of the day, and I didn't want to risk being accused of making shit up for attention, which is what the administration liked to say anytime a student pointed out an issue.

"Do you like it?" Emily asks. "Working there?"

"Hate it." I exhale, brushing hair out of my eyes. "I'm treated like a piece of meat."

Something I should be used to by now.

"I get hit on at least once every shift. I've seen men purposely spill their drinks on other servers to try to see through their shirts. Last shift, someone grabbed my friend's ass." I shake my head. It makes me sick to think about going back there. "But the money's good."

Chapter 13

FORD

BREE AND ARLO are working on a jigsaw puzzle at the kitchen table when I get home.

"Oh, hey, Principal Hawthorne." Bree lights. "Found this in one of your closets. Hope that's okay."

"It's fine." It's a thousand-piece puzzle of a lighthouse, a white elephant gift from many Christmas parties ago. Forgot I even had it.

"Arlo was an angel today," she says, rising and slipping her hands into the back pockets of her shorts, pressing her chest forward. I keep my eyes on hers. "I was going to tell you, I was junior class president last year, and I know all the ins and outs at Rosefield. I know pretty much everyone too. If you ever need anyone on the inside, I'm your girl."

"Thank you, Bree."

"I do cheerleading in the fall," she continues. "For football. And also in the winter. For basketball. I'm in madrigal choir and art club, too. Dad says it's good to stay busy. Looks good on college applications."

"It's true."

"Dad wants me to go to Northwestern next year," she says. "His alma mater."

"Good school."

"Where'd you go?" she asks, lashes batting.

"Rutgers," I say, swallowing the hard ball in my throat.

"Never heard of it." She shrugs. "I'm sure it was a good school though. Oh, hey. I was going to tell you, I think I want to go into higher education administration, like you and my dad. Would it be okay if you mentored me for a bit? I'd stay out of the way. I just want to maybe shadow you for a while? See if it's really the job for me?"

"Of course." Like I can say 'no' to my boss' daughter.

Her mouth pulls wide at the corners. "Really? Thank you so much!"

Retrieving some cash from my wallet, I pay her for her time and walk her to the door before she squeezes any more favors out of me.

Chapter 14

HALSTON

"ABOUT DAMN TIME. Guys, Halston is here!" Courtney loops her arm around my shoulders and pulls me into her apartment in downtown Rosefield Friday night. Vic and Tab think I'm sleeping over at Emily's tonight, and she's covering for me. I should be in the clear. "Look at you!"

She points at my outfit, a skimpy tank top and short shorts I wore underneath my other outfit, changing in the bathroom of a nearby gas station on my way over. I shoved my other clothes in my bag, touched up my makeup, changed into some heels, and trekked over to the Mayflower Apartments on Hillside Drive.

Courtney's place is nice—which I guess she can afford since she "makes the big bucks" at Big Boulders. It's a two-bedroom on the ground level overlooking the complex's sparkling pool, and everything is new. The carpet. The cabinets. The building itself.

"Guys, this is Halston." Courtney leans on me, her words slurring. "She works with me."

About twenty unfamiliar faces fill the place, but I don't let it rattle me.

When Court gets distracted by the newest guest, I head to the kitchen, rummaging through the bottles on the counter.

"I can make you a drink." I glance up. A tall drink of water with sandy brown hair and pale brown eyes stands on the other side of the granite island.

"I'm good." I force a smile. He looks at me the way the customers at Big Boulders do, like I'm on display for their personal enjoyment.

"You don't recognize me, do you?" he asks.

I study his face. "Should I?"

"I work at Big Boulders. I'm the weekend bartender." He starts clearing out the empty bottles and cans, tossing them in Courtney's trash. "I'm always coming when you're going. You've probably never noticed me before."

"Yeah, you're right. I haven't. I'm sorry."

We both reach for a bottle at the same time, an open bottle of whiskey.

"You can have it," he says, turning to grab me a red plastic cup. "Would probably taste better with Coke. That's the cheap stuff. It's going to burn going down. And you want ice. This has been sitting out for hours."

"You're the expert."

"Just let me." Within thirty seconds, the tall drink of water mixes my drink and hands it over. I take a small sip, a trick I learned years ago. If you drink too much at one time, it could make you sick or send you into a coughing fit. "You like it?"

I nod. "Not bad ... what's your name? I'm sorry."

"Gage," he says. "And you're Halston. Is it weird that I know that?"

"Yeah." I take another sip, fighting my smile. He's cute. But I'm not in the market for trouble. "Kind of."

"Nah." He shakes his head. "I just heard them talking about you, that's all. You don't forget a name like that. Or those green eyes."

"Talking about me?" I ignore his flattery. "Hope it was juicy, whatever they were saying."

Gage laughs. "It was nothing bad. They were just saying that you could be very good for business and they hope you didn't quit."

"Good for business ..."

"Look, sometimes we scrape the bottom of the barrel when it comes to servers," he says. "Not a lot of, uh, beautiful women, aspire to work at Big Boulders. Not that there's anything wrong with it, but, like, you're one of the prettiest ones we've had in a long time."

I take a bigger drink this time, willing myself not to cough. "Can you please stop saying I'm pretty?"

His expression falls. "I'm sorry. I thought girls liked to hear that kind of thing."

"Let's cut the bullshit, all right? You want to fuck me tonight," I say. "And it's not going to happen."

Gage freezes, saying nothing for a second. I've sucked the words right out of his mouth, but that's the only thing I'll be sucking tonight.

"Look, you're cute. And you're nice. But you're still not getting laid," I say. "What kind of girl would I be if I gave it up to the first guy who approached me?"

He's still silent, but at least he's blinking.

"I'm on the money, aren't I?" I laugh, eyes scanning the room, and I find myself wondering what Kerouac's up to tonight.

The alcohol turns warm in my veins and suddenly my cares drift away on a cloud of nothingness.

Gage mutters something under his breath before shaking his head and walking away. I don't 'do' the nice ones anyway. I have standards, damn it.

Standing alone in the kitchen, I watch people come and go, grabbing drinks and making messes. Checking my phone a few minutes later, I press the Karma app.

Congratulations! You've reached thirty Karma points! You may now communicate with Kerouac using our Karma-issued phone numbers! Press here to make your first call!

My heart pounds in my ears, whooshing and rushing the way it does when I'm about to do something I know I shouldn't be doing. With heated skin and wicked intentions, I push my way through the partygoers and end up on the patio outside. The air is chilly for an evening in July, but I'm too distracted by what I'm about to do to care.

Pressing the flashing green button, I take a seat when the line begins to ring.

I cross my legs, ankle bouncing as I bite my thumbnail.

"Hello?"

Holy shit he sounds hot.

"*Kerouac*," I say, my voice low and breathy.

He's quiet.

"*Absinthe.*"

"Hi." I chuckle. This is weird.

"Hey. What are you doing?"

I check the time. It's almost ten o'clock. "Hope it's okay I'm calling so late."

"It's fine. I'm in bed."

"On a Friday night?" I ask.

"Family's still in town," he says.

"And if they weren't, where would you be tonight?" I ask.

"I feel like you're looking for an exciting answer, but I don't have one for you." Kerouac sighs. "I just moved to a new place. Don't really know anyone yet. I'd probably be drinking a glass of Macallan 18, enjoying the fuck out of a Cuban cigar, and reading James Joyce."

"Sounds magical."

"You're making fun of me."

"I'm not." I sit up, chin resting on my hand. I could listen to him talk forever, his voice worldly, experienced, confident. It's deep but not too deep, relaxed yet cadenced. "It's exactly the kind of answer I hoped you were going to give."

"What are you doing tonight?" he asks.

"I'm at a party."

"Having fun?"

"Not really. It's a bunch of work people and people they know. Not sure why I thought it sounded like a good idea. Really not in the mood to be social." I take another sip of my drink. It's almost gone. There's not an ice cube's chance in hell I can get Gage to hook me up with another. "Kind of want to leave."

Maybe in another version of our lives, he'd ask me to meet him somewhere. We'd walk around at night, under the cover of a moonless sky, discussing literature and basking in our insane chemistry. He'd kiss me. Then he'd take me home. Fuck my brains out—but *not* break my heart—and in the morning, I'd make him pancakes before going for round two.

In a perfect world, I suppose …

"Why don't you want to be there?" he asks.

Dragging in a lungful of heavy, night air, I contemplate my response. "I don't even have an answer for you. Didn't feel like hanging out at home tonight but now that I'm here, it's kind of lame."

"Do you need a ride?" he asks.

My heart gallops. I was thinking of calling Emily a second ago.

"Why? You offering?" My response sounds more eager than I intended.

"I'm offering to call you a Lyft." He chuckles. "I feel the need to remind you that we're never going to meet. I have this idea of you, and it's perfection. I want to keep it that way. Now get back to your party, Absinthe. Make some bad decisions for me. Try to have some fun. I'll call you tomorrow."

"Such a fucking tease," I say with a smirk before hanging up.

Chapter 15

FORD

THE SATURDAY MORNING news fills the silence of an empty, Arlo-less house as I unpack the last of my boxes. It's kind of lonely without that little guy, but I'm glad to be done with Bree invading my space—literally and figuratively. Each day, her clothes would get progressively skimpier, her smile would get progressively sultrier, and her pathetic attempts at flirting would get progressively bolder.

Not to mention Arlo couldn't stand her. He said she was on her phone the entire time and when she wasn't, she was grilling him about me.

So much for the superintendent's daughter being a safe choice.

Never. Again.

I'm mid-reach for my coffee when the Karma app on my phone begins to vibrate, telling me I have a call.

"Good morning, Absinthe," I answer. "I was just thinking of you."

"Liar." God, I love her voice. Picturing this voice coming from those sultry lips in her photograph makes me hard as a rock.

"How was the rest of the party?"

"Fun," she says. "I made some bad decisions, just like you told me to."

"And what did you do?"

"I fucked a guy in the bathroom," she says, her tone matter-of-fact. "He was big, and he fucked me so hard, Kerouac. I thought he was going to split me in two. And when we were finished, he ate my pussy until I came *three times*."

"Bullshit."

She laughs. "I know. You believed me for a second though."

"I did." So much so that it was beginning to make me envious of the faceless, big-cocked stranger who got to devour my Absinthe.

"I like your voice," she says after a silent lull. "It's sexy. You should read to me sometime."

"That's a strange request."

"Just do it. Grab the nearest book and read to me," she pleads. "Come on. My hand is down my pants right now, fingering my pussy. I want to cum to the sound of your voice, Kerouac. Please?"

My throat is tight, my cock straining against the fabric of my sweats. Grabbing a book from the coffee table beside me, I flip to an open page and begin to read, taking my time, keeping my voice steady and rhythmic. "*And I know I am deathless, I know this orbit of mine cannot be swept by a carpenter's compass, I know I shall not pass like a child's carlacue, cut with a burnt stick at night. I know I am August ...*"

Absinthe exhales a sweet, soft moan, her breath quickening with each word I utter.

"Keep going," she whispers, and so I do.

I turn to the next page, and I read another line, and another. Her breath grows forced and impatient and then quiet altogether.

"Walt Whitman." Her breathy rasp mixed with her intelligence is like sexual napalm. "Very nice."

For the first time in weeks, I find myself wanting to touch her—physically touch her. And knowing it's an impossibility makes me want her even more.

The ache in my cock is a distraction that refuses to go away, and while I'd love nothing more than to lie around on this lazy Saturday, waxing poetic with Absinthe and getting lost in the sound of her sweet, sexy voice, I've got a little problem to take care of.

"I should shower. Work and all," she says. The image of her in the shower does nothing to help my current situation. "Thanks for … that."

Absinthe ends the call, and I close my eyes, slipping my hands down my shorts and jerking the length of my throbbing cock while a fantasy plays out in my head. In my mind's eye, I'm punishing her for teasing me about fucking another guy at the party. And I'm showing her how good I can make her feel, how she'll never need another man but me so long as she lives. I gift her with demanding kisses, animalistic thrusts, her ass cheeks red and warm from the slap of my palms.

And in my reverie, she gazes at me, her green eyes full, and she declares that it's only me.

I'm the only thing she wants.

The only thing she'll ever need.

Chapter 16

HALSTON

I COUNT THE WEEKENDS.

There are five.

Five more Saturdays, five more Sundays, then I'll be done with Big Boulders. I'll have saved around three grand, purchased my car, and burned my uniform.

My back and feet are throwing themselves a pity party, but at least I have tomorrow off. Mondays and Tuesdays are officially my off days now, though I'm not opposed to picking up a few shifts here and there. So far, no one's asked. I think they know I hate working there, but no one's actually come out and asked me yet.

That said, I think I do a pretty decent job at hiding my true feelings. I've learned to smile on command, walk with enough bounce in my step that my breasts bounce, and I've yet to screw up anyone's order, which apparently puts me in the running for this month's top server bonus.

Not to mention gratuities are getting better by the hour.

Who knew I was such a hustler?

Tugging my pajama drawer open, I reach for my vinyl makeup bag to add today's tip money to my growing collection. Last week I asked Vic about my birth certificate so I could open a bank account, but he said he knew nothing about its whereabouts, that I'd have to request another copy from the state, so I submitted my request online and received an email stating it could take three to twelve weeks unless I paid two hundred bucks for a rushed copy.

But tonight the cherry red pouch feels lighter than usual ...

Yanking the zipper, I'm seconds from throwing up when I see it's empty.

Bree.

That fucking twat.

Marching toward my door, I pull it open so hard it slams against the wall. Storming down the hall, I burst into Bree's room. She's lying on her stomach on her bed, earbuds in her ear as she does homework, her feet bopping to the music.

I yank the earbuds.

"Hey!" She rolls over to face me, resting on her side. "Oh. It's just you."

"Give me my money." I try to appear intimidating, keeping my shoulders lifted and my hands on my hips, but my eyes are burning and my mouth feels wavy and I'm seconds from simultaneously puking, crying, and screaming. "*Now.*"

Bree leers. "No clue what you're talking about."

"Yes, you do. You stole my tip money."

"Oh, you mean, your tip money from the Waterfront

Sea Food Restaurant?" She sits up, her blonde lashes fluttering as she fights a bitchy smirk.

"What'd you do with it?"

She shrugs.

I want to smack her. I want to rip her hair from her scalp, one handful at a time.

"I thought it was odd," she says, brows furrowed. "You were making so much money waitressing, like even for a nice restaurant. So, I did some checking. I went into Waterfront for lunch one day, when you were supposedly working, but the manager there said she'd never heard of you. So, then I asked myself ... is she selling drugs?"

Rolling my eyes, I tune her out, rifling through her drawers and closets, looking under her bed, turning over pillows.

"You're never going to find it," she says, admitting what I already knew. "It's gone."

"What. The fuck. Did you do with it?" My jaw tightens, aching.

I've never hated anyone this much in my life.

All those weekends. The aching feet. The tired backs. The grease-scented skin. The disgusting customers. The blatant stares. The selling of my soul.

All of it was for *nothing*.

"You know, you really should've kept it in a bank account," she says. "That's what normal people do. They put their money in a safe place, where no one else can touch it. Guess your parents didn't teach you that, did they? I bet they never even had bank accounts."

Before I can stop myself, I lunge at Bree, pinning her scrawny body beneath mine. She's screaming, but the house is so big I doubt her parents can hear her.

It's only when I have my hands around her throat and

her lips are turning a mottled shade of blue that I realize I've gone too far.

I let her go, my chest rising and falling as I struggle to breathe with all the adrenaline coursing my system.

She reaches for her neck, coughing, choking on spittle as she scrambles toward the head of her bed like I'm some serial killer about to murder her.

I've scared the hell out of her, but to be fair, I've just scared the hell out of myself as well. I'm not a violent person. I don't have these tendencies. I've never wanted to hurt anyone in my life. But I want to hurt her. I want to inflict pain. Teach her a lesson. Make her sorry.

This is fucking *war*.

"You're paying me back." I point a shaking finger at her. "Every last fucking dime. And if you don't? I'll make your senior year a living fucking hell. That's a promise."

Bree looks like she's about to cry. "I told you. It's … gone."

"Where is it?!"

"I donated it to a charity," she manages to squeak.

My gaze falls to the diamond pendant around her neck, then to the Gucci watch on her left wrist. Come to think of it, her entire outfit is new. And this morning, I spotted her carrying a little Louis Vuitton handbag.

"You lying bitch," I growl. "Hope you kept the receipts."

Bree scoffs. She doesn't need to answer. I already know. She destroyed the evidence, and since she paid with cash, it'll be impossible to return those items without any proof of purchase.

Refusing to look at her disgusting face a second more, I run back to my room, slip on the first pair of shoes I can find—pleather ballet flats—and get the fuck out of here.

I walk until my heels throb with the threat of blisters,

down several tree-lined blocks, past beautiful houses with manicured lawns and expensive cars in the driveways, and finally past the iron gates that guard this stupid neighborhood from the rest of the world.

I'm not sure how long I've been walking, but I manage to find a little park at the end of a cul de sac in an older part of town.

It's dark now, the end of another shit-tastic day in my shit-tastic life. I'd sleep here if I knew I could get away with it. The thought of going back to Uncle Vic's and being under the same roof as that fucking bitch makes me want to gouge my eyes out with rusty pliers. But if I don't come home, Tab will freak out and say to Vic, "I told you this was a bad idea!" and then I'll be on the streets.

A group of teenage boys in baggy t-shirts pass me on skateboards. They're way too young to be out this late, and they smirk when they see me, circling, swarming.

"Hey," one of them says to me, slowing down. "You lost?"

"Fuck off."

"Suck my dick." He spits at me, missing.

"I would if you had one." I glare.

His friends laugh. They skate away.

That's what I thought.

Continuing, I make my way to the park, tucking myself in a plastic tunnel like I used to when I was little and my parents were screaming at each other over missing drugs.

I feel safe in the tunnel. Cut off from the outside world. As a young girl, it was my armor.

I stay as long as I can, but Vic and Tab will freak if I'm not home before ten, and it's already half past nine.

Sucking up my pride and refusing to let this be the end, I tell myself tomorrow's another day. I'll work harder, flirt more, pick up extra shifts. I'll make that money back and then some. I'll get my fucking car. And then I'll get the hell out of here.

———

"TODD WANTS to see you before you start your shift." Courtney doesn't smile when she sees me the next morning. Her mouth is pulled into a frown and her eyes carry pity.

"What's wrong?" I ask.

She shrugs, pretending not to know.

She knows.

My heart races, and I can't help but feel I'm marching to my death as I head back to the door with the crooked "manager" plaque.

"You wanted to talk to me?" I stand in his doorway wearing a hopeful smile.

"Hey there. Why don't you have a seat?" His lips press into a straight line. He won't make eye contact. "Shut the door too, will you?"

"Am I being fired?" I can't breathe. I can't fucking breathe.

"It's been brought to my attention that you'll be attending Rosefield High this fall." His voice is flat, and today he's wearing a plain blue polo and khakis, a departure from his usual jeans-and-quirky-t-shirt uniform.

"Yeah? So? I'll be nineteen in early December."

"We have a strict no high school students policy," he says. "It's straight from corporate. It's nothing personal. Frankly, I wish we could make an exception for you."

"Why didn't you ask me that when you hired me?" My words are terse, my skin hot.

Todd places his hands in the air. "I know, Halston. It's my fault. I just ... you look so much older than you are. I figured you were at least twenty, twenty-one. You checked the box saying you were over eighteen. To be honest, I don't look at the paperwork or any of that. That all goes to HR at corporate."

"So, there's nothing you can do? I'm one of your best servers, and I've only been here a few weeks."

"I know you are. You're a great addition to the team and the customers really like you. You were our most-requested last weekend," he says. "But a policy is a policy. I'm sorry."

I turn to leave, eyes stinging. The smell of the greasy kitchen wafts down the hall, making me nauseous.

"Oh, HR wanted me to have you sign this waiver really quick before you go," he adds.

"I'm not signing a damn thing."

Maybe I should accept half the blame. Maybe I should sign the damn form and walk out of here with my head held high, but I'm not in a good place.

And right now, I'm in the mood to burn my life to the ground.

It's the only way I'm ever going to be able to rise from the ashes.

Chapter 17

FORD

"I WANT TO MEET YOU." Absinthe's smooth cadence purrs into the earpiece of my phone.

I'm in the office early today, trying to get things in order before Bree shows up. She told her father about our mentorship agreement and he insisted that we get started right away so she has time to decide on a major before filling out her application to Northwestern.

"I know you do."

"So?"

"It's not going to happen." I exhale, rifling through some leftover paperwork the previous principal had tucked away in the bottom of a seldom-used drawer. "Not that I don't think about it every fucking minute of every fucking hour of every fucking day."

She sighs. "You have no idea what it does to me when you say shit like that."

"You're right. I don't. Enlighten me."

"I don't even know what you look like, Kerouac, and I know with one-hundred percent certainty that I would fuck the shit out of you if you asked me to. If you named the time and the place, I'd be there with fucking bells on. Tied to my nipples."

I laugh at the image.

"Seriously though," she continues. "You're such a mind fuck, and it drives me wild."

"Mission accomplished."

"I got fired from my job yesterday." She changes the subject.

"Congratulations."

"Heh." She releases a breath into the phone. "If only I shared your sentiments."

"You hated your job."

"I needed my job," she says.

"Find another. There are hundreds of restaurants in this town."

"Yeah, but this one was a cash cow. I'll have to work twice as hard for half as much anywhere else."

"Then maybe you're in the wrong profession. Did you go to college, Absinthe?" I assume the answer is yes. She speaks with intelligence and grace, and she's the most well-read woman I've ever had the privilege of chatting with.

"Nope."

"That's surprising." I come across another stack of papers. "Why not?"

"It's complicated."

"It's never too late," I say. "What's your dream job?"

"I just want to marry some rich guy, have a couple of his babies, and spend my days catching up on *Real House-wives* between spin class and Botox touch ups."

I cock my head, my mouth pulled up at one side as I formulate a response.

"I'm fucking with you, Kerouac," she says.

"Good. I was about to lose all respect for you."

"I don't know what I want to do with my life."

I begin to offer her words of comfort when Abbott's daughter stands at my door, dressed in a skirt much shorter than what's appropriate and a white blouse that's damn near transparent.

"I have to go." I hang up on Absinthe, shoving my phone in my pocket. "Bree. Come in."

Bree tucks a strand of hair behind one ear before placing her purse on the edge of my desk. Taking a seat, she crosses her legs, letting her panties flash—not that I'm looking, but they're hard to miss out of my periphery when they're neon fucking pink.

"So excited." She claps her hands together, and I imagine she's the girl who tries too hard to fit in. She's the girl who doesn't get invited to parties, doesn't get asked to prom, but latches onto the "cool" crowd because she refuses to believe for a second that those people don't want to be friends with her. Girls like Bree don't take social cues like everyone else does. They see what they want to see, believe what they want to believe.

She's completely unfit to be an administrator in this field.

Leaning forward, she tilts her non-existent cleavage in my direction. "What are we working on today?"

"Just going through some old paperwork Principal Waters left behind," I say, avoiding eye contact with any part of her body.

"Anything I can do to help?"

"These are confidential." I shove them aside, working on another pile. "Thought you just wanted to shadow me?"

"I do."

"Then you'll need to sit back and watch. That's what shadowing is."

"Oh?" She sits up, frowning. "I thought I'd be helping you with stuff?"

"That would be an internship."

"Where does the mentoring come in then?" she asks.

"After you've completed your masters' degree." And hopefully I'm long gone by then.

"Oh." Her shoulders slump, but I feel her watching me. "I like your watch."

"Thank you. It was my grandfather's."

"My necklace belonged to my grandmother." She tugs on the little pearl pendant around her neck, only the clasp snaps and the dainty chain falls between her breasts. "Ha. Whoops."

She giggles, digging around, nearly exposing her tits in the process.

"Excuse me for a moment, Bree." I show myself out, needing physical distance from her so she gets the hint.

I'm disinterested.

Wandering the halls for a few minutes, I pass a maintenance worker and a teacher using the computer lab. When I get back to the main office, I stop outside the door and get a drink of water. Whatever kills time.

Bernie, the custodian I met at the staff meeting a while back, passes by, pushing an empty trash can, and I ask him to step inside the office with me and wait outside my door while I deal with a student. One of the things that's been instilled in me since the beginning of my career is that it never hurts to enlist a witness when you're approaching a formidable situation.

Bree Abbott is, without question, a formidable situation.

Returning to my office, I stop in my tracks when I find

her perched on the edge of my desk, legs crossed and her little skirt pulled to her upper thigh.

I called it.

"Principal Hawthorne." She hops down. "I was wondering if you were coming back."

"Does your father know you left the house like this today?" I force a breath through my nostrils, arms crossed.

Bree rolls her eyes. "Negative. He had a seven AM tee time."

"One of the things we need to go over if you wish to continue shadowing me, Ms. Abbott, is professional dress," I say. "As well as a professional code of conduct. Sexuality has no place in the school."

"So, I take it you like my outfit?" She pretends to be shocked, placing her hand over her breasts before giggling. "About time you noticed."

"Absolutely not," I say. "And it's not like you gave me a choice."

"All those things I wore when I babysat your nephew," she says, "those were for you. And you didn't even act like you cared."

She pouts like a sullen child.

"This is highly inappropriate," I say, jaw flexing. "I'm going to have to ask you to leave."

Bree exhales, sauntering toward the door. "Fine. I guess I'll just tell my father you don't want to work with me because you're having difficulty maintaining professional boundaries in my presence."

Stepping outside my office, I motion for Bernie to come closer. Bree's jaw falls when she sees him.

"Just making sure you're hearing this entire conversation," I say.

"Haven't missed a single word," he says, arms folded as he gives her a hard stare.

Her eyes turn glassy, and she glares at me, as if *I've* committed the ultimate act of betrayal, and without saying another word, she pushes past me and disappears out the door.

"Thanks." I place my hand on his shoulder. His thick gray hair and hunched posture suggest he's pushing closer to retirement with each school year.

"Wasn't the first time. Won't be the last," he says, showing himself out. Before he leaves, he stops and turns to me. "That one's trouble. I'd keep your distance."

"Thanks for the head's up, Bernie." I close my door. Returning to my desk, I hold my head in my hands and breathe out. "Fuck, fuck, fuck."

Chapter 18

HALSTON

"WHAT ARE YOU READING?" Kerouac asks. It's a rainy Tuesday night in August, three weeks until school starts.

"*Rebecca*." Lightning flashes outside my window. "For the fourth time. Started it again a couple weeks ago, then I got busy. It's crazy how much time you have when you're not working though. I might read it a fifth time just for the hell of it."

"A classic. Read to me."

"Why? So *you* can jerk off this time?" I chuckle.

"No," he says. "I did that a half hour before you called."

"Were you thinking about me?"

"You and only you," he says in such a way that I wholeheartedly believe him.

I smile, cracking the spine of *Rebecca*. "*I am glad it cannot happen twice, the fever of first love. For it is a fever, and a burden, too, whatever the poets may say.*"

"Have you ever loved anyone, Absinthe?" he asks.

"Not in any remarkable kind of way." The roll of thunder in the distance rattles the windows.

"Has anyone ever loved you?"

"Not in any remarkable kind of way," I echo, chuckling once. "Plenty of guys have claimed to have loved me. I've yet to say it back to anyone. I don't want to say it until I know for sure that I mean it. What about you? Have you loved anyone?"

"Not so much that I couldn't live without them," he says. "So, in a way, no. Because if you truly love someone, you can't stand to be without them. I've never felt that about anyone."

"Mr. Complicated."

"Always." He sighs. "Love is overrated anyway. But sex? Sex is … everything."

"My thoughts exactly." I play it cool, neglecting to inform him that on the nights when my body refuses to rest, I lie in bed thinking of the two of us. And when I think of us, I think of the prospect of love—something I've yet to think about with anyone else.

And maybe it doesn't make sense. But it means something. I just don't know what.

"As much as I'm at odds with the idea of love, I can't help but find myself in love with the idea of you," I blurt.

It comes out of nowhere. I didn't rehearse it, didn't give it a second thought before allowing it to leave my lips. It felt like the right time to bare my soul, a decision I may come to regret in the immediate future because my words are met with dead silence.

"Absinthe," he says an endless moment later, speaking the way a teacher would scold a student for talking out of turn. "You're idealizing me."

"And what's wrong with that?" I ask.

"You shouldn't idealize anyone. That's how people get hurt. Hearts get broken."

Pretty sure my heart is titanium or elastic or whatever Sia sings about.

"You're giving yourself too much credit, Kerouac," I say, trying to cover the quick bruising of my ego. Rain beads gentle on my window. Outside the storm is passing, but inside it's only getting started. "You're just a voice on the other end of a phone. A faceless man with a dirty mind and a love of books. I might be in love with the idea of you, but trust me, you could never break me."

Many have tried.

None have succeeded.

If he only knew what I've been through, he'd know it would take a lot more than an innocent crush on an Internet stranger to damage this heart. My entire life, nothing's ever come easy. The kinds of simple luxuries afforded to everyone else seem to have skipped over me.

Some people are born with silver spoons. I was born with a rusted paring knife.

And still, it didn't break me.

"Maybe we've crossed a line." He exhales.

I sit up.

His single sentence takes this entire conversation in a completely different direction.

"No," I say. The room begins to tilt.

"This was supposed to be phone sex and meaningless conversations," he said. "I think we took it too far."

"Why are you saying this?" My chest burns, swells. A moment ago we were talking about *Rebecca*. I want to go back. I want to go back to that so I can take back what I said.

"Because I feel the same way about you—I'm falling in

love with the idea of you, of you I've dreamed you up to be."

I exhale, sinking into my pillows, relief washing over me. He feels the same way. We can work with this.

"So what now?" I ask, drawing in a cleansing breath. My mouth curls into a gentle smile. "I'm in love with the idea of you. You're in love with the idea of me. Sounds like the premise for an amazing F. Scott Fitzgerald novel, don't you think? Now we just need a good twist and a couple of complications."

"This is the end, Absinthe." He says the last words I expected to hear, going in a completely different direction than the one I anticipated.

My eyes blur, fat tears dripping down my cheeks, leaving cold, itchy tracks. I'm at a complete loss for words for the first time with him. In fact, I can't even breathe right now.

"Absinthe," he says after a bout of silence.

"Seriously? Just like that ... you don't want to talk to me because you're *feeling* something?" I manage to fire back at him. "This is bullshit."

"I told you I was complicated."

"You're not complicated," I say, teeth gritted. "You're a coward."

"I'd only hurt you." Kerouac exhales. "I hurt everyone. That's just how it is."

"So, we can't even talk on the phone? You just ... you just want to cut ties? Walk away like this never happened?"

"No." His voice is louder. He's never taken this tone with me. This man, this Kerouac, I don't know him. "That's not what I want. But if we keep talking, one of these days I know I'm going to give in. I'm going to meet you somewhere. I'm going to fuck the hell out of you. I might even convince myself that I'm in love with you after a while. And then I'm going to break you. And I don't want to do that to you. You mean too much to me."

"You're so full of shit." I release an incredulous laugh. "And you don't know that's how it would go."

"I do," he says. "You're not the kind of woman I could just fuck and not think twice about the next day."

"And that's a bad thing?!"

"It's a bad thing if you're me." He's quiet for a moment. "I don't do commitment, Absinthe. Never have. And even if I did, I'm not in a place in my life where I have the time to dedicate to a relationship."

My heart sinks. It feels like a breakup, but it hurts a hell of a lot more. The physical sting radiating through my body, the gasps of breath in my lungs, the weight on my chest … it's all too much.

"Fine." My voice shakes with that one little word. "Goodbye, Kerouac. It's been nice talking to you. I hope someday you find exactly what you were looking for. I'm sorry I couldn't be your exception."

Kerouac says nothing, but I hear him breathing on the other end, almost as if he's second-guessing his decision, not yet wanting to end the call.

So I hang up first.

Because … fuck him.

It takes a moment for me to catch my breath, to accept what just happened. When I finally come to, I add him to the long list of people who've left me, people who've decided for whatever reason that they want nothing to do with me.

My parents, a long list of foster families, a few friends here and there along the way, and now some faceless internet stranger I had no business fancying into the man of my dreams.

The tiniest fraction of my heart squeezes as it clings

onto what might have been, refusing to accept that it's over, that I meant nothing to Kerouac, and that everything he ever told me was probably a lie.

But the rest of me wants to move on, pretend like he never happened.

Besides, what choice do I have? It's not like I have a face or name. It's not like I'd even know him if we ever did cross paths. The fact of the matter is, Kerouac doesn't exist.

He's not real, at least not in my life.

And not anymore.

Pressing my finger against the little green Karma app, I wait until it begins to shake and then I press the little 'x' in the corner.

Goodbye, Kerouac.

Chapter 19

FORD

3 WEEKS Later

"YOU WANTED TO SEE ME, Principal Hawthorne?"

I know that voice. I'd know it anywhere.

Glancing up from my desk, I find a girl in skintight athletic leggings and a low-cut tank top standing in my office doorway, her full lips wrapped around a shiny sucker and a familiar electric jade gaze trained on me.

It's *her.*

The woman I spent most of all summer chatting with under the anonymous veil of a dating app—one specifically meant for adults seeking connections but not commitment. I purchased a stock photo for seven dollars, chose a pseudonym, *Kerouac,* and messaged a woman by the name of *Absinthe* who quoted Hemingway in her bio when everyone else quoted Nickelback and John Legend.

Fuck.

Me.

"You must be Halston." My skin is on fire. I stand, smooth my tie, and point to the seat across from me. I never knew her name, but I'd know that voice anywhere. I can't even count how many times I came to the sound of her breathy rasp describing all the wicked things she'd do to me if we ever met, reading me excerpts from *Rebecca* and Proust. "Take a seat."

She takes her time pulling the sucker from her mouth before strutting to my guest chair, lowering herself, cleavage first, and crossing her long legs. The tiniest hint of a smirk claims her mouth, but if she knows it's me, she's sure as hell not acting like it.

"You want to tell me what happened with Mrs. Rossi?" I ask, returning to my seat and folding my hands on my desk.

I may be a lot of things; overconfident prick, allergic to commitment, red-blooded American man …

But I'm a professional first.

"Mrs. Rossi and I had an argument," Halston says. "We were discussing the theme of *The Great Gatsby*, and she was trying to say that it was about chasing the elusive American dream. I told her she missed the entire fucking point of one of the greatest pieces of literature in existence." She takes another suck of her candy before continuing, then points it in my direction. "The real theme has to do with manipulation and dishonesty, Principal Hawthorne. Everyone in that book was a fucking liar, most of all Jay, and in the end, he got what he deserved. They all did."

My cock strains against the fabric of my pants. It's her voice. It's her goddamned sex-on-fire voice that's doing this to me. That and her on point dissection of classic American literature. Sexy, intelligent, outspoken. Three elusive qualities I've yet to find in another human being. Until her. And knowing that now, I couldn't even have her if I wanted her, isn't doing me any favors. If I don't compose myself, I'm going to be hard as a fucking rock.

"Language," I say. The room is growing hotter now, but I keep a stern, undeterred presence.

She rolls her eyes. "I'm an adult, Principal Hawthorne. I can say words like *fuck*."

"Not in my office, you can't." I exhale. "And not in class either. That's why Mrs. Rossi sent you here."

"The jackass behind me was drawing swastikas on his notebook, but I get sent down here for saying 'fuck.'" Her head shakes.

"I'll discuss that with Mrs. Rossi privately." I scribble a note to myself and shove it aside.

"You're really young for a principal." Her charged gaze drags the length of me. "Did you just graduate from college or something?"

Six years of school and two years of teaching place me in the budding stages of a career shaping and educating the minds of tomorrow's leaders, but I refuse to dignify her question with a response.

"My age is irrelevant," I say.

"Age is everything." She twirls a strand of pale hair around her finger, her lips curling up in the corners. The cute-and-coy shtick must work on everyone else, but it's not going to work on me. Not here anyway. And not anymore.

"I said *my* age is irrelevant."

"Am I the first student you've ever had to discipline?" She sits up, crossing and uncrossing her legs with the provocative charm of a 1940s pin up. "Wait, are you going to discipline me?"

I take mental notes for her file.

- *Challenges authority*
- *Difficulty conducting herself appropriately*
- *Possible boundary issues*

"I'm not going to punish you, Halston. Consider this a verbal warning." I release a hard breath through my nose as I study her, refusing to allow my eyes to drift to the soft swell of her breasts casually peeking out of her top. Knowing her so intimately over the phone, and being in her presence knowing she's completely off limits, makes it difficult to maintain my unshaken demeanor. "From now on, I'd like you to refrain from using curse words while on school grounds. It's disruptive to the other students who are here to actually glean something from their high school education."

"I don't know." Her lips bunch at the corner, and she fights a devilish grin. "I mean, I can try, but 'fuck' is one of my favorite words in the English language. What if I can't stop saying it? Then what?"

"Then we'll worry about that when the time comes," I say.

"You could always bend me over your knee and spank me." She rises, wrapping her lips around the sucker before plucking it out of her mouth with a wet pop. "Or maybe you could fuck my brains out and break my heart."

"*Excuse me?*" My skin heats as she recites my words, but I refuse to let her see that she's having any kind of effect on me.

"You're him," she says, as if it's some ace she's been keeping up her sleeve this entire time. "You're *Kerouac.*"

I'm at a rare loss for words, trying to wrap my head around all the ways this could go very fucking wrong for me.

"Don't worry. Your secret's safe with me." Halston rises, her gaze lingering on me one last time, and then just like that, she's gone.

Chapter 20

HALSTON

THE LAST BLOCK of the day is taking for-ev-er, so I ask for a hall pass and make my way around the school, loitering at every drinking fountain and every bulletin board. The teacher's probably wondering where the hell I am, but I'm not afraid to tell him I got my period. That usually shuts them up.

Rounding the corner by the front office, I'm making a beeline for drinking fountain number six when the door swings open and out walks *Kerouac*.

Or rather, Principal Hawthorne.

We both stop so as not to bump into each other, though he'd be so lucky.

I saw the way he looked at me in his office this morning, the way his body responded to my voice. I knew the instant he started talking that it was him, though it took all the strength I had to ignore his chiseled jaw, dimpled chin, thick, dark hair, and hooded, honey-brown eyes.

Principals are supposed to be old with gray hair, glasses, and dad bods.

They're not supposed to look like fucking supermodels.

Our eyes lock, and I smirk. To think, all those times I was talking to *this*.

This is what was on the other end. That stock photo doesn't even hold a candle to the striking Adonis standing before me. No wonder he doesn't want to commit. For a man like that, the world is one giant, all-you-can-eat buffet of beautiful women.

"Excuse me," he says, stepping out of my way like a gentleman.

God, that voice. That gentle, low rasp of a voice. I about creamed my pants when he did the overhead announcements earlier. Almost had to excuse myself from class so I could finish the job in an empty bathroom stall.

It doesn't help that all anyone can talk about lately is how fucking hot the new principal is. I overheard a group of senior girls earlier making a wager to see who could sleep with him before they went off to college. The winner was to get a thousand bucks.

Ha. Stupid girls.

If they only knew who they were dealing with.

But I'm no better than they are. I know the man that lies beyond the carefully crafted exterior, behind those dark, hooded eyes and that confident stride. The man on the inside is a million times sexier than any of them could begin to imagine.

"You're excused." I make my way to the fountain, press the button, and lower my mouth to the jet stream of fresh water. His stare is heavy, weighted, and I'd give anything to know what he thinks when he looks at me.

The halls are empty and quiet. It's just the two of us.

Across the way a male teacher drones on about World

War I and the Lusitania, and when I glance into the classroom, I spot Bree sitting in the front row, gnawing on the tip of her pen as her eyes wander in our direction.

I move out of her line of sight. Ford follows.

"I'd like to talk to you sometime," he says. "About—"

I rise, turning to him. "About what? Nothing happened."

He squints, studying me. He must think I'm planning to blackmail him, but he'd be mistaken. While his rejection stung at the time, I'm over it and I've got bigger fish to fry —specifically a bottom-feeder by the name of Bree.

"I tried to reach out to you after we last spoke," he says, keeping his voice down. "I wanted to make sure you were okay. Couldn't find you on the app."

"I deleted it."

His lips press, and he nods. All those long phone calls and messaging sessions this summer, and the man can't find more than a handful of things to say to me now. He must still be in shock. I can't say that I blame him. He'd have a hell of a lot more to lose than I would. The stakes are higher for him. I might be legal and an adult, but there isn't a single red-blooded soul in this entire school district who'd be okay with a principal striking up a sexual relationship with one of his students.

On paper, it would seem atrocious. Scandalous. Disgusting.

But it doesn't keep me from wishing we could've made it work, as insane as that is.

"You know, we're going to be seeing a lot of each other around here, so let's do ourselves a favor and get the fuck over what happened," I say, arms folded as I maintain my icy demeanor. My ego may be bruised, my heart may be longing for him, but I'll be damned if I run away with my tail tucked like some rejected schoolgirl. "If you're going to look at me like that every time you see me——"

"I'm sorry." He won't stop staring. "I just … I can't believe it's *you*."

"Believe it." I begin to walk backwards, distancing myself from him.

He may have closed the door a few weeks ago, but I'm the one who locked it.

Chapter 21

FORD

PULLING INTO MY DRIVEWAY, I kill the engine and exhale.

I read her file today.

After she left my office this morning, I contacted the school guidance counselor and asked her to send me anything and everything she had on Halston Kessler.

By the time lunch was through, I had a thick file on my desk with "Confidential" stamped over each and every page.

I'm not exactly sure what I was looking for, but whatever it was, I found it.

And then some.

Bree's silver Prius pulls into the Abbotts' driveway, parking outside the third stall of their garage, and I watch from my car as a passenger climbs out the other side. The girl has wild blonde hair, and she flings a bag over one shoulder as she heads inside, not waiting for Bree.

Bree yells something.

The girl turns back.

It's her. Halston.

I'd have never paired the two of them as friends—they couldn't possibly be more different, but high school's a trying time and stranger things have happened.

Halston comes back to the car, retrieving something from the back seat. Bree spots me, waving, and Halston glances in my direction. I've no choice but to get out and say hello. Sitting in the car, staring, would be inappropriate at this point.

Exiting my car, I walk toward them, doing my best to be a friendly principal and not a man who spent the entire school day obsessing over a woman he has no business so much as thinking about.

"Hi," I say, hands resting on my hips. Halston keeps back, staring. Bree smiles, acting like nothing happened.

We're all just fucking acting like nothing happened.

"How was your first day, Principal?" Bree asks.

Glancing toward Halston, because I can't help myself, I nod. "It went well, thank you."

Halston smirks, taking a sip of her iced coffee, her red lips wrapped around a green Starbucks straw.

"I didn't know you lived here." Halston moves my way.

Bree watches us. "How could you not know? He moved in two months ago."

Well shit. Halston must be Abbott's niece.

Halston shrugs, electric jade eyes trained on me. "Guess I was a little too … preoccupied to notice."

"We should probably head in," Bree says, still observing.

"You go ahead." Halston takes another sip. "I'll be in in a sec."

She loiters for a moment before disappearing inside,

though I fully expect her to watch us from behind a pulled curtain.

"We couldn't really talk earlier," I say, closing the space between us. "I just want to make sure you're okay."

Halston rolls her eyes. "Good god. You must think I'm weak or something."

"That's not true." I look at her, but all I can think about is her file.

Everything she's been through.

Everything she's overcome.

"The good news is, guys like you are a dime a dozen," she says, shrugging.

"Guys like me?" I smirk. "What's that supposed to mean?"

"You know, the ones who're afraid to commit, afraid to limit their options."

"It was never about limiting my options." I exhale, pinching the bridge of my nose. Every person I've ever loved has left me in some capacity or another. Over the years, I've found it easier to separate emotions from sex, to swear off commitment altogether. The only time I ever found myself second-guessing that decision was the last time I spoke to "Absinthe" on the phone.

But she hung up before I had a chance to say it.

"Anyway," she says, wrapping her lips around the straw and smiling. "I don't know about you, but I find this entire situation to be fucking hilarious."

"I don't."

"You're worried." Halston adjusts the slipping bag on her shoulder. "And you shouldn't be."

My gaze holds hers, and I wonder what it must have been like for her to grow up in a meth house. To miss years upon years of school. To know what it was like to go to bed hungry, to not have heat in the wintertime.

But there was one case note, specifically, that broke my heart in fucking two.

At thirteen, her father pimped her out to one of his friends in exchange for drugs. She lost her virginity, her innocence. And it wasn't just once. It went on, according to the notes from the social worker, for the better part of a year.

How she can stand here with her head held high and a resilient gleam in her eye is beyond me.

"Okay, if we're just going to stand here staring at each other ..." Halston lifts her brows.

"Sorry." My brows meet. "I was just thinking."

"Thinking what?"

About how beautiful she is inside and out, how genuine and unapologetic she is, and how fucking much I'm going to miss talking to her, knowing her in an intimate way that goes beyond the physical.

"Have a good night, Halston." I say her name, a reminder that my bittersweet, addictive *Absinthe* is real.

And then I watch her walk away.

Chapter 22

HALSTON

"WHAT THE HELL kind of name is Thane?" I ask my Chem II lab partner on the second day of school. If we're going to be working side by side the rest of this semester, I need to know if he can handle me. I need to prepare him.

"What the hell kind of name is Halston?" he zings back.

I smile. "Touché."

Our teacher passes out beakers and blue fluid and some form we're supposed to work on together, but we're not paying attention.

"I hope you're good at chemistry," I say, "because I'm not."

"My dad's a pharmacist," he says. "Scientology runs in the family."

"You did not just call it 'scientology.'" I laugh, rolling my eyes.

"I'm messing with you." He bumps his arm against

mine, and I'm suddenly aware of his sweeping height and the faint, agreeable scent of his crisp cologne. "My dad's a pharmacist. And I'm amazing at chemistry. You've just won the lottery of lab partners. Congratulations."

I try not to pay attention to who's who around here. I could give two shits about popularity or whether or not anyone likes me, but Thane Bennett is the guy who walks the halls of Rosefield High School with a dimpled smile, leaving throngs of swooning girls in his wake. He's an all-star quarterback. The star forward on the basketball team. And last year, he broke three state records on the track team.

But more important than any of that, Thane Bennett is the love of Bree's life. She's been crushing on him since they were kids. I used to hear all about him when we could actually tolerate each other enough to endure a sleepover here or there. I'll never forget her practically making out with his school picture, tongue and everything.

"Lucky me." I wink.

Our hands brush when he reaches for the assignment sheet.

I feel him staring, but I pretend not to notice.

When the first half of the block is over and the bell rings, our teacher lets us take a five-minute break. Thane disappears, returning with two chocolate bars from one of the vending machines. He slides one in front of me.

"What's this?" I inspect it before looking at him like he's insane.

"I was hungry. Didn't want to eat in front of you, so I got you one too."

Popular, athletic, intelligent, *and* polite.

I suppose I see the appeal …

"You don't have to do shit like this," I say. "I feel like you're trying to win me over or impress me or something."

"And what if I am?" His mouth curls at the sides, accented with two centered dimples, and his messy, sandy brown hair falls in his crystalline blue eyes. "What if I think you're pretty and funny? What if I want to ask you out?"

"Then I'd say you're blind, deaf, delusional, and wasting your time." I rip the wrapper of the chocolate bar, snapping off a tiny square and letting it melt on my tongue.

He's undeterred, still wearing that panty-melting smile that works on all the other girls. Unfortunately for him, it doesn't have the same effect on me.

"I'm taking you out Friday night," he says.

I choke on my chocolate, sputtering and coughing into my elbow.

"You are, are you?" I finally manage to ask a minute later.

"I am." He stands closer to me than before, so close his body heat merges with mine. Or maybe I'm imagining it because it suddenly got twenty degrees hotter in here.

This isn't supposed to happen. Preppy, popular boys with dimples aren't supposed to ask girls like me out, and girls like me aren't supposed to get fucking butterflies in their stomachs over this kind of shit.

"I'll check my schedule and get back to you," I say.

"I'll pick you up at six. We'll do dinner. And a movie. And after that we can just hang out somewhere and talk."

"Why?"

He scoffs, though his eyes are smiling. "Why what?"

"Why do you want to hang out with me?"

"I don't want to hang out with you. I want to take you on a date," he says. "And I want to take you on a date because I think you're beautiful. And interesting. And different."

"You've known me all of forty-five minutes."

"So?"

"What if we go on a date and you try to kiss me and I knee you in the balls and then we're stuck being lab partners for the next four months and it's really fucking awkward?" I ask.

Thane chuckles. "What if we go on a date and have an incredible time and I get to spend the next four months being lab partners with my girlfriend and it's really fucking amazing?"

"Whoa, whoa, whoa." I hold my hand up, backing away. "Slow your roll."

"My bad." He slips his hand around my wrist, pulling me back to our table. Our assignment is untouched, and glancing around, most everyone around us is nearly finished. "One step at a time. A date this Friday. Another one next Friday. And then I'll take you to homecoming the weekend after that."

I pretend to gag myself with my pointer finger. "Gross. I don't do school dances."

"Then we'll just do something else that night."

My scrutinizing stare flicks to him. He can't be serious. "But you're probably going to be in the homecoming court and all that. And you're playing in the game. You can't not go."

Thane shrugs. "I don't need a stupid crown. I'll take myself out of the running. And the game is Friday, the dance is Saturday. I'll still play."

"I have an extremely hard time believing you don't have some ulterior motive right now," I say. "Did you and your football buddies make some kind of wager? See who can snag me first?"

"Football *buddies*?" He laughs. "And no. No wager."

"That's exactly what someone who made a wager would say."

"Halston and Thane." Our teacher, Mr. Caldwell, clears his throat, standing in front of our table, the buttons of his shirt about to pop. "Let's stay on task or I'll be reassigning both of you to different partners first thing tomorrow."

Thane reaches for a beaker, measuring out fifty milliliters. I have no idea what we're supposed to do, but I grab a pen and try to look busy until Caldwell waddles away. As soon as his back is turned, we exchange looks and bite our lips to keep from laughing.

Thirty minutes later, the final bell rings.

"You want me to walk you to your car?" Thane asks as I load my notebook in my bag.

"I don't have one, but if I did, my answer would be no." I walk away, he follows.

This nicey-nice stuff is weirding me out. I'm not used to it. I don't know how to accept it with grace and a giddy smile like all the other girls. No one's ever been this sweet to me before.

"How do you get home from school? You take the bus?" he asks, walking beside me in the hall. Everyone who passes stares at the two of us like we're some kind of spectacle. This time tomorrow, the whole school is going to know Thane Bennett has a thing for the new girl, I'll suddenly be cool by association, and I still won't give a flying fuck.

"God, no," I say. "I ride with my cousin."

"What if I drove you home today?"

"Stop." We stop in the middle of the hallway, two rocks in the middle of a stream of people, all of them moving around us. "I get it. You think you like me. But you're coming on way too strong."

Thane offers a lust-drunk half-smile. "Sorry, Halston. I'm not usually like this. I just … really want to be around you for some reason."

"No, thanks." I keep walking. He follows. My rejection of his offer doesn't faze him in the slightest. "What are you doing?"

"It's just a ride," he says. "You act like I'm asking you to marry me or something. I just think you're cool. Want to get to know you, is all."

Exhaling, I think of Bree and how much she likes Thane. How much it would irk her to know he's showing interest in me: her insubordinate, ne'er do well cousin.

"Fine. You can give me a ride home." I try to pretend like I'm not thrilled, but the idea of rubbing this in Bree's face pleases me to no end. "But only because I feel sorry for you."

He chuckles. "Sorry for me?"

"Yeah." My gaze flicks onto his. "This whole lost puppy thing is kind of sad. You must be really lonely."

I pretend I don't know he's the most popular boy in school, his smile capable of melting even the coldest of panties. Except for mine. Of course.

Following Thane to his locker so he can grab his bag, I compose a quick text and send it to Bree, hearts and all:

DON'T WAIT FOR ME. GETTING A RIDE WITH THANE BENNETT!!! <3 <3 <3

FUCK THAT BITCH.

Chapter 23

FORD

"PRINCIPAL HAWTHORNE?" Bree stands in my doorway after school on Wednesday.

"Yes?" I try to hide my disdain for this girl, but I'm sure my face has given away all my cards.

"You have a second?"

The coy, coquettish act doesn't fool me. This girl would still be throwing herself at me had I not nipped it in the bud a few weeks back.

I motion for her to come in, and she takes the chair across from me.

"As senior class president, we're going to be working closely together this school year. I chair a lot of committees, and my goal is to implement at least ten new policies this year, which you will have to sign off on."

"All right." I fold my hands across my desk, my bored gaze drifting out the window to my right where throngs of students make their way to the parking lot like a herd of sheep, only the moment I see Halston standing next to another student, I can't pay attention to a word Bree is saying.

The other student, a tall, athletic type with sandy hair and the kind of smug smirk that tells me he's used to getting whatever he wants, puts his arm around her, pulling her against him.

She laughs, pushing him away before pretending to hit his arm.

I know his type.

I know his tricks.

Hell, back in high school, I *was* him.

"Principal, are you listening?" Bree asks, frowning.

"Yes," I lie.

"Then what did I just say?"

For fuck's sake.

Bree whips around, staring out the window just in time to see Halston walk off with the boy.

"Oh, yeah." She rolls her eyes. "Thane Bennett asked my cousin on a date. He just wants to use her for sex."

"Excuse me?"

Turning to face me, Bree shrugs. "He uses everyone for sex. Everyone knows that. He's already slept with half the school."

My jaw tenses. "You should warn her."

She scoffs. "Not going to waste my breath. Halston doesn't listen to anyone. And she's probably only hanging out with him to get back at me."

"Why do you say that?"

"Why are you so interested in our girl drama?" Her face is pinched, confused. "Can we get back to talking about committees? Specifically, the homecoming committee? Since the dance is in three weeks?"

"Right. Continue."

"Okay, so I'm going to have a sign-up sheet posted on the …"

I tune her out again, watching as Halston and Thane disappear behind a row of waxy, shiny imports.

God help him if he so much as thinks about *using* her.

She's been used her whole life.

I refuse to sit back and let it happen again.

```
┌─────────────────────────────────┐
│                                 │
│          Chapter 24             │
│                                 │
└─────────────────────────────────┘
```

HALSTON

HE'S A GOOD KISSER.

Too good, if I'm being honest.

I try not to think about how many girls his tongue has tasted before, how many Victoria's Secret-covered tits and asses he's groped and grabbed because the girls at our school seem to sacrifice themselves to him willingly and without question.

I try not to think about anything at all.

Crammed in the backseat of Thane's BMW on a Friday night, my legs straddle his lap and my shirt is somewhere in the front seat. We're in the middle of some barren cornfield outside of town, the moon gleaming through the sunroof above us as some California punk pop band plays from his speakers.

Aunt Tab and Uncle Vic think I'm staying the night with Emily, who just so happens to be out of town this weekend and is none the wiser. Thane's parents think he's staying the night with one of his friends. We were going to camp out here tonight, under the stars, talking and listening to music.

It was supposed to be innocent. Just "hanging out" as he kept calling it. But flirting at dinner turned into hand-holding at the movies and when he started kissing me out here twenty minutes ago, I found myself actually enjoying it, enjoying the distraction from my everyday life, and somehow, we've migrated to the backseat.

My hips grind against his, his hardness straining against his jeans.

I'm wet and aching, but I'm not going to fuck him.

Yet, at least.

If he wants this, he's going to have to work for it.

I may be a lot of things, but easy isn't one of them.

Thane's hands are in my hair, his soft lips working mine. If I grind hard enough, fast enough, I might be able to make myself cum.

"You're so fucking hot," he whispers, his mouth grazing mine before traveling lower. He presses hot kisses into my neck, his hands traveling to my breasts, untucking them from the silky cups of my satin bra. Thane takes a nipple in his mouth, gently dragging his teeth across the swollen bud. "I can't wait to fuck you, Halston."

"You're going to have to," I whisper, smirking in the dark, my hands draped over his broad shoulders. If he's this big and built for an eighteen-year-old, I can only imagine what he's packing below.

"I don't know if I can," he moans. "You're so sexy I can hardly stand it." He kisses me, running his thumb across my bottom lip, our eyes meeting. "Your mouth. This bangin' body."

"A week ago, you didn't know I existed," I say, my

words breathy and playful. "I think you can wait a little while longer."

His hands grip my hips, pressing me against him as he rocks our bodies, teasing me with the promise of a rock-hard cock.

"You keep putting up walls, and I keep tearing them down. I'll tear this one down, too. Just watch," he says, smirking. "You like me. And you don't want to wait any more than I do."

"Don't flatter yourself, Thane Bennett." I bury my face in his shoulder so he can't see me smile. We've spent the better part of the week doing more flirting than chemistry assignments, and when he takes me home after school, he takes the long way so we can talk.

Every part of me has no intentions of liking him.

Yet it's happening anyway.

And there's not a damn thing I can do to stop it.

"I like when you say that," he moans, gripping my ass.

"Say what?"

"My whole name," he says, "like you just did."

I laugh. "Thane Bennett?"

"Yeah." He cups my chin, kissing me again. "You should practice. You're going to be saying it a lot."

Chuckling, I shake my head. "I don't say anyone's name during sex, and if I did, it sure as hell wouldn't be their full name."

I ponder, for a second, the possibility that Thane gets off on girls going gaga for him, on his name being synonymous with popularity and good looks. Thane Bennett is practically a household name at Rosefield. A brand with an air of exclusivity.

He's completely lost touch with reality.

"I think you've let your popularity go to your head," I

say, leaning back as much as I can. His lips are still parted, his eyes half open.

"What are you talking about?"

"I couldn't give two shits about how many girls want to date you or how many passes you caught at the last game," I say. "If I let you fuck me, it'll be because I like you. And I mean *you*. Not Thane Bennett, *you*."

I expect his face to light. I expect to see some kind of sign, an acknowledgement that this is a good thing, a realization that I'm not like most girls.

Instead, he exhales, running his palms up and down his face and groaning.

"Well, shit." Thane sighs, turning his head toward one of the back windows and refusing to look at me. His hands rest useless at his sides, like he's done touching me.

"I'm more work than you thought I was going to be, huh?"

His hands slide down my lower back as he pulls my hips harder against his, pinning me to him. "Don't be like this. Come on. We're having a good time."

My palms flatten against his chest, and I try to push myself off of him, but he's too strong. He won't let me go. The second his grip loosens, it travels to the straps of my bra, tugging them down my shoulders. I try to yank them from his fingers, only he won't let go and one of them snaps and breaks.

"Oh, shit." Thane's eyes study mine as he waits for my reaction.

Saying nothing, I climb over his console and into the front seat, searching in the dark for my shirt. I'm leaving.

"What are you doing?" he asks.

"Take me home." I'm a fucking moron. "I actually believed for four straight days that you were into me."

"What are you talking about? I *am* into you."

If he truly liked me, he'd have taken my hands in his, kissed me, and said he'd wait until I was ready. Guess the whole gentleman shtick was nothing more than a ruse.

"No. You brought me out here because you thought I was going to fuck you, and the second I said I wasn't, you got all pissy about it. So, take me fucking home."

"What did you think we were going to do, Halston, huh? You and me, alone, out here? You didn't think it was going to come to this?"

"Shameless." My arms tighten across my chest. "You're a real fucking winner."

"Stop overreacting."

"I'm not overreacting. I'm over *you*." I say, pulling my shirt over my head.

He's still in the backseat, cozied up in the middle and not so much as moving an inch.

"You going to drive me home or what?" I ask.

"Your aunt and uncle think you're staying at Emily's," he says. "What are you going to tell them?"

His question is rooted in nothing more than concern for his own self. He's afraid he'll get in trouble if I tell them the truth.

"Don't worry," I huff. "I won't be telling anybody about this."

"What's that supposed to mean?"

Rolling my eyes, I tug the hem of my shirt down. "That this was a mistake. One I'd like to forget."

His expression is bathed in genuine shock. I'm sure I'm the only girl he's ever "hung out" with who has so much as dared to imply that getting hot and heavy in the backseat of Thane Bennett's BMW is something they'd sooner forget.

Yanking the door handle, I step out of the car, which sends him scrambling to get out of the backseat. Finally.

"Where are you going?" he asks, his athletic body squeezing out from behind the backseat of his coupe.

"Home." With my bag hanging across my body and my arms folded, I trudge through a muddy cornfield, toward the twinkle of city lights in the distance. My feet sink into the soft earth with each step, and I'll be trudging down gravel roads and through weedy thickets, but home is just a few miles from here.

I'd rather walk for the next hour than spend another minute next to Thane.

Chapter 25

FORD

I'M half asleep on the sofa Friday night when the faintest knock on my door has me convinced I'm dreaming.

Until I hear it again.

Peeling myself up, I finger comb my hair into place and shuffle to the door. If it's Melissa fucking Gunderson, I'm going to scream.

But it's not Melissa.

Quite the contrary.

"Halston." She's the last person I expected to see standing at my doorstep at eleven thirty on a Friday night, but there she is, her clothes and hair disheveled, and her shoes covered in mud.

"I need a place to stay."

"And your principal's house seemed like the best option?" I lift a brow, pretending that's the more pressing concern when really I want to know why the fuck she looks worse for the wear.

"Yeah." She pushes past me, showing herself in. Halston slides her dirty shoes off and leaves them on the rug by the door. "Believe it or not."

Glancing outside, I make sure no one saw her come inside, and then I lock the door. "What happened? You okay?"

Halston rolls her eyes before taking a seat in my chair. "Don't want to talk about it."

"If I'm taking you in, I need to know why," I say, a million scenarios running through my head. Every part of me knows this is wrong, and if anyone caught us, they'd never believe that my intentions were noble. But every part of me knows I can't shut her out.

"My aunt and uncle think I'm staying with a friend. I was really going to stay with a guy." She exhales, running her tongue along her full lips. They're swollen, like she spent the last several hours making out. Her elbows rest on her knees, her body hunched forward. "Long story short, he thought he was going to fuck me, and I asked him to take me home. When he wouldn't, I got out of the car and walked ... through a muddy cornfield ... down a gravel road ... and into town."

Exhaling, I hide my relief.

"Smart," I say.

Her emerald gaze flicks to mine. "I don't need your validation."

Smirking, I place my palms up. "All right."

Reaching for a book on my coffee table, she examines the cover. "*A Wrinkle in Time*. Why would you read this depressing shit?"

"It's a classic."

"It's sad as fuck." She tosses it aside, reaching for another book, making faces when she doesn't find one that suits her liking.

"I have more upstairs," I say. "In my library. But you can't go up there."

She arches a brow. "Why not?"

"It wouldn't be appropriate."

Tossing her head back, she laughs. "Nothing about me being here with you right now is appropriate. I think we passed that a long time ago, don't you?"

"I'm sitting here." I drag my teeth along my lower lip, watching how she brushes her hair over her shoulder and tilts her head as she checks out my living room. "You're over there. I'd say we're being pretty fucking appropriate right now."

"Then can I see your library?"

"No."

Her brows meet. "What are you worried about?"

That I'll get her upstairs, mere feet from my bedroom. That I'll want to kiss her. That I won't be able to stop. That I'll lose all fucking control. That everything I've ever worked for will go down in flames because of a young woman named Halston Kessler.

"I'm not worried about anything," I lie. "But you're still not going upstairs."

"You're really high strung. Explains why you're such a control freak."

I shrug, refusing to apologize for my inherent need for power over every situation.

"When was the last time you got laid?" she asks.

"I'm not discussing my sex life with you. Not anymore."

"I don't know what the difference is between now and a few weeks ago," she says. "I'm still Absinthe. You're still Kerouac. Only this time we're in the same room, sitting here trying to pretend we're not ridiculously attracted to each other and that you haven't wondered what it would feel like to touch me."

I exhale, refusing to dignify her with a response.

"Admit it. You've thought about me." She drags a fingertip down the front of her twisted lips, fighting a chuckle. "My mouth on your cock. Your fingers in my pussy. I know I've thought about it. So much."

Glancing away, I pull in a tight breath and let it go. "I'm your principal and you're my student. I would never touch you. I would never cross that line."

"But what if you could? What if you knew with one-hundred percent certainty that we would never get caught?" She crosses her legs, angling her body toward me. "Would you do it?"

"No."

"I would." Her bee stung lips tug up at one side. "I don't mean to make you uncomfortable, I'm just being honest."

"You're not making me uncomfortable." I sigh, covering my face with my hands. I've thought about fucking her. I've thought about how her curves would feel under my palms, ample and soft, how her lips would taste, like cherries or cinnamon, how her body would feel pressed warm against mine, how safe and protected I would make her feel. "I'm going to bed. Goodnight, Halston."

"You were my best friend this summer," she says, her voice softer, quieter. "I told you more than I've ever told anyone before. I was myself with you, unfiltered, unedited. For whatever it's worth, I just wanted you to know that."

"Likewise."

"It's too bad we can't be friends." Halston leans back in my leather chair, her hands resting on her stomach. "But I understand. I don't want to jeopardize your career or anything. Just miss talking to you, is all."

"I miss talking to you too."

Her eyelids flutter, and she flashes a sleepy smile. Rising, I grab a pillow and blanket from a hall closet and make the sofa into a bed. I'd let her have the guestroom, but having that extra floor between us feels safer tonight.

"Here," I help her to the sofa, keeping back as she makes herself comfortable.

Spreading the covers over her body, she reaches toward me, her hand resting on mine. "Thank you. If you didn't answer your door tonight, I was probably going to sleep at the park."

She says it like it's no big deal, like she's done it hundreds of times before.

"You're fearless," I say. "That's not always a good thing."

Halston lets her hand fall from mine before rolling to her side. "I know."

Within seconds, she's out, and I switch off the lamp beside her.

Every time I closed my eyes this week, I saw her. Every waking moment of every hour of every day, I thought of her. And now that she's here, in my house, it takes everything I have to walk away, when all I want to do is stay all night by her side, devouring books, reading our favorite lines to each other until we give in to the inevitable.

But the inevitable can't happen.

I won't allow it.

⸺

SHE'S GONE before the sun comes up, her blanket neatly

folded at the end of the sofa and a scribbled note left on the coffee table.

KEROUAC,

You're a good man, maybe even the best one I've ever known.

xoxo—

Absinthe

PS – "I love sleep. My life has a tendency to fall apart when I'm awake, you know?" – Ernest Hemingway

PPS – Those are friendly and "appropriate" x's and o's.

I FOLD the paper in half and press it between the pages of Philip Roth's *Goodbye, Columbus*.

If things were different, she could be mine.

And we could be happy.

Chapter 26

HALSTON

MY HEART POUNDS in my ears as I head to Chem II. I've been dreading fourth block all day, knowing I'll have to spend ninety minutes next to Thane Bennett, asshole extraordinaire.

He tried calling me Saturday. Texted me Sunday.

I ignored him the entire weekend.

Walking into class, I feel his eyes on me. I'm seconds from asking Caldwell for a new lab partner when a substitute takes the desk up front.

Shit.

Finding my seat, I fish my pen and notebook from my bag and face forward.

"So you're just going to keep ignoring me?" Thane breaks the silence with a stupid question.

"Mm-hm."

"I'm sorry. I screwed up," he whispers, leaning close. His cologne invades my space, but I secretly like the scent so I don't say anything. "I like you. And I'll wait for you. I'll wait as long as you want."

His hand reaches under the desk, his fingers interlacing with mine.

"Think about it at least?" he asks.

The sub writes her name on the whiteboard up front, and I focus on the red ink and her terrible handwriting. Thane leaves me alone for the next forty-five minutes, but when the mid-block bell rings and the sub tells us to take five, he follows me out to the hall.

"What are you doing?" I ask, stopping short outside the classroom.

"I thought we could talk for a minute."

"There's nothing to talk about." My arms fold.

His hand drags along his jaw, and he wears a sad, pathetic expression which unfortunately almost makes me feel sorry for him.

"I spent all weekend thinking about how I screwed up," he says. "I stayed home. I didn't go out. I just lay around, thinking about you."

"Sounds like you wasted a perfectly good weekend."

"I'm serious, Halston. Give me another chance and I won't screw it up this time."

My lips part, and I'm seconds from giving him a resounding "no" when Kerouac comes around the corner.

"Is this student bothering you, Miss Kessler?" he asks, jaw flexing.

Rolling my eyes, I shake my head. "We're just talking."

He glares at Thane, sizing him up and looking down his nose. I didn't give him any details Friday night other than telling him Thane wanted to fuck me, but clearly that rubbed Kerouac the wrong way.

"Okay. You can go now," I say, shooing him away.

His head cocks, eyes narrowing in my direction this

time. "Miss Kessler, I'm your principal, and you will speak to me with respect in my school."

My brows lift. I can't tell if he's joking, so I laugh until his jaw flexes and his nostrils flare.

The halls empty just as the tardy bell rings.

"We should get back," Thane says, reaching for my hand.

"I need a word with Miss Kessler," Kerouac's voice is stern yet impossibly sexy. I wonder if he has any idea how badly he's turning me on right now?

As soon as Thane's out of earshot, I whisper, "It's really hard to take you seriously when you talk to me like that."

"Talk to you like what? The way I'd speak to any other student in this school?" he asks. "I really hope you're not expecting preferential treatment."

"I've learned never to expect anything from anyone," I say.

His expression softens. "Was he bothering you?"

"No. He was actually apologizing."

Kerouac's face hardens, like it's a bad thing Thane apologized. "Just be careful."

"Thanks, *daaaad*," I say in a slow, schmoopy voice.

"And don't call me that. I'm not nearly old enough to be your father." He releases a heavy breath like I frustrate him. "The emotional health and welfare of my students is one of my top priorities as an administrator."

"So you're invested in every relationship in Rosefield High? Ensuring nobody gets hurt and everyone lives happily ever after?"

Sara Bliss, Rosefield's notoriously ditzy art teacher, passes us in the hall, smiling when she sees Kerouac and nearly tripping over her faded Birkenstocks.

"Get back to class, Miss Kessler," he says, watching with folded arms as I walk away.

He cares about me.

And he *likes* me.

He won't admit it—not even to himself.

But I know.

———

"BEFORE I FORGET," Uncle Vic says at dinner that night, "I ran into Ford Hawthorne earlier. Invited him over for dinner this Friday."

I almost choke on my mashed potatoes before reaching for my glass of water.

"Wonderful! I'd love to finally meet him. Bree talks about him so much, I feel like I already know him, but I've been dying to put a face with that name." Aunt Tab flitters about. She'll do just about anything for a chance to play hostess.

"I have a date that night," I say.

Bree's attention lands on me, though she says nothing.

"You're still seeing that Bennett boy?" Tab asks. "He seems very nice. We'd love to meet him sometime. You should bring him over for dinner! You could eat here and then afterwards, have your little date."

I mean, I hadn't decided if I was going to forgive him yet, but I'm not in the mood to explain the intricacies of the past week to my aunt and uncle over a plate of quiche Lorraine.

"That's a great idea." Vic nods. "Bree, you're awfully quiet over there."

"I have a headache. May I please be excused?" she asks, monotone.

"Of course, darling." Tab places her hand over Bree's.

I'm finished as well, so I excuse myself, only by the time I round the corner by the front door, Bree's standing at the bottom of the stairs, arms crossed.

"I saw you come home Saturday morning," she says, lips puckered like the asshole she is.

"So?"

"You weren't walking from Emily's house. You were coming from a different direction."

"And your point?"

Bree huffs. "You lied about where you were that night."

"You lie about shit all the time." I point at her chest. "Your entire fucking bra situation is a lie."

She covers her chest, jaw hanging, and I push past her, heading up to my room, but she follows.

"I'm going to find out what you're up to."

"Is that a threat?" I ask, keeping my voice down. "Because you don't want to go there with me." Stepping back, I smirk. "Wait, this is about Thane. You're jealous."

Duh.

"No, I'm not," she says, chin tilted up.

"You are *so* jealous." Chuckling, I shake my head. "Doesn't quite make up for the money you stole from me, but it's somewhat vindicating."

"I stopped liking Thane years ago, when he dated one of my best friends. We don't double dip in my group." Her nose lifts in the air.

"Best Friend? As in one of those girls you follow around like a lost puppy because you don't actually have any real friends because you're a boring little poser that nobody wants to hang out with?"

"*I have friends,*" she says, her words staccato and brusque, like she's trying to convince herself as well.

"How come you don't ever hang out with them outside

the cafeteria? Why aren't they blowing up your phone on the weekends?"

Her eyes water and her slender lips quiver. For a sliver of a second, I see Bree as a human being with feelings and not a humanoid Stepford daughter with a heart as black as coal.

"You're such a bitch," she says, wiping tears with the back of her hand. "I hate you."

"For once we have something in common."

"I wish you would just leave!" Bree runs to her room, slamming the door.

I don't get the chance to tell her that the money she stole would've helped with allowing me to leave at will, but that's neither here nor there.

Ambling toward my room, I lock the door behind me and yank my phone off the charger.

I miss talking to Kerouac.

On a whim, I reinstall the Karma app and unblock him just to see if he's still around. Lo and behold, his profile is still there and the app tells me he hasn't been active in four weeks … since we last spoke on the phone.

Settling into my bed, I compose a message:

TO: Kerouac@karma.com

From: Absinthe@karma.com

Subject: Oh, you.

Time: 6:35 PM

Message: Uncle Vic says he invited you to dinner on Friday. My aunt then suggested that we make it a thing and I bring Thane because everyone's under the impression we're still dating. I don't know why I'm telling you this. Guess I thought maybe you'd get a kick out of it. I know you don't like him, and now you get to sit across from us at supper later this week while we hold hands and play footsy. Just kidding. I don't do that shit. But don't think I won't be eye-fucking you every chance I get. Okay, kidding about that too. Kind of. You know I like to tease. Anyway. I don't even know if you still get push notifications from this stupid app. For all I know I'm talking to dead air.

TO: Absinthe@karma.com
    From: Kerouac@karma.com
    Subject: Re: Oh, you.
    Time: 6:38 PM
    Message: I *really* don't like that guy.

I LAUGH OUT LOUD, my stomach fluttering when I read his email.

TO: Kerouac@karma.com
    From: Absinthe@karma.com
    Subject: Re: re: Oh, you.
    Time: 6:41 PM
    Message: I know you don't. I don't either. I'm just using him to piss Bree off. No intentions of screwing him if that makes you feel better. Boys use girls for worse things than that all the time, so I figure it's okay.

TO: Absinthe@karma.com
    From: Kerouac@karma.com
    Subject: Re: re: re: Oh, you.
    Time: 6:43 PM

Message: You're better than that. Not sure why you're wasting your time.

TO: Kerouac@karma.com
    From: Absinthe@karma.com
    Subject: Re: re: re: re: Oh, you.
    Time: 6:45 PM
    Message: Is there a reason your responses are only one or two sentences? You know this app is 100% anonymous. There's no way our conversations could ever be traced back to us.

TO: Absinthe@karma.com
    From: Kerouac@karma.com
    Subject: Re: re: re: re: re: Oh, you.
    Time: 6:46 PM
    Message: Well aware. But we shouldn't be conversing at all.

TO: Kerouac@karma.com
    From: Absinthe@karma.com
    Subject: Re: re: re: re: re: re: Oh, you.
    Time: 6:47 PM
    Message: Then stop responding!

I BITE MY THUMBNAIL, my lips overtaken by a mile-wide grin as I await his response.

But it never comes.

It's all right. I got my Kerouac fix for tonight.

Chapter 27

FORD

"YOU HAVE SOMETHING ... RIGHT HERE." I point to my mouth, then to Sara Bliss' as we eat lunch in the faculty lounge.

She giggles, dabbing her fuchsia lips with a napkin. I didn't invite her to sit with me, but we were the only two in here eating lunch at two thirty in the afternoon, and it would've been weird to sit at different tables.

"What do you think of the school so far?" she asks, dragging her fork around the mushy frozen entrée she's picking at. There's a smudge of something on her hands, chalk or pastels or paint perhaps. "Liking it?"

"I am." I uncap my water, glancing at the clock. In twenty-five minutes, the final bell will ring. I haven't seen Halston all day, our paths taking us in different directions apparently.

The silence between us is awkward and stifling, and I still have half a sandwich left to finish.

"Read any good books lately?" I ask a minute later.

Sara smiles, eyes crinkling as she quickly chews her bite. "Not much of a reader. Sorry."

If I were a lonely man, looking for a companion and some decent sex on a regular basis, I could easily bag Sara Bliss. She's a free-spirited twenty-something art teacher who probably keeps a cluttered house and doesn't own a watch or a calendar. She's attractive in a Tinkerbell sort of way, pixie-sized and fine-featured. But she's boring. She doesn't read. Keeps her opinions to herself. Smiles way too fucking much.

And she's not Halston.

Sara finishes her meal, which smelled way better than it looked, and washes her hands in the sink. "Oh! I was going to ask you if you wanted to chaperone the home-coming dance next weekend? I was supposed to do it with Connie Seltzer but she threw out her back, so I need a replacement. If you don't want to, no worries."

Running my lips together, I consider it for a moment, weighing my options. Chances are Halston's going with Thane, at least if her intention truly is to make her cousin jealous. And if that's the case, I should be there to make sure he keeps his hands off her.

"Just get back to me by tomorrow or something if you want to think about it." Sara gives a nervous titter before heading for the door.

"I'll do it."

"Really?" Her expression is lit. "Awesome. It'll be fun. You'll like it."

I doubt I'll like it.

I'm just going for the peace of mind.

Chapter 28

HALSTON

KEROUAC SITS ACROSS FROM ME, with Bree on his left. She's in heaven right now, finding it impossible to remove that shit-eating grin off her face. I'm sure in her warped little mind, she's pretending he's there with her. That they're together.

But whatever.

She won't look at Thane.

It's like she couldn't care less that he's there, which is truly bizarre. I'd been thinking about this moment all day, practically reveling in how good it was going to feel to shove Thane in her face. Maybe she *is* over him?

Kerouac and Uncle Vic do most of the talking, Aunt Tab nodding and "mm, hm-ing" every so often between running back and forth to the kitchen to bring out the next course.

By the time we finish dessert, my aunt's famous crème

brulee, the buttons on my jeans are threatening to pop, and I'm wondering if anyone would notice if I disappeared for a little while and changed into something else.

"This was amazing, Mrs. Abbott. Thank you." Thane pats his washboard abs. "Mr. Abbott, thank you for having me."

"You're so welcome, sweetheart," she says, smiling with every feature on her face. "Ford, was everything okay?"

"Absolutely. Can't remember the last time I ate like this," he says, gaze resting on mine. My mind goes to a dark and dirty gutter for a half of a second, picturing his tongue between my thighs as he devours me.

Thane threads his hand through mine, standing and pulling me up. "Our movie starts in a half hour. We should probably head out."

I follow Thane to the foyer, leaning against the stair rail as he slips his shoes on, and when he's finished, he rises, strutting toward me and resting his hands on my hips.

"I'm so glad you decided to give me another chance," he whispers before his mouth grazes mine. He cups my cheek, pressing his lips harder onto mine before slipping me the tongue. I close my eyes, pretending it's not Thane I'm kissing in this moment.

The clearing of a throat pulls us out of the moment, and thank god for that. Turning, I spot Kerouac standing in the doorway, keys in his hand.

"Don't mind me." His tone is displeased, and he directs his attention to me, his stare hard and unforgiving with a hint of something else entirely in his gaze. Jealousy? Resentment?

Passing us, he reaches for the door handle and shows himself out.

"You ready?" Oblivious, Thane checks his phone,

firing off a quick text to God knows who. He's always texting. I don't tend to care.

"Yeah," I say. From inside, I see Kerouac trekking across the driveway, heading home.

I'd much rather be with him tonight.

I just hope he knows that.

———

ABSINTHE: Hey, you there?

Kerouac: Aren't you supposed to be at the movies?

Absinthe: I am. Hiding in the bathroom. He took me to some CGI hot mess that has absolutely no plot and terrible dialogue. I'm dying. SOS.

Kerouac: You made your bed.

Absinthe: So you don't feel sorry for me?

Kerouac: No.

Absinthe: :(

Kerouac: You should get back to your movie.

Absinthe: I know. But I'd rather chat with you. Side note: I've decided my type are really attractive, literature-obsessed intellectuals.

Kerouac: Like me?

Absinthe: No! Like me.

Absinthe: I'm basically looking for a guy version of myself. The one I found doesn't reciprocate my feelings, so …

Kerouac: I know what you're doing. Stop.

Absinthe: Saw right through that one, huh?

Kerouac: Just because I'm chatting with you doesn't mean I'm going to make you an exception to my rule.

Absinthe: I saw the way you looked at us earlier … when you saw him kiss me in the foyer. You were bothered by it.

Kerouac: Your point?

Absinthe: The whole time he was kissing me, I was wishing it was you. Just thought you should know.

Kerouac: Get back to your movie.

Kerouac has signed off.

Chapter 29

FORD

"WHOA. I'm surprised you answered. I was just going to leave you a message. Why are you up so late?" Nicolette's voice chuckles through the receiver just past eleven o'clock Friday night.

"What am *I* doing up late? You're the one with a five-year-old who wakes up before the sun."

"You know I have insomnia. Anyway, check your email."

"Why?" I ask.

"I sent you an article."

Retrieving my laptop from the coffee table, I prop the lid open and pull up my email. A moment later it loads, and I sort through dozens of junk messages to find the one with her name on it.

"Is this going to piss me off?" I ask before clicking the link.

"Yes."

Groaning, I tap the trackpad and pore over an article detailing the recent success of our stepbrother, Mason Foster. According to the write up, his tech company was started when his mother gifted him ten million dollars (of my father's money), and over the past five years, he's started a software firm, a wildly popular gaming app universe, and an up-and-coming social network; the latest of which he sold to Facebook for over two billion dollars.

"You done reading yet?" she asks.

I see red. It's not about the money—I do just fine without it. It's about the entitled, undeserving bastard and his conniving wench of a mother.

There's a photo of Mason, perched on the edge of a desk in jeans and a blazer, the views of his office over-looking Silicon Valley as he wears a smug grin. But he's sitting on a throne built by my parents' time, money, and dedication. He didn't earn any of this.

"I fucking hate him," Nicolette says.

"Not as much as I do." I press my phone against my chest when I hear a faint knock at the door. "Let me call you back."

Ending the call, I peer out the window next to the front door and see the outline of a young woman standing in the dark.

Yanking the door open, I exhale. "Why?"

Her full lips curl. "Not exactly the reaction I was expecting."

Hooking my hand into her arm, I pull her inside before anyone sees her. "Aren't you supposed to be on your date?"

Halston's eyes roll to the back of her head and she makes a gagging sound. "I was about to die, it was so fucking boring. I made him drop me off early. Told him my curfew was eleven but it's really midnight. Now I have an hour to kill."

"You've got to stop doing this." I rest my hands on my hips, shaking my head before releasing a deep breath. All I keep seeing is that picture of Mason, perched on his desk like some self-made man who started from the bottom. And when I glance up at her, all I see is my future going down in flames because I want nothing more than to feel her naked body on mine, her hips grinding on my cock, her full breasts bouncing with each thrust as her mouth finds mine in the dark. "You can't keep coming over like this."

"Okay, this is the second time. Ever. And you've got nothing to worry about. Tab and Vic are asleep. Bree's babysitting overnight for some doctor's family, and when I leave, I'll sneak out the back door."

She smirks, stepping toward me and clearly not taking this seriously.

"You really need to lighten up," she says, eyeing my liquor cart in the corner. "Let me make you a drink."

Before I have a chance to stop her, she's pouring two fingers of Scotch into a crystal tumbler. I take a seat in the middle of my sofa, rubbing my eyes and sinking my head back.

"Here you go." She taps my knee.

When I open my eyes, I find Halston on her knees between my legs, holding up a glass of liquor with a smile on her fuckable mouth. My cock throbs, swelling against my jeans.

"You need to leave," I say. "Before I do something I'm going to regret the rest of my life."

Halston's expression fades. "What did I do? All I did was make you a drink. Now you're kicking me out?"

"It's not you," I say.

"Of course it is." She rises. "God, I'm an idiot."

"What are you talking about?"

"I thought we had a real connection." She grabs her bag from the floor by the front door, flinging it over her shoulder. "And I thought maybe you were different, that we had something genuine. But now that you know you can't fuck me, you just want to be done. So, fine. I get it. I'll leave you alone from now on."

The notion of watching her walk out the door and never talking to her again, seeing her parading around the halls at school with that pencil dick boyfriend, sends a fire through my veins unlike anything I've ever felt before.

This woman—this young woman—is everything I never knew I wanted in another person, everything I never knew was possible to have.

And I want her.

I want her so fucking bad it's unreal.

"Halston." I move toward her with steady, confident strides. "You have it all wrong."

She rolls her eyes. "You're all talk, Kerouac. It's all you've ever been and all you'll ever be. I know that now."

Cupping her face, I realize this is the first time I've ever touched her—really touched her. I let my palm linger, my thumb running over her pillowed lips.

"I'd give anything to kiss you right now," I say, my voice a remorseful whisper. My heart thrums at a dangerous pace, the distance between our mouths closing.

But I won't kiss her.

I can't.

Her green eyes are lost in mine, holding for what feels like an eternity. Her scent fills the space between us, soft and wild at the same time. I'm seconds from telling her I'll wait for her, that there'll be a day when we can be together —until her mouth grazes mine.

Halston kisses me, pressing her lips into mine harder, slinking her arms over my shoulders and rising on her toes.

For a brief moment, I lose myself, relishing in this kiss like it's the only one that's ever mattered in my life.

And then I push her away.

"Why the *fuck* did you do that?" I'm seething, jaw clenched and shoulders rising and falling with each breath.

"Wh-what?" She's somewhere between laughing and crying as she floats back down to earth.

"This is bad. This is really fucking bad." I pace the living room before stopping in the center, massaging my temples and refusing to look at her.

"Kerouac," she says. "You're overreacting. It was just a kiss."

Turning to her, I shake my head, lips pressed into a hard line. "You don't understand. I could lose my job over this."

"No one's going to know." Her eyes widen. "I'll take it to the grave."

"You say that now." I cock my head before dragging my hand across my cheek. "One day I might piss you off and—"

"God, no. I would never do that." She approaches me gingerly at first, then rushes to my side, placing her hand on my chest. I brush it away. "I'm not like that. At all. I would *never*."

"You shouldn't have done that."

Halston shrugs. "Okay, fine. I'm sorry. But your hand was on my cheek and we were standing so close. I thought … I thought that's what you wanted."

I can see how she would've been confused, how passion and wanton lust would've overtaken her in that moment.

"You have no idea how lucky you are that I stopped," I say.

"Funny. I feel the exact opposite."

"You shouldn't come here anymore," I tell her, though

it breaks my heart. If she continues to stop by like this, we're going to keep skirting the line. And one of these days, we're going to cross it. And once the line is crossed, we'll never be able to go back.

Halston's emerald eyes gloss with tears, and I imagine she's not accustomed to crying over much of anything. She's tough, fearless, with thick skin and a resilient spirit.

But I may have just broken her.

"You should go now," I say.

She does.

And the moment she's gone, it's as if someone's blown a cannon-sized hole through my chest, heavy and gaping. I take a seat in my chair, facing the window and watching her shadow move across the yard in the dark, her arms folded across her chest and her chin tucked.

The berry-sweet taste of her full mouth lingers on mine, its taste turning bitter the second I refuse to allow myself to enjoy it a second longer. I should never have placed myself in that position—standing so close.

I knew better.

And while every part of my body craves hers with an invigorated intensity, I know deep down, I did the right thing.

Chapter 30

HALSTON

"GIRLS? You ready? Your dates are here!" Aunt Tabitha calls to us from the bottom of the stairs, and I give myself one last look in the full-length mirror on the back of my bathroom door.

I didn't want to go to homecoming, but Thane managed to talk me into it, and when Bree miraculously landed a date, her parents insisted we go as a group. Besides, focusing my time and energy planning for this student dance all week has helped to take my mind off Kerouac … somewhat.

It doesn't help that I see him every day, multiple times a day at school, but lately I've been learning his schedule and taking alternate routes to class, mixing it up sometimes so I can be sure I won't have to see him.

Bree knocks on my door. "Come on. They're waiting."

Tonight we have to pretend we like each other, but I'm hoping after dinner and a little bit of time at the dance, I won't have to see her at all the rest of the night. Vic and Tab gave us a 12:30 AM curfew, and Thane's older brother rented us a block of hotel rooms at the Embassy Suites in downtown Rosefield. Thane was elected homecoming king yesterday at the afternoon pep rally, and last night the Rosefield Tigers won their game against their unrivaled Cherry Dale Cardinals, so everyone's expecting Thane to be there. He promised we'll make an appearance and then we'll bounce.

"Yeah," I call out. "One sec."

I graze my palm along a pressed wave. Tabitha insisted we get our hair done at her salon today. While my hair looks soft and bouncy and neatly done, it's hard as a rock and covered in hairspray.

A gold sequined bodice hugs my waist and lifts my breasts, and the peach tulle skirt hits just above my knees.

I look like Peaches-n-Cream Barbie.

I look exactly like the kind of girl who goes to homecoming with Thane Bennett.

The squeal of my aunt and uncle downstairs tells me Bree went on without me, which is fine. Grabbing my matching sequin bedazzled clutch, I head downstairs.

Nobody makes a big deal out of my entrance ... except for Thane. His face lights as he stands there in his suit, holding a corsage in a plastic box and wearing the biggest grin I've ever seen.

"Halston," he says, brows lifted. "You look beautiful."

I wave my hand, brushing off his compliment. "Anyone would look beautiful with this much hair and makeup and a dress that shines like the top of the Chrysler building."

"Don't be so modest, you look incredible," Aunt Tabitha says, and it just might be the first compliment she's ever paid me.

Glancing out the front window, I spot a black limo in

the driveway, and a man in a black tux and white driving gloves standing beside the passenger door.

"So, dinner reservations are at seven at Maestro's Little Italy, but they want us to check in ten minutes early," Bree says. Leave it to her to be the mother hen of the group tonight, though I'd expect nothing less. "I have our tickets in my bag. I also have gum and a phone charger if anyone needs it."

Rolling my eyes when no one's looking, I loop my arm through Thane's and pull him toward the door.

"No, no, wait," Aunt Tab says. "I want to get some pictures. And you need to do the flower thing."

Exhaling, I turn back toward the group and suffer through no fewer than a hundred snapshots, smiling and posing and pretending to gush over the pink rose and baby's breath corsage Thane chose for me. By the time we're done, my cheeks are stretched and my jaw aches.

This very well may be the longest night of my life.

But I'll get through it.

Always do.

Chapter 31

FORD

"I'VE ALWAYS LOVED HOMECOMING." Sara Bliss clasps her hands, watching as students begin to fill the gymnasium. Music pumps from the speakers, a mix of songs, some new and unfamiliar, some nostalgic. "There's just something magical in the air. The weather is cool, the leaves are changing. Everyone's excited for a new school year."

Her small talk is like a splinter, slivering its way beneath my skin.

"I was homecoming queen my senior year, believe it or not," she says, leaning closer and bumping me with her shoulder. If she's trying to impress me, she's wasting her time.

A Black Eyed Peas song comes on next and she starts dancing some weird, dorky little dance, and I don't know if she's trying to be funny and quirky or if this is just how she is, but I can't take my eyes off the door.

Any minute now, Halston's going to wander in on Thane's arm, and while I have no intentions of stoking the fire that took all the self-control I had to put out last weekend, I want to make sure she's okay.

All week, she avoided me.

She'd see me and she'd walk the other way.

Clearly, I hurt her, and while I'm sorry, I did what I had to do.

If only I could find the chance to tell her that.

The song changes, something slow and unfamiliar, and couples filter toward the dance floor, wrapping their arms around each other and trying to pretend their moments are more enchanting than awkward.

Hate to break it to them, but one of these days, they'll barely remember this night. All they'll have are their filtered-to-death Instagram posts and saved Snap Chats.

The crowd is thicker than it was a moment ago, and the students begin to stir a bit.

"Elvis has entered the building," Sara says.

Peering across the gym, the sea of well-dressed high schoolers parts and Thane Bennett struts, peacock proud, with Halston Kessler in tow. His crown rests on his head, cocked to the side, and he wears the proudest smirk I've ever seen.

Everyone cheers for him, even Sara. But I just stand here, arms folded, watching their every move.

I swear there's a halo around Halston. She radiates, her skin warm and tan, her dress glimmering under the flashing lights. He places his hand on her hip and pulls her close just as the song changes, and then he kisses her.

He kisses the sweetest lips I've ever known.

And in this moment, I'm sunk.

Being jealous of an eighteen-year-old means I've officially hit rock bottom.

I stand behind the refreshments table and observe the two of them, ensuring his hands don't travel lower than they should while nonchalantly watching for any cues that suggest she'd rather be anywhere else but here, with him.

But she's acting as if I don't exist, pretending not to feel my penetrating stare from across the room.

They dance to another song before a crowd of brawny football players surround him. He wears the limelight like couture, basking in his moment. Guys like Thane tend to peak in high school, but I won't be the bearer of bad news. He'll find out someday. The second he leaves Rosefield High, no one's going to give a rat's ass how many track records he's shattered or how many girls he fucked before he even knew how to properly fuck.

Halston squeezes away from the crowd, heading toward the punch bowl ... toward me.

We lock eyes, and I wear a solemn expression, though my heart is thundering harder with each step that brings her closer.

When she stands on the other side of the table, maybe two feet from me, I want to tell her how beautiful she looks. How radiant and stunning. But I can't.

"Principal Hawthorne," she says, filling her cup. "Had no idea you were chaperoning tonight."

I'm not sure how to respond with Sara beside me, but I know what Halston's insinuating.

"I'm filling in for someone," I finally say.

She takes a sip, staring up at me through thick, dark lashes. "Okay."

Either she doesn't believe me or she doesn't care. I'm not sure which is worse.

"Are you enjoying yourself tonight, Miss Kessler?" I ask.

"Wouldn't you like to know." Halston lingers for a second, and then she's gone, disappearing into the crowd.

The DJ asks the king and queen to take the dance floor while he spins some God-awful pop medley, and the second it's over, I spot Thane and Halston slipping out the side door.

It's only nine. They weren't even here for a half hour.

Pulling in a deep breath, I force it through my nostrils. Every muscle in my body tightens. I don't know where she's going or what his intentions are with her tonight. Not being able to talk her out of it is killing me.

"Uh, oh. I think I see a flask." Sara taps me, pointing toward a girl with wild red hair and a purple dress that goes to the floor. "You want to take care of it or do you want me to?"

Storming off, I do my fucking job.

And the second the dance is over and the last student has left the building, I sit in my car and message Halston. I'd promised myself I'd leave her be. I swore on my life that I'd never contact her again, but in this case, I'm truly concerned for her safety. Leaving the dance early with Mr. Popular can only mean one thing: the pencil-dicked douche wants to get her drunk and fuck her.

Not on my watch.

Pulling out my phone, I tap on the Karma icon and shoot her a message.

KEROUAC: Where'd you go?

Absinthe: Seriously??

Kerouac: You left after twenty minutes. I assume you went to a party?

Absinthe: WTF is wrong with you?!

Kerouac: ???

Absinthe: You tell me to leave you alone. You kick me out of your house after we kiss. You watched me like a fucking hawk at the dance—which made an already unenjoyable evening that much more unenjoyable, so thanks for that. And now you're messaging me like it's any of your business what I'm doing?!

Kerouac: Just because I can't be with you doesn't mean I can't care about you.

Absinthe: Yes, it does. That's exactly what it means. You don't get to care anymore.

Kerouac: I'm trying to do the right thing. Morally. Ethically. Professionally.

Absinthe: How valiant.

Kerouac: I think about you all the time. I go to bed, you're on my mind. I wake up, you're the first thing I think about. Seeing you in the halls drives me fucking insane because all I want is to have you to myself, for you to belong to me. You're right there, so close, and I can't go anywhere near you. I may not be able to control my thoughts, but I can control my actions. I'm not going to touch you. I'm not going to cross that line.

Absinthe: You could've had me, but you're too chicken shit. I thought you were like me, but turns out you're nothing but a fucking coward.

Kerouac: I'm a professional, not a coward.

Absinthe: You're a big, fat fucking coward.

Kerouac: Where are you right now?

Absinthe: LOL

Kerouac: Are you drinking?

Absinthe: Duh.

Absinthe: And don't worry. I won't come a-knockin' on your door tonight.

Kerouac: I just want to make sure you're safe and that you have a ride home.

Absinthe: I've got it covered. I'm a responsible adult … too bad you don't see me that way.

Kerouac: That's not true. I think the world of you. And I see you as an adult, just not one that I can be with at this point in time.

Absinthe: I'm so bored with this. You sound like a broken fucking record. And you know what the worst part is? I'd still come over and fuck you if you asked me to. I'd leave right now.

Kerouac: Don't say that.

Absinthe: It's the truth.

Absinthe: And that's the difference between you and me … I'm not afraid of the truth.

Absinthe: You want to be with me, Kerouac. And it terrifies you. And because of that, you lost the one chance you had. The only chance you'll ever have.

Absinthe: I have to go.

Kerouac: Wait.

Absinthe has signed off.

Chapter 32

HALSTON

"OH MY GOD." The hotel room is dark as midnight, the blackout curtains drawn tight with a hint of daylight around them. The sensation of cool sheets against my naked body mixed with the pounding throb in my head wasn't exactly how I planned to wake up this morning. "Thane. Wake up."

He's out cold, but I shove him until he begins to rustle, and when he rolls closer, he wears a dreamy smirk.

"You were supposed to take me home last night." I wrap the sheets around me, climbing out. "And where the fuck is my dress?!"

"You said it was uncomfortable. You took it off." He sits up, clicking on the bedside lamp and running his fingers through his messy hair as he watches me scramble around the room.

"I don't remember saying that."

"You were plastered last night." He chuckles. "Never

seen a girl put it down like that before. You didn't get sick once. We were shocked."

I tug my dress on, thinking back to last night. All I remember is leaving the dance, climbing into Thane's brother's car, and heading to the hotel to party a little.

"You were pacing yourself at first, then you were outside on your phone. When you came back in, you slammed a couple more shots of tequila and passed out."

I don't remember any of that.

He climbs out of bed, and the first thing I notice is the fact that he's not completely naked. "We didn't screw. Just so you know."

Thank god.

Although I wouldn't know for sure, I suppose.

"You have to take me home," I say. By some miracle I manage to find my phone buried under a mountain of empty beer cans.

Twelve missed calls.

All of them Uncle Vic, and all of them spanning one o'clock in the morning until as recently as fifteen minutes ago.

Fuck. Fuck. Fuck.

I may not have screwed Thane, but I'm still screwed.

———

THE SILENCE of the house when I step inside Sunday morning sends a chill to my veins. There's no television humming in the background. No clinking or clamoring coming from the kitchen. Not so much of a hint of Aunt Tab's Sunday morning cinnamon rolls in the air.

Sliding off my heels in the foyer, I reach for the stair railing and begin my quiet ascent to my room so I can change out of this scratchy dress.

"Halston." Uncle Vic's voice booms, echoing off the two-story ceiling and sending a quick shudder through my body. Turning, I see him standing at the bottom landing, arms folded and mouth bunched tight.

"Uncle Vic. I'm so sorry. I fell asleep and—"

"This is completely unacceptable." He doesn't give me time to explain. "We trusted you. We extended your curfew. We gave you a chance to show that you could be respectful and responsible. We've opened up our home to you, Halston. We want to see you succeed and become a productive member of society. The last thing we want is for you to end up like your parents."

I glance away. He didn't need to bring them into this.

I'll *never* be like them.

"You know, I was so proud of you this past summer when you started working," he says. "And then you just quit one day. For no reason." He shakes his head, but if he only knew … "And then school starts. You get this new *boyfriend*." He says boyfriend like it's a dirty word. "It's like that's all you care about now. Going out on the weekends. Messing around with boys. This is exactly what I was afraid of."

I'm not half as bad as he's making me out to be, though I suppose if he's comparing me to his virginal prodigy, Bree, I'm going to come out looking like the devil himself.

"I'm sorry," I say again. "It won't happen again. I swear."

"Damn right it won't happen again." His face is red, his nostrils flaring as he steps toward me. I've seen my uncle get worked up about things in the past, but I've never seen him like this. "Give me your phone."

"What?!"

"And your computer." He holds his hand out, eyeing my clutch.

"Why are you doing this?" It's not like he's crossing some line. He gave me the phone. He bought me the computer. He has every right to take them from me.

"What's the passcode to your phone?" he asks.

I freeze, unable to speak. If he logs onto my phone, if he digs deep enough into everything I do, he'll find my activity on Karma. All those opportunities I had to delete our conversations … I never wanted to because I loved going back and re-reading them, especially on the days when I missed him.

"Your passcode, Halston." His voice is louder this time. He has zero patience, and there's not a chance in hell he's going to calm down and change his mind anytime in the impending future.

"Eight, two, nine, six, two, eight," I whisper the numbers, it's all I can do to force myself to speak.

"And the password on your laptop?" he asks.

"A farewell to arms," I say softly, adding, "All one word."

"Bring it to me."

Turning, I take the steps, biding my time. And when I make it to my room, I close the door, crack open the laptop, and drag the Karma app to the trash. If I'm lucky, he'll shove my phone in a drawer and never look at it again, and no one will know about the Kerouac and Absinthe saga.

Wrapping the charger around the computer, I carry it down in my arms and hand it over.

"When will I get these back?" I ask. "I have homework due this week."

"You're not getting them back, Halston," he says. "Where you're going, you won't need these things."

"Where I'm *going?*" I squint.

"Pack your things. We're leaving first thing in the morning."

"Wait. You're kicking me out because I came home late after homecoming?" I've never spoken back to my uncle before, but I can't keep my mouth shut this time. He's over-reacting.

"It's a culmination of several things," he says. "There's a place that's better equipped to handle girls like you."

"Girls like me?" I spit his words at him. "Uncle Victor, I'm your niece. I'm not some wayward soul, some problem child."

He exhales, head tilted. "I see you going down the same path your mother did at your age. I'll be damned if I let it happen to you. You have a future, Halston. But if you continue on this path, defying authority and abandoning your responsibilities and obligations … you're going to end up just like her."

"You won't give me another chance?"

"We've been giving you chances all year." He shakes his head. "You're family and we love you, but having you here has been a big adjustment for everyone."

My jaw falls. "I sit in my room ninety-nine percent of the time. I don't make a sound. I clean up after myself. I do my chores. You're making me out to sound like some kind of heathen, Uncle Vic, and it's not fair."

Vic's nostrils flair, and he squares his shoulders. "I wasn't going to say anything. I promised Bree."

"What?" My brows twist. Oh, god.

"Bree told us you were working at an adult restaurant," he says.

That fucking traitor.

"It wasn't an *adult* restaurant," I say with air quotes. "Not the way you're making it sound."

"Not to mention the alcohol bottles Bree found under your bed last month," he adds.

My jaw falls, and it may as well hit the floor. "Alcohol bottles? She's lying to you, Uncle Vic. She's jealous and she's making this up to—"

His hand lifts in the air, cutting me off. "Since you've lived here, Bree's come to us on a number of occasions to report missing items. Jewelry. Clothes. That sort of thing. We've kept our mouths shut because we knew you needed our support to turn your life around, but enough is enough, Halston."

"This isn't fair! Bree just gets to say whatever she wants about me and I don't get to defend myself?" My voice shrivels in my hot throat. "You're just going to take her word for this?"

"We have no reason to believe she'd make any of this up," he says. "She's a good girl. She gets straight A's, does what she's told. She's never lied to us."

My hand claps across my mouth, and I breathe in through my nose to keep from hyperventilating as I pace the small space at the top of the stairs.

This isn't happening. This isn't happening. This isn't happening.

"The decision's been made. Tabitha and I have already decided. I made the phone call to an old colleague of mine this morning." Uncle Vic pulls in a hard breath. "You'll be finishing your senior year at Welsh Academy in Brightmore, New Hampshire. It's a reform school. You'll live there in the dormitories with a roommate."

"You're sending me to boarding school? No. Absolutely not. I'll just ... drop out and get my GED and—"

"If you refuse to finish your high school education the proper way, I'm afraid my offer to pay your tuition will be off the table." His chin lifts as he peers down his nose. I know that look. It's his way or nothing, and I don't exactly have eighty grand lying around to pay for college. "Eight months and then you're done. You'll emerge a better person, with more discipline, more respect, more poise and grace."

"I can't believe you're doing this." My eyes burn, but I refuse to cry. "You're all I had. And you're just shipping me away, like I'm not your problem."

"You were never my problem to begin with," he says. "But I took you in because you're family. And I love you. I know it may seem harsh, Halston, but I'm doing this for you. This is going to change the entire trajectory of your life. And someday, you'll thank me for it."

Chapter 33

FORD

SWEAT BEADS down my forehead Sunday afternoon, my shoes pounding the pavement as I push forward, running harder, faster, rounding the corner to my house. I pass the Abbotts' place, slowing down once I reach the foot of my driveway. Slowing to catch my breath, I stretch my arms behind my head before heading inside.

I couldn't sleep last night.

Hell, I couldn't function this morning.

The run was a last-ditch attempt to do something productive with my day, but none of it matters. All I keep thinking about is how I lost her. And how fucked up it is to even think of it that way because she was never mine to lose in the first place.

Five minutes later, I'm standing motionless under the spray of a cold shower, the water harsh and unforgiving. But I'm not sure what I expected. If a sleepless night and a long run couldn't quell the maelstrom raging inside, a frigid shower isn't going to help.

When I'm finished, I accept my defeat.

With a towel wrapped around my hips, I give myself a long, hard look in the mirror.

And then I find my phone.

TO: Absinthe@karma.com

From: Kerouac@karma.com

Subject: Please read

Time: 1:21 PM

Message: If things were different, I'd have made you mine the moment we met. Wait for me, Absinthe. Eight more months and I'll make you mine forever. I love you.

PLACING THE PHONE ASIDE, I change into clean clothes. When I return, the message shows as 'read,' but there's no response.

Chapter 34

HALSTON

"WHO'S KEROUAC?" Bree barges into my room Sunday afternoon, my phone in her hand and a smug sneer on her thin lips.

I'm pretty sure my heart stopped beating for a second, but I manage to keep my shit together. Closing my copy of *East of Eden*, I sit up on the edge of my bed and shoot her a dead-eyed stare.

"Who?" I play dumb.

"Apparently the two of you have had a lot to talk about over the past couple of months." Her thumb scrolls up and down the screen, her mouth twisting into a wicked grin. "Who is he, Halston?"

"Nobody I've ever heard of." I exhale, lying back down and unfolding my book.

Her dull blue eyes flick up. "If he's nobody, then I probably don't need to read you this email he sent about ten minutes ago."

My heart races.

"It was really sweet too," she adds, her tone mocking and saccharin.

"You're bluffing," I say. Kerouac doesn't do sweet. He never has.

She flips the screen toward me, though from here I can't read it.

"No, no. It says right here. Sent today at one twenty-one PM." Bree presses the phone against her chest. "I'll show it to you if you tell me who he is."

"It's an anonymous dating app. We've never met."

"I knew it. And you're such a liar." Her face is pinched, yet there's a satisfied gleam in her eyes. "Just last night you two were chatting about a kiss. Fess up."

"I'm not telling you a damn thing." My fingers twitch, my skin boiling just below surface level. I'm tempted to lunge at her and rip the damn thing from her bony little hands.

"What's eight months from now?" She glances up at the ceiling, counting on her hands as she whispers, "October … November … December … January …"

May.

Eight months from now is May.

The end of the school year.

Oh, god.

I need to see that email.

"May," she finally says. "What's so special about May?"

"How should I know? Guys say a lot of shit that doesn't make sense."

Lifting the phone to her face, she smirks. *"If things were different, I'd have made you mine the moment we met. Wait for me, Absinthe. Eight more months and I'll make you mine forever. I love you."*

He loves me …

176

Kerouac *loves* me.

My stomach flutters, yet at the same time all I see is red.

"Give me my phone," I say, teeth clenched. "*Now.*"

"Never." She shoves it in her back pocket. "It's no longer your property."

"Give it to me!" I'm not one to scream. I generally find it pointless and weak, a last resort that does nothing more than declare to the other person that you've lost all control, but I do it anyway. I don't recognize my voice like this, but it's me, screaming at the top of my lungs like a crazy person.

I suppose love makes you do crazy, insane, lose-all-control-of-yourself things.

He loves me.

And fuck. I love him too.

Charging at Bree, I reach around, attempting to take it back, but in the process, I push her against the wall, knocking down a gaudy abstract portrait that falls to the ground and shatters on the hardwood floor, sending the two of us to our knees.

We're surrounded by glass. Tiny invisible shards dig into my stinging palms.

"If you don't tell me who it is, I'm going to show this to my father," she says, carefully flicking broken glass off her bloody knuckles. Bree's out of breath, but she doesn't seem deterred. "If you tell me who it is, I'll delete the app. Nobody will ever know."

"I'm not negotiating with you." I will not be black-mailed by this bitch.

"Fine," she says, pushing herself to a standing position. Brushing the hair out of her face, she holds her head high. "Eight months from now is May. May is … Mother's Day, Memorial Day, and … graduation. This guy says he can't be with you until May, so … is it a *teacher*?!"

I say nothing.

"Oh, god," she says, expression fading. "It's Principal Hawthorne."

My nose wrinkles. "No, it isn't."

"He couldn't stop staring at you that night at dinner. He got all weird watching you and Thane, and then he left when you guys left. And that one time, after school, when he needed to talk to you alone … and I saw you two talking at the drinking fountain that day …" She paces the room, stepping over the shattered art. "Wow. Oh my god. Wow. This is … this is major."

"Aren't you a real fucking Nancy Drew." I roll my eyes. "Too bad you're still wrong. You'll never figure it out."

"It's absolutely Hawthorne. I see it on your face. Your nose twitches and your voice gets a little higher. You're lying," she says. "As a future education administrator and mandatory reporter, I need to report my suspicions to the appropriate authorities."

"*Bree*." The broken, guttural tone in my voice is both a plea and a threat, though in this moment she doesn't appear to care either way.

"I'll tell my father what I suspect and let him take it from there." She heads to the door, only it swings open, banging against the wall and startling us both. "If he's innocent, as you say he is, then he'll have nothing to worry about."

My uncle stands in the doorway, eyes bugging. "What's going on up here?"

His gaze lands on the shattered frame, and I suspect he senses the thickness of contempt in the air.

"We were just talking about her little love affair with Principal Hawthorne." Bree slides my phone from her back pocket, handing it over. "Sorry. *Alleged* love affair with Principal Hawthorne."

"Why do you have this?" he asks, taking my phone, my entire life, with a single impatient grab.

"It was going off earlier," she says. "I went to shut it off, but a message popped up on the screen. I think you should take a look. Just press that green app right there. You can see every email and message they've exchanged since summer."

"It's not Hawthorne," I say. I'm a terrible liar, but I'm not going down without a fight. I'll fight for him. He doesn't deserve this. He did nothing wrong. It was all me. I pushed him. I wanted him, and I recklessly crossed the line every time he told me not to.

Victor's gaze moves between the phone and my bewildered expression. How one botched homecoming night could go from bad to worse over the span of a few hours is beyond me, but there's no going back.

I'd say the damage has been done, but I have a feeling it's only just begun.

Chapter 35

FORD

"VICTOR, HI. COME ON IN." I pull the door wide and step aside, instantly regretting my decision to let a man with murderous eyes set foot in my house. But when my boss pounds on my door in the middle of a Sunday evening, there's got to be a good reason. "Everything okay?"

"I need a word." His tone is brusque and impatient, his eyes narrowing and his complexion ruddy.

Exhaling, I point toward the living room.

Victor stands dead center, not sitting, not making himself at home. With arms folded, he examines me from head to toe.

"When I first interviewed you, I was impressed with your professionalism," he says. "Several candidates made the short list, many of them with impressive job histories and Ivy League educations, reference lists a mile long, extraordinary recommendation letters. They gave all the right answers. They knew exactly what I wanted to hear.

They exceeded my expectations in each and every way. And then there was you. You were well-spoken and efficient. You didn't bullshit. You had full control of yourself, a commanding presence. You were easy to respect, Ford. It was easy for me to overlook the fact that you're new at this. It was easy for me to make an exception for you."

Victor pauses, moving toward the window and glancing outside at a passing family of bicyclists. I really wish he'd get the fuck on with this.

Turning back, he lifts his brows. "So, tell me, Ford, what the *hell* you were thinking when you decided to involve yourself with my goddamned *niece*?!"

I knew it.

I fucking *knew* it.

All those times Halston swore up and down she'd never let it slip, that she'd never tell a soul …

She lied.

When we messaged last night, she was furious with me.

This is her retaliation.

I imagine her reading my email, laughing at my ridiculous declaration of love, and then running off to Uncle Vic so he can give the knife a final twist.

If she wanted to get back at me, if she wanted to hurt me for hurting her …

… mission fucking accomplished.

I hope she's happy.

"Because this involves my family, we're going to keep this quiet," Abbott says, chin tilted down, voice low. "But I expect your resignation on my desk first thing tomorrow. And if you so much as *think* about contacting my niece again, I'll make sure you never set foot in a school ever again. In fact, I'm going to recommend you find a new career altogether. There's no way in hell I'm going to recommend you for any job in the education field after this. I was wrong about you."

The disgust in his voice is unnecessary. I'm already disgusted with myself. I knew better.

I nod, saying nothing because there's nothing more to say.

I'll resign tomorrow.

I'll leave Rosefield.

And as for Halston, she better hope we never cross paths again.

Chapter 36

HALSTON

NOBODY SMILES HERE.

I walk behind the headmistress Tuesday morning as she spouts impressive facts to Uncle Victor, reassuring him he did the right thing.

"Our success rate is second to none," she says. "Many of our girls go on to be doctors, lawyers, and CEOs. Of course, most of those girls started with us in their younger years, but I just know Halston will do wonderfully here. We'll be sure to make the most of the short time we have with her."

She doesn't look at me when she speaks, and she seems quite smitten with Vic. He's wearing his power suit, his gray hair slicked back.

He keeps a stern presence, rarely making eye contact with me. I didn't speak to anyone Sunday, refusing to leave my room. It wasn't until my stomach was growling at two in the morning and hindering my sleep that I finally snuck down for a bowl of cereal.

Aunt Tabitha tried to hug me goodbye Monday afternoon when we left for the airport.

I kept on walking.

And as for Bree, I hope I never see her again.

The headmistress is still schmoozing as we pass the cafeteria. Girls glance up at us with dead eyes, their mush breakfasts resting on beige trays, mostly uneaten. This place feels like a bad dream and a horror film all mixed into one with its limestone, Gilded Age exterior, the weeping willows lining the circle drive, the sconce-lined walls, and the sweeping ceilings that make every footstep echo. The only thing it's missing are bars on the windows and ravens quoting "nevermore."

"The rooms are this way," the woman says, pointing down a long corridor lined with oil portraits. "Each girl has one roommate and each hall has one communal bathroom. Twenty girls to one bathroom. The curtains rise at five o'clock each morning and lights are out by eight PM sharp. We have one hour of recreation before bedtime each night, and we encourage our girls to work on their homework between dinner and their final class of the day."

We pass an exit with glaring red letters. It seems out of place in a home that appears to have frozen in time one hundred years ago, and for half of a second I think about walking away.

But I have no money. No car. Nowhere to go.

And I'd be throwing away a free college education, my only shot at a decent future.

Girls in gray dresses begin to fill the hall, all of them walking in a straight line, eyes forward as they disperse to their rooms.

"Would you like to meet your roommate, Halston?" the woman turns to me, her pencil-thin mouth curling.

Victor turns to me. I nod.

Stopping outside a room labeled "The Katrina Howell Suite," the headmistress tells Uncle Vic about "Our dear, sweet Kat, who went on to become the US Ambassador to Norway before meeting and falling in love with the Duke of Pendleton ..."

When she finally stops rambling, she raps on the door three times before barging in.

A girl with shiny dark hair and deep set aquamarine eyes gazes up from a thick book. She doesn't seem the least bit startled about anyone barging into her room. Didn't even flinch.

"Lila Mayfield, I'd like you to meet your new roommate, Halston Kessler," the woman says.

The room is small, the two twin beds maybe five feet apart, but the ceiling is sweeping and the windows run from floor to ceiling. We each have a desk and a wooden wardrobe but nothing else. This is nothing more than a glorified prison cell in a gilt mansion.

"I'll leave you two to get acquainted." The headmistress places her hand on Victor's forearm. "If you'd like to come with me, we have a few forms we'll need signed. I'll send someone for her bags shortly."

She leaves the room first, and Victor's eyes meet mine.

I've never known him to be an emotional man. He holds his cards close, his heart forged of tungsten and coal. But his eyes shine, glassy.

"We'll visit in—," he says.

"Don't bother," I cut him off. I don't want them to visit. I don't want them to call or write. I don't want to see them a month from now and have to pretend like everything's kosher, like he didn't just toss me to the side like I'm someone else's problem now.

He stops, lingering for a moment, and I can't help but wonder if he's regretting his decision, though even if he were, it wouldn't matter. Victor Abbott doesn't apologize for anything, and he never admits he's wrong.

Turning my back, I wait for the shuffle of his footsteps and the gentle click of the door catch.

Lila's quiet, observing me, and I hope to God she's not another Emily Miller.

"You're going to hate it here," she says after a moment of silence.

I stand, feet planted in the center of our tiny room and arms folded across my chest. "How long have you—"

"Eight years," she answers, exhaling as she draws her knees against her chest and rests her back along the headboard. "Eight fucking years of this bullshit. You know they actually have a class here called *Charms and Graces 101*? We have to walk around with books on our heads and learn to make tea like we're some British fucking aristocrat."

I glance at her nightstand, a thick, leather-bound book catching my attention. "You read?"

Lila laughs. "I do. Here."

Grabbing the book, she tosses it to me. "Great Expectations."

"No. Open it up."

Flipping the cover open, I see where the inside has been hollowed out and a Harlequin paperback is tucked neatly inside. The woman on the cover is half-naked, her dress barely containing her ample bosom, and the long-haired, broad-muscled man holding her looks like he's seconds from devouring her.

"Oh, honey, we need to fix this." I shut the cover, tossing the book back.

Lila shakes her head. "I like my smut."

"Read *Fanny Hill* or *Lady Chatterley's Lover*. I promise you'll never touch one of those again."

"Anyway," Lila sits the book back. "What's your story? Why'd your parents ship you off?"

I move to my new bed, taking a seat on the edge. The mattress is springy and thin, and my palms trace the lumps beneath the coverlet.

"My aunt and uncle sent me here because I was becoming too much of a burden or some shit like that," I say. "And I don't have a story. I'm just the girl that nobody ever wanted."

Lila pouts, placing her hand over her heart. "You say that like it's not the saddest thing in the world."

"It's not sad. It's a fact." I shrug. "Got over it a long time ago. What about you?"

She rolls her eyes. "I was an oops baby. My parents were in their forties when they had me. Their first three kids were already grown and off to college and they were looking forward to retiring early and traveling the world when I came along. They kept me around the first ten years or so, hiring nannies and all that. Then one day they just decided I should come here."

"Just like that?"

Lila nods. "Pretty much."

"Were you sad?" I imagine how difficult it would be as a ten-year-old girl, being left here while your family carries on without you.

"Not really." She glances down, focusing on the rug between our beds. "Honestly, I barely know my parents. They were never around growing up … maybe holidays and stuff but nothing else. As far as I'm concerned, they're just a couple of spoiled rich assholes who gave me their last name and these dashing good looks."

Lila smirks, lashes fluttering. She's kidding, but she doesn't need to. It's true. She's beautiful, striking really, even covered in a drab gray dress and sitting in this dimly lit dungeon of a dorm room.

"Look at us," Lila says. "Just a couple of girls nobody wanted. God, I can't wait to get the fuck out of here."

"What are you doing after graduation?"

"Reinventing myself," she says without hesitation. "I'm going to be the girl that everyone wants. The girl no one wants to be without. I refuse to spend the rest of my life as someone else's afterthought."

I cross my legs, leaning back on my palms. "And how are you going to do that?"

She laughs. "I don't know. I'll figure it out. But I'm going to do it. I'm going to be that girl."

"I want to be that girl too," I say.

My mind returns to Kerouac for the millionth time today, unexpectedly and out of the blue like it does, only this time I'm not wondering what he's doing today or when he'll find out I was shipped off or if he's been searching for me in the halls at school.

I'm thinking about that last email, wishing I could talk to him and tell him I'll wait because he's the only person who's ever truly wanted me.

And now I have no way to reach him.

Uncle Victor took my electronics. The headmistress says we're an 'electronics-free' school, save for the computer lab, which has no Internet access. I never knew Kerouac's real phone number or real email. We only ever communicated through Karma.

"You're thinking about someone," Lila says, squinting. "Who is it? You have a boyfriend back home?"

"No boyfriend."

Her mouth pinches, like she's unsure if she believes me. "Some guy you love?"

"Something like that."

"You're not going to wait for him, right?" she asks, chuckling.

I search for the right words, something that won't make me seem lovesick or pathetic. No one could possibly understand what we had, why I loved him, or why I would wait a hundred lifetimes for him if I had to.

"Oh, god. Please. No. We're way too young to wait around for these assholes. I did that my sophomore year. Met a boy on summer break. Told him I'd wait for him so we could be together the following summer. Found out later on that he had three different girlfriends during the school year." She makes a gagging sound. "They lie. They always lie. Especially the hot ones."

"My situation is different."

"Everyone says that." Lila rolls her eyes. "I promise you it's not. Boy meets girl. Boy charms girl. Boy says he loves girl. Boy asks girl to wait for him. Boy fucks other girls."

"We never dated … we just talked."

Her head tilts, like a confused toy poodle. "So, you're hung up on some guy back home that you only ever *talked* to?"

"We had a connection." I don't know how to say this without sounding trite. Saying we had a connection makes it seem so much less than what it was when it was so much more than that. "We wanted to be together, but we couldn't."

"Oh, god. Married man?"

"No. Principal." My gaze flicks to hers. I expect to get a reaction from her, judgement or disgust or something. Instead she climbs off her bed, walks toward me, and places her hand in my face, palm-side up.

"High five, Halston. That's fucking awesome," she says. "I knew you were bad ass, but this takes it to a whole other level. Love a girl who's not afraid to go after what she wants in a world that doesn't want us to have anything."

I laugh, slowly lifting my hand. I hate high fives, but I like Lila.

Chapter 37

HALSTON

ONE YEAR LATER...

WHAT A DIFFERENCE A YEAR MAKES.

Fall leaves crunch beneath my boots as I lug my backpack over one shoulder, hauling ass across the campus of Greatwood University, the only state college that accepted my application, and only after Uncle Vic pulled a few strings.

Eight months at Welsh Academy turned out not to be so bad. There was no Bree. There was no Uncle Vic or Aunt Tabitha. There were no BMW-driving rich kids to contend with. By all accounts, it was a fresh start. A clean slate.

It didn't take long for me to get used to the rigorous schedule or the ridiculous classes we were forced to suffer through, but Lila made things palatable. She knew all of the best hiding spots, all of the little nooks and crannies of the house. She knew where all the cameras were and how not to trip the alarms in the library and pantry.

The summer before college, I went home with Lila, spending those warm months at her family's vacation cottage in Portland, Maine, just the two of us in a little house by the shore. She'd planned to attend Brown in the fall, her father's alma mater, but at the last minute, she decided to go to GU with me.

I couldn't have been happier … but I played it cool.

I didn't want to seem *that* desperate.

"Hey, stranger." Lila walks toward me from Curtis Hall, shoving the rest of her peanut butter sandwich between her pink lips. "Want to go to Friday After Class at The Oxblood Taproom? Two for one wells?"

Within a month of moving into our dorm, Lila somehow managed to find us both fake IDs. I haven't asked. She hasn't explained. It's probably safer that way.

"I have a ten-page paper due Monday." I bite my lower lip.

"Oh, my god," Lila groans. "You're almost twenty. Come get one drink with me. Live a little. You're killing me here."

If someone had told me years ago that I'd turn into a studious, college embracing nerd, I'd have never believed them, but for the first time in my life, I feel like I've finally found my groove.

I wake up when I want to wake up. I take classes that actually interest me. High school cliques and politics don't seem to be an issue here because there are literally tens of thousands of students, and last but not least, I don't need a car. The extensive bus system gets me where I need to go, and anything else is within walking distance.

I've also managed to land a part-time retail job on the

weekends, which pays for most of my clothes and extras.

All things considered, I'm doing really fucking well.

Glancing over Lila's shoulder, I spot Emily Miller in the distance, laughing and walking in a group of girls who all look alike: mousy and tiny. She finally found her people. I saw her at the food court the first week of school. She pretended like she didn't know me, which at the time, caught me off guard. But the more I thought about it, the more I realized Bree probably spent the remainder of our senior year trashing my reputation to anyone who would listen.

I can only imagine the kinds of things circulating the halls of Rosefield High.

"Lila, hey." Two guys with khaki shorts, neon polos, and backwards visors approach us, their gazes darting between us as they wear mischievous grins. "Didn't see you in Econ this morning. What gives?"

"Overslept." Lila bites her bottom lip. "I can't do eight AM classes."

"Ah, well. I took notes. Let me know if you want them," the first guy says.

"What? No way. That's so sweet of you." Lila's mouth pulls wide and she tilts her head. The note-taker blushes. She's so good at playing the charm card it's disgusting.

"Anyway, we're going to grab some drinks at Oxblood if you and your friend want to join us?" he asks.

Her face lights. "We were just talking about going to FAC. We'll totally join you."

I shoot her a look, which she proceeds to ignore, and the second the guys leave, I jab my elbow into her ribcage.

"I cannot believe you just did that," I say, my voice hushed.

"What?" The legitimate confusion on her face is concerning. "We were going anyway, what's the big deal?"

All those years spent away at a girls' only prep school have done some serious damage to this woman. We've only been here a couple of months and already she's doing everything she can to make up for lost time.

I'm pretty sure if I looked up "boy crazy" in Webster's dictionary, there'd be a cross-reference to Lila Mayfield.

Folding her arms, she squints. "When are you going to move on?"

"Excuse me?" I ask.

"This is about that guy, that principal guy," she says.

"No, it's not." I try to sound convincing, but I don't even convince myself.

Her jaw hangs. "That's exactly what this is about. That's why you've been acting so weird since we came here. All you do is study and hide up in our room, and when you're not studying, you're reading books, and when you're not studying or reading books, you've got a million Google tabs going at once."

Busted.

Trying to find Kerouac has become a compulsive obsession that occupies ninety-nine percent of my study-breaks.

"When are you going to move on, babe?" Lila asks, one hand on her hip. "It's been a year."

"It feels like yesterday," I say, my voice narrowing to a whisper.

She places her hands on my shoulders, almost shaking me as she gets in my face. "I promise you, Halston. Where ever he is? He's not sitting around waiting for you to walk back into his life. So why are you?"

I let her words replay in my mind, hoping they might actually sink in for once. It's not like I haven't had the exact same thought a million times before …

My heart just isn't ready to accept it.

Chapter 38

FORD

ONE YEAR LATER ...

"NOT THAT YOU'RE not welcome to live out the rest of your days on my living room sofa," Nic stands over me, a mug of coffee between her palms, "but it's been a year now, and I feel like you should probably start thinking about figuring your shit out."

I lost everything.

My job. My career. My house. My livelihood.

Everything.

Nicolette takes the spot beside me, pushing my feet out of the way, and I sit up, dragging my palms down my scruffy face.

"You're a shadow of your former self, Fordie," she says with a half-hearted chuckle, though there's concern in her eyes.

I never told her what transpired last year. I was too ashamed. Too proud to admit I'd fucked up and thrown away everything I worked for over a girl.

"Have you thought about talking to someone?" my sister asks.

Tossing my blanket off, I rise. I should shower. I can't remember the last time I showered. It's not that I don't shower every day, I just literally don't remember any of it. I couldn't begin to tell you what I had for dinner last night or what day of the week it is.

I'm simply existing in this weird little bubble with no concept of space or time. I don't think about tomorrow. I try not to think about yesterday. Everything blurs and blends together. It's easier that way. It's easier to avoid mirrors and calendars and anything else that might lure me out of this limbo headspace and back into reality.

"No," I answer her. "I don't need to talk to anyone."

"Then maybe try to get out of the apartment a little more?" She shrugs. "Sometimes you don't leave for days. I go to work and I come home and you're in the exact same place you were when I left you."

"You don't have to say anything else." I wave my hand to silence her. "I know I'm pathetic. I know you feel sorry for me. I know you're worried about me."

"Damn right, I'm worried about you. This isn't you. You are not my brother. You're not Ford Hawthorne," she says, voice pitched. "And it scares the hell out of me."

Her easygoing demeanor fades, and for the first time since our father passed, I see tears in my sister's eyes.

Sinking down into a chair across from her, I hold my head in my hands. "Fuck."

She's right. This isn't me.

And maybe deep down, I already know that.

Maybe that's why I avoid my reflection like the plague.

Maybe that's why I spend my days holed up in this shoebox apartment, hiding from the rest of the world.

"Go for a run or something," she says. "You used to run all the time. Go run. Go to the coffee shop every morning so you can at least have some human interaction. Just do something. You can't sit around here anymore."

"Are you kicking me out?" I half-chuckle, though I know she's fully serious.

"I don't think I have a choice, do I?" She worries her lower lip. "I love you, Ford. You're my brother. My best friend. But I want you to be happy. And at this point, I'm enabling your unhappiness. I love you too much to do that."

"So, it's settled." I sit up, my eyes locking on hers from across the tiny room. "I'll be out of your hair by the end of the week."

Her nose scrunches. "Where are you going to go?"

"Not sure yet." Shrugging, I add, "As far away as possible."

Chapter 39

HALSTON

TWO YEARS LATER ...

I'M GOING to call him, "Judd the Dud."

The guy sitting across from me at the cheapest pizza place in Campus Town checks football scores on his phone, laughing and nodding to himself before firing off a text message.

I yawn, cursing Lila's name for setting up this blind date.

Judd Johnston is the epitome of a Hollister-wearing Joe Anybody, who has lived in Illinois his entire life, has a perfectly boring family, is majoring in 'Business' and can't carry on an interesting conversation to save his life.

And the worst thing about him?

He doesn't fucking read.

Hates books.

"I've never been into reading," he told me five minutes ago. "Books are just boring to me."

"Wonder what's taking our pizza so long?" I ask, spinning my napkin ring and resting my head in my hand. I've already rearranged the parmesan cheese and red pepper flake shakers, and I've taken a field trip to the bathroom just to get away from Judd, but it's been twenty-minutes and we're still sitting here, staring at each other with dead eyes.

He adjusts his visor, which must be a thing here at Greatwood. All the guys wear backward visors and boat shoes and they all have messy, long-ish hair. To the untrained eye, these guys would be cute. They'd be worth the random fling or hookup.

But my tastes have matured since Kerouac.

And none of these boys hold a flame to what I really want.

When our waitress finally delivers the goods, I wolf down three pieces before he finishes his first, and then I tell him I have a test to study for the next day.

"But it's a Friday," he says.

"It's an online class." I try to sound remorseful. "Thanks for the pizza though. See you around!"

Before he has a chance to contest my early termination of this God-awful date, I'm already out the door, practically jogging toward the bus stop to catch the next one. When I get back to the off-campus apartment I share with Lila, she's curled up on the sofa with her newest flavor-of-the-month watching some cheesy reality show on the DVR.

Springing up, she's all smiles, resting her hands on the small of her back as she follows me to my room.

I kick off my heels, yank out my earrings, and strip

down, changing into a thin white tank top and a pair of pajama shorts.

Lila's smile fades when she checks the time on her phone. "It's only seven o'clock."

"Yep."

"So it didn't go well with Judd?" Her frown borders on a pout.

"To say the least." I plunk myself down on my bed, shoving a pillow behind my neck. "I just want to Netflix and chill right now. By myself."

"Lame." She exhales, taking a seat on the edge of my desk. "What was wrong with him? Why didn't you like him?"

Resting my forearm over my eyes, I say, "I don't know. He was boring."

She's quiet for a beat. "He's not Kerouac. That's what you're trying to say."

Sitting up, I roll to my side, facing her. "Not true."

"Bullshit." Crossing her arms, she rolls her eyes. "Look, I know Judd isn't Kerouac, but that's the whole point. You need to move on. You need to see that there are other guys out there who aren't *him*."

"Regardless, he's not my type."

"Fine. Whatever. Don't date Judd. Who the hell cares? Just stop comparing every guy you meet to Kerouac because there's only one of those, and he moved on a long time ago."

Rolling to my back, I close my eyes. I know Lila's right.

But it doesn't change the way I feel.

He's the only one I want.

The only one I'll ever want.

Chapter 40

FORD

TWO YEARS LATER …

"YOU'RE AMERICAN, RIGHT?"

I'm sitting at the end of a bar in Milan when a leggy brunette sidles up to me, a martini glass in her left hand. Her wide mouth forms a smile and she tosses her thick waves over one lanky shoulder.

Glancing toward her for a split second, I turn my attention back to the whiskey sour I'm nursing.

"Sorry. I thought you were American," she says, biting her lip.

"I am," I finally respond.

"Oh, jeez." The woman clasps a hand at her chest. "Thank God. I don't speak any Italian. I'm here for a modeling job, and I'm new at all of this."

I take a sip, staring straight ahead at the backlit

shelving unit before me and the shiny bottles of liquid amnesia.

I was never much of a drinker until the last couple of years, always opting to do so socially or with a good book and an even better cigar. But lately, I've found a strong drink takes the edge off, and as long as I don't overdo it, I manage to straddle the line between the past and future just enough to function.

"Where are you from?" she asks, elbow resting on the bar, her entire body facing me.

I'm not sure how to answer her. As of right now, I'm not really from anywhere. Ever since my sister kicked me off her couch last year, I've been drifting around from country to country, taking in the sights with nothing but a backpack on my back. Contract work pays my bills, mostly writing or translating academic write ups into English. Sometimes I'll teach some ESL classes. I take what I can get, and so far, I've been getting by just fine.

"You're seriously just going to ignore me?" she asks. "I'm just trying to make conversation, not hit on you. It's been a week since I've spoken to someone without an accent, and I heard you order your drink, that's how I knew you were American. I'm homesick. And you looked nice. Guess I was wrong."

I smirk, taking another sip. "Yeah. You were."

From the corner of my eye, I watch as she lifts her martini glass, contemplating whether or not she wants to splash her drink in my face. The emerald green liquid sloshes in her hand, threatening to spill over the rim before she takes a step back then trots off in her sky high stilettos.

Absinthe.

She was drinking absinthe.

Even thousands of miles away, I can't get away from her.

Chapter 41

HALSTON

THREE YEARS LATER …

"I'M SORRY HALSTON. The trail ran cold as soon as I got to New York," the private investigator I hired to locate Kerouac fills me in over the phone. "Looks like he left Rosefield three years ago, moved to Brooklyn, then after that … nothing."

"How can there just be nothing?" I ask. My stomach churns when I think about the student loan I took out to pay the investigator, and the fact that it was all for nothing.

"I'm guessing he went overseas," he says. "For all we know, he could be backpacking in Europe. He wouldn't have an address there. That's the only thing I can think of. There's no death certificate, so he's still alive. He's just … not anywhere we can find him."

Hunched over my computer desk, I rest my palm

against my forehead, trying to think. "So there's nothing else we can do?"

"Not unless you want to pay me to go overseas, but no offense, sweetheart, but even I wouldn't recommend that. It'd cost you a small fortune. No ex-boyfriend is worth that," he says. His voice is wise and sharp, and he reminds me of a father figure. "If you were my daughter, there's no way in hell I'd have let you hire a PI in the first place. A man who walks off like that, leaving you broken hearted? Not worth an ounce of your time or money."

"You're sweet to say that, but our situation wasn't that simple."

"Oh, hey." His tone perks. "One other thing. He's got an ex-stepbrother who lives in the Silicon Valley area. Name is Mason Foster. He's some tech billionaire. I tried calling him several times, but he never would get back to me."

I lift a brow. I had no idea he had a step-brother. In fact, he never really spoke about his family at all.

"I can give you his number if you'd like. Maybe you'll have better luck?" He clears his throat, rattling off ten digits that I scribble down as fast as I can.

"Thank you, Kent," I say. "I appreciate your help."

"Good luck, Halston."

Ending the call, I perform a quick Google search on Mason Foster—my last remaining avenue to Kerouac.

Chapter 42

FORD

THREE YEARS LATER ...

"I CAN'T GET over how different you look," my sister says. I've been back in Brooklyn forty-eight hours now and she hasn't stopped staring once. "The longer hair, the scruff. The styled, casual outfits. You remind me of a high fashion model. It's like you left the states and came back someone else completely."

"Are you saying I look like shit?"

"No. I'm saying it's taking some time to get used to," she says. "When you left here, you looked like shit. Now you look like you should be walking runways in Paris."

She folds her arms, leaning back against the bench we share outside a little park in her neighborhood. Arlo climbs across playground equipment, stopping to wave when he sees us both watching.

"Hey, buddy!" Nic yells.

I give a quick wave and a short smile. I've missed this kid something fierce, but Nic's been good about sending pictures and videos.

"You doing okay though?" she asks a second later.

"Of course. Having the time of my life."

Shielding her eyes with her hand, she cocks her head. "Really, Ford?"

I nod, concentrating on my nephew. "Yes, Nic. Really."

"I call bullshit."

"That's fine. You can call bullshit."

"You're lonely," she says. "I can see it in your eyes, the way you talk."

"How does the way one talks suggest loneliness?"

"You sound sad." Nic shrugs. "And you look sad."

"I can assure you you're wrong," I say. "I'm not sad. Quite the contrary. I'm free as a fucking bird, living life without a care in the world. That means I'm happy."

"Maybe you're not sad, but you're definitely lonely," she says.

"Why are we talking about this again?" I adjust my position, crossing my legs wide and leaning away from her.

"Because I'm a good big sister, and I care about you."

I say nothing. I can't argue with those facts.

"Do you ever think about finding someone and settling down?" she asks. "I mean, we're both in our thirties now. I'd love to find someone special and share my life with them. I can't imagine you don't want the same thing."

"My mind doesn't even go there, Nic," I lie. "Settling down couldn't be further from my mind."

"I don't mean right now. I'm talking someday," she says. "Do you want to settle down someday?"

Someday is a concept that no longer exists for me. When I think about "someday," I think about missed opportunities, a future in ruins, and everything I've had to sacrifice.

"Uncle Ford, can you pitch for us?" Arlo runs up to the bench, red-cheeked and out of breath, a ball and mitt in his hand. He points toward a group of boys all his age, setting up a makeshift baseball diamond in a grassy area.

"Sure," I say, rising. He runs ahead.

"What are you going to do, Ford?" Nicolette asks.

"Right now? I'm going to play baseball with my nephew. Tomorrow? I'm going to Amsterdam."

Chapter 43

HALSTON

FOUR YEARS LATER ...

"YES, CAN I HELP YOU?" A narrow-eyed receptionist with jet black hair pulled into a tight, low bun glances up from a reception desk.

This is Mason Foster's administrative assistant.

His gate-keeper.

The woman who, allegedly, hasn't been relaying my messages for the past month.

"I'm here to see Mason Foster," I say with gumption.

She reaches for her phone. "Is he expecting you?"

"He should be," I say. "I've been trying to reach him for weeks."

Placing the phone back in the cradle, she bites her lip. "I'm sorry. Unless you have a scheduled appointment, he can't see you. We have a strict, no-soliciting policy."

"I'm not a solicitor," I say.

"Then what's this meeting in regards to?" She bats her thick, dark lashes.

"I'm going to change his life," I say, knowing full well I sound insane, but one of the top rules of marketing is to hook the customer within the first several seconds, and I'm already running out of time.

The girl laughs. I don't blame her. I would laugh at me too.

"Trust me, all I need is five minutes of his time," I say with a wink. "Then I'll stop with the phone calls and the emails and crazy ex-girlfriend behavior."

Her smile fades the second she glances over my shoulder, and when I turn, I see a tall man, a few years older than me, with sandy blond hair and an overwhelming air of arrogance in his step.

"Mr. Foster," the receptionist says, sitting straighter.

"Ming." He approaches her desk, glancing over the ledge. "Everything all right?"

"This is the woman that hasn't stopped calling all month," she says. "Says she's going to change your life if she has five minutes of your time."

Mason takes a step back, eyeing me from head to toe before a devilish smirk claims his mouth. "I'm not sure whether to have security escort you out or to insist you join me for sushi so I can get to know you better."

I think he's hitting on me.

Extending his hand, he says, "And you are?"

"Halston Kessler," I say. "Owner of Fusion PR. We specialize in promoting tech companies."

"Beautiful name," he says, "for a beautiful woman."

"Flattery is not necessary, Mr. Foster," I say, releasing his handshake and trying to imagine Mason and Kerouac side by side at Thanksgiving dinner, wondering how they interact and if they keep in touch.

"So tell me, Halston," he asks, "would you care to join me for lunch?"

If it means getting his attention, then yes. "I'd love to."

"Perfect. I'll drive." Mason nods toward the elevator, and I follow. "We're in the market for a new PR firm."

"I know. I saw the ad in the Silicon Register." Two months ago, Lila and I graduated from Greatwood, loaded up our little cars, and road tripped it to Silicon Valley to start up our PR firm. We figured a specialized firm in a location with loaded locals was going to be a recipe for success, and with my degree in Public Relations and her degree in Information Technology, our business plan practically wrote itself.

For now, we work out of a two-bedroom basement apartment we share in a shitty side of town, but our lease is month-to-month and as soon as we land a few contracts, we're going to upgrade our digs and get an actual office.

The elevator deposits us in a basement parking garage, and Mason leads us to a parked Ferrari. Bright red. The shiniest thing I've ever seen, even in dimly lit surroundings.

"Hop in," he says with a wink.

This was almost too easy.

My heart races when I think of Kerouac and how insane it is that I'm spending time with his stepbrother or ex-stepbrother or whatever their dynamic is. I'll figure it all out soon. I don't want to rush this, don't want to make it obvious.

I'll work for Mason, get to know him, and maybe one of these days I'll see Kerouac.

Even if it's just in passing, even if it's a photograph or a conversation … I'll settle for that because it's better than nothing.

The never knowing is what kills me.
And as soon as I know, I can finally move on.

Chapter 44

FORD

FOUR YEARS Later

IF I'M LUCKY, I won't remember any of this tomorrow.

My vision blurs as I scroll through Halston's Facebook page, one finger on the trackpad of my laptop and the other hand wrapped around a long neck bottle of Guinness as I recline against the headboard of a Belfast hotel bed.

For four years I've held strong.

I haven't so much as Googled the woman who ruined my life—despite the fact that I've thought about her every single fucking day. It has taken all the power I had not to dig anything up on her since leaving Rosefield, not to go down that rabbit hole.

It was always for the best.

No good could come from that, from ruminating in what-might-have-been.

But tonight, on the eve of her twenty-third birthday, I find myself missing her more than usual, unable to stop myself from seeking the answers to the questions I've asked for the past four years: What is she up to? How is she? Is she happy? Did she find someone new?

My self-control is pathetically non-existent, and six beers later, I've typed her name into a search engine and found a few limited results.

Her social media is pretty sparse, her pages private and locked down so tight I can't even see her friends list or where she lives. Her Facebook profile picture, a photo of her with a grinning dark-haired girl draped around her shoulders, hasn't been updated in fifteen months, and the rest of her photos are pretty non-telling.

Halston smiling in front of some sculpture.

Halston standing in the middle of a group of friends at someone's wedding.

Halston volunteering at a soup kitchen.

She seems happy in all of them, and fuck, is she still just as gorgeous as before, if not more so.

Her hair is longer, her jade eyes brighter, her bombshell figure just as curvaceous. I can almost taste her berry-sweet lips on my tongue, can almost feel her soft hair in my fingers.

I take another swig of Guinness, emptying the bottle. My eyes blur, my vision darkening. In a few minutes, I'll pass out.

Erasing my internet history, I slam the lid of my laptop down and place the empty bottle on the nightstand. She may have ruined me, but I still love her, and that's what hurts the most.

Closing my eyes, I try to relax until I'm overcome with a heavy stupor that sinks me into a black oblivion.

Here's to forgetting, if only for a little while.

Chapter 45

FORD

FIVE YEARS Later

"LIGHTEN UP, FORDIE." My sister straightens my tie and dusts specks of invisible lint from my shoulders before smiling.

We're in Sag Harbor for our cousin Bristol's five-day wedding extravaganza, which isn't exactly my idea of a good time, but she made me an usher and made Arlo a junior groomsman, and she happens to be our only cousin on our father's side, so here we fucking are.

"I don't know how you can be so flippant right now." My jaw tightens, throbbing as it has been all week. "It's going to take all the strength I have not to punch him in the face the second I see him."

Nicolette laughs. "Not true. I know you, and you're not going to do that because this is your favorite cousin's wedding that your favorite aunt and uncle are spending a small fortune on, so you're not going to cause a scene."

"Aunt Cecily ceased to be my favorite aunt when she decided to become best friends with Catherine." I haven't said our former stepmother's name in I don't know how long.

Nic rolls her eyes. "Still. You're a class act, Ford. You always have been. Just go out there, catch up with our old friends and family. And in a few days, you'll be free to go back to … where are you staying now?"

"Prague." I groan. "I've told you this. And after that, I'm going to London."

"I can barely keep track of my ten-year-old. You expect me to keep track of you?" she asks. Nicolette steps back, inspecting my suit and tie. "You look nice, brother. Still hard to get used to you with the longer hair."

I run my fingertips along the sides of my head, combing my hair into place. I've grown out my classic crew cut in favor of something a little more relaxed, something I can muss into place in the morning and go. Plus, the shorter hair was a reminder of the life I left behind, and the last thing I need is to be reminded of everything I lost …

My house. My job. My reputation. My career.

Her.

I'm not sure why Bristol's wedding has me thinking of Halston, but today she's particularly prominent in my thoughts. And sometimes those thoughts are so heavy, I can feel them. Physically feel them.

They're heavy today.

"Arlo, you ready yet? We gotta go." Nic yells toward the hotel bathroom. "God, he takes forever in there and he's only ten. What's it going to be like when he's sixteen?!"

The lock on the door pops and Arlo steps out in slacks

and a cashmere sweater, his blond curls combed straight and parted on the left.

"My *baby*." Nicolette strides toward him, cupping his face in her hands. His eyes widen and he looks to me for help, but all I can do is fight a smirk. "You're so grown up. Oh, my goodness. Stop growing. Stay little forever."

Arlo tries to squirm away when my sister wraps him in her arms.

Checking my watch, I clear my throat. "We should head down. The mixer started a half hour ago."

Only Aunt Cecily could extend an hour-long wedding into a five-day event. Tonight's the mixer, tomorrow's the clam bake, Friday's the rehearsal dinner, Saturday's the wedding and reception, and Sunday is the wedding brunch, which I didn't even know was a thing.

Nic checks her reflection in the mirror, smoothing her hands down her sides before turning to check her ass.

Shameless.

"You trying to meet someone tonight?" I ask as we head toward the hallway.

"You never know who you're going to meet at these things," she says. "Five of my friends met their future spouses at other people's weddings."

We stand in front of an elevator bay, watching Arlo press the down button repeatedly.

"I didn't know you were looking," I say. My sister and I are close, but we seldom discuss her love life. I suppose I've always assumed she was content to be Arlo's mom because she never alluded otherwise.

"I'm always looking, Ford," she says as the elevator doors ding and slide open. "Isn't everyone?"

I frown for a second before shaking my head. "I'm not."

"That's right. You have impossible standards," she says,

exhaling and staring up at the mirrored ceiling as we ride to the bottom floor. "Hate to break it to you, but the girl of your dreams? She doesn't exist. I've yet to meet a feisty, opinionated blonde who reads Proust and swears like a sailor."

The elevator slows to a gentle stop and the doors part. Nic and Arlo step off, making a beeline for a table covered in hor d'oeuvres.

Ahead stands none other than Mason Foster with a beautiful woman draped on his arm. Her curved body wears a slip dress that plunges low in the back and shimmers like diamond dust, and her hair, smooth as glass and the color of melted chocolate, hits just below her collarbone. A champagne glass rests lightly between her delicate fingertips, and she nods when Mason leans close and whispers in her ear.

But when she turns toward the elevator, her expression disappears the second her wild green gaze lands on mine.

It's Halston. All grown up.

My heart thunders in my chest, but I walk past her. I don't stop. I can't.

I keep moving.

I may have loved that woman once, but that was a lifetime ago—before she destroyed me. And how she ended up with Mason is none of my fucking concern.

Removing my gaze from her womanly curves and her juicy mouth the color of ripe strawberries, I make my way to the end of the bar, order a double vodka, and lose myself in the crowded ballroom the rest of the night.

Chapter 46

HALSTON

IT WORKED.

I found him.

I finally found him.

My skin is flushed, the room is hot, and Mason won't stop touching me. He pulls me from aunt to uncle to cousin to grandmother, introducing me as "My Halston" despite the fact that we're not together.

I'm simply his wedding date, a work colleague he's been chasing for the better part of a year.

"Uncle Roger," Mason says, pulling me by the hand to a cozy corner of a giant ballroom. "Have you met my Halston?"

Roger is a tall man with slick, silver hair and a devious smirk. He takes my hand from Mason, lifting it to his mouth and depositing a kiss, like I'm some noblewoman.

"A pleasure to meet you, Halston," he says. "We hope you're enjoying yourself so far? I know my daughter, Bristol, was looking forward to meeting you. She's around here somewhere."

"This is a beautiful venue," I say. "And I look forward to meeting her as well."

Mason rests his hands on my hips. I brush them off without making a scene.

Every few seconds, I can't help but to scan the room, looking for Kerouac again. I'm not entirely convinced I wasn't daydreaming a little while ago.

He was there, stepping off the elevator in a navy suit, his hair slightly grown out. Our eyes locked for an endless second. And then he was gone.

My body's acting like I just finished a marathon, heart racing, adrenaline pumping, mouth dry, so I take another sip of champagne to quell my nerves, but I'm going to need something stronger.

"Mason!" A girl with long auburn hair, dressed in head to toe Lilly Pulitzer, squeals before running toward us and wrapping her arms around him. "How have you been? Oh my gosh. Is this her?"

I lift a brow while maintaining a graceful smile.

"Hi, I'm Bristol," she says, hesitating before giving me a hug. "I've heard so much about you."

Shooting Mason a look, I pretend to be amused. "And what exactly has he been saying?"

"Oh, Aunt Constance!" Bristol rises on her toes, waving to another guest across the room. "I'm so sorry. I'll catch up with you guys later, okay?"

With that, she's gone, and I reach for Mason, pulling him close so I can whisper in his ear.

"Why the hell does everyone think I'm your girl-friend?" I ask. "I'm your *wedding date*, Mason."

He wears a shit-eating grin, smoothing the lapels of his suit coat and straightening his shoulders.

"It's not funny." My brows narrow. The last thing I need is for Ford to hear through the grapevine that I'm a taken woman.

I'm not taken. At all.

I've been waiting for him all these years.

"It is funny," Mason says, taking my hand and placing it on his chest. "And it'll be even funnier fifty years from now when we're telling our grandkids about it."

Pulling in a sharp breath, I let it go and finish the rest of my drink. "You promised you wouldn't do this. I agreed to come with you as your friend, your *date*. Had I known you were going to pull some stunts—"

"Forgive me." He moves closer, placing his greedy hands on my waist and tucking his chin against his chest. His hooded eyes relax. "I am completely and utterly obsessed with you, and not being able to snap my fingers and get exactly what I want isn't something I'm used to. I don't mean to be aggressive, I just find it difficult to contain myself when I'm with you."

If my sympathy is what he's looking for, he's not going to get it.

I don't particularly have a soft spot for spoiled tech-y billionaires. And his Mexican beach house, his New York brownstone, his Silicon Valley estate, and his fleet of Italian sports cars might be enough to win over most women, but not me. I need more than good looks, a nice wardrobe, and a bottomless bank account.

Take all of that away, and Mason is mind-numbing, clichéd, and uninspiring at best.

He hasn't read a book since college, and my research on him has led me to conclude that he didn't get to where he is because he's gifted or inventive. He got there because he's resourceful. And lucky.

There's nothing sexy or extraordinary about a man

whose mother gifts him ten million dollars in his early twenties, which he then uses to pay some of the world's most in-demand software developers to whip up a bunch of apps and games for a flat fee, which he then goes on to sell and take all the credit for.

"I'm going to grab another drink." I step away before I say something I'm going to regret. The weekend is too young to go there with him, and I've got more important things to worry about.

Like finding Ford.

A few minutes later, I walk away with a gin and tonic, heading into a sea of unfamiliar faces. Men stare when I walk past, old and young, single and married. Over the past five years, I've completely transformed myself, graduating at the top of my class at Welsh Academy, finishing my bachelor's degree at the University of Illinois two semesters early, and starting a PR business with my best friend, Lila Mayfield.

And in the process, I traded in my wild blonde mane for something sleek and more refined. I learned how to do my makeup, dress for my body type, and walk in six-inch heels. I know how to eat lobster and oysters, how to prepare challenging French dishes with perfection, how to make the perfect pot of tea, and entertain guests with polish and poise.

I'm still me. I'm still Halston. I'm just older and wiser. More confident.

Unstoppable.

I grew into my skin. I reinvented myself. I became the girl that everyone wants instead of the one that everyone wants nothing to do with.

And for that, I'll never apologize.

"There you are." Mason takes me by the arm, catching

me off guard and nearly spilling my drink. "Thought maybe you'd dodged back to your room."

Stirring my drink with a little straw, I take a sip. "Not yet. But I will soon."

"We've only been here an hour." He pouts, because Mason Foster does that. He's a thirty-three-year-old man who pouts when he doesn't get what he wants.

"I'm exhausted and my head is pounding," I say, scanning the room for the millionth time.

He's here. I know it. I saw him.

I *feel* him …

… that electric charge in the air.

Mason exhales, lifting his hand to my cheek before smiling. "All right. You get your rest. Tomorrow's the clam bake at Aunt Cecily's. You'll meet everyone else then."

Before I get the chance to rebuff him, he presses his lips against my forehead.

Fucking jackass.

"Mason." I say his name through gritted teeth, trying not to make a scene and keeping my hands gripped tight around my tumbler so I don't accidentally wring his neck.

"It was an innocent peck," he says, sweeping my hair over my shoulder and drinking me in like I'm a work of fucking art.

And I am.

"The more you push me away, the more I want you," he says, head tilted as he studies me. "You're the only woman I've ever met who hasn't thrown herself at me." Mason exhales. "You drive me crazy, Halston. I'd give you the world if you asked me to."

"I know."

He could give me the world and it still wouldn't be enough.

It still wouldn't be Kerouac.

Chapter 47

FORD

"YOU'RE NOT EATING. Why aren't you eating?" Nicolette pushes my breakfast plate closer, as if that could possibly bring my appetite back. "You're going to be starving later. The clam bake takes all day with all those stupid games and stuff they make us play. We won't be eating until later."

"I'll live."

Arlo digs at his soggy Frosted Flakes. The hotel boasts a five-star restaurant with a celebrity-chef prepared menu, but this kid wanted cereal.

Nicolette clears her throat. Then again. Her eyes darted over my shoulder as if to point in that direction.

"Mason," she says under her breath.

"So?" I shrug, trying to ignore the palpitations reverberating against my chest wall at the thought of seeing her again.

When I first saw her last night, I was angry. All those

emotions I'd buried so long ago, the ones that had settled to the bottom in hopes they'd someday be forgotten, were stirred, rising to the surface to be experienced all over again.

A couple drinks later, my breathing had returned to normal, but I was still seeing red, still ensuring I kept my distance if only because I didn't trust myself not to say something—or do something—I'd later regret.

There were things I wanted to say to her, things I'd harbored for years. Things I'd written a hundred times in letters that were eventually torn into a hundred pieces, burned in fireplaces and left in trash cans in hotels around the world.

"Ford. Nicolette." Mason's arrogant burr fills my ears. I don't turn to face him. If he wants to speak to me, he can stand in front of me. I refuse to so much as crane my neck in his direction. He moves around the table, lowering himself to my nephew's level. "And you must be Arlo."

Arlo glances at his mom, silently asking who the hell this jackass is.

"How are things?" Mason wears an enormous smile, like he's biding his time, waiting for the perfect opportunity to rub his success in our faces. Growing up, he was always jealous of us, of our intelligence and our hardworking drive and ambition. Those things came natural to us, they were effortless. He hated us for it, but only because we made him look bad.

Guess he sure showed us.

"Did you need something?" I ask, refusing to make eye contact. I butter a slice of toast from my plate to make the simple point that a piece of warm bread is more deserving of my attention than he is.

"Just saying hi." He shrugs, not getting the hint that he's not wanted. "It's been, what, ten years or so?"

"We're not really keeping track …" Nicolette hides her smirk behind a glass of fresh squeezed orange juice.

"I'll have to introduce you to my girlfriend," he says. "You're going to love her. Smart as a fox. Beautiful too. Hoping she's the one."

My fist clenches around my fork, my jaw tightening.

Maybe I've moved on. Maybe I don't want her anymore. But I sure as fuck don't want him to have her. He deserves some vapid Brazilian supermodel, not the woman of my goddamned dreams.

"Best of luck to you, Mason." Nicolette locks eyes with me. "See you around."

Mason lingers, and I imagine he's disappointed that he couldn't stand around and brag a little more, but I don't particularly give a shit.

"Heyyyy." Nic kicks my leg under the table. "What was that about? I know we hate that bastard, but for a minute there I thought you were going to drive a butter knife through his carotid artery."

Drawing in a long breath, I shake my head. "Nothing. It's nothing."

Nic is my best friend. I've always told her everything.

But I never told her about Halston.

I was ashamed. Humiliated. A fucking disgrace to everything we've ever stood for.

All she knows is it didn't work out.

She doesn't know why.

Tossing my napkin over my plate, I excuse myself. I need a run, a cold shower, and a whole lot of self-restraint before we head to Aunt Cecily's.

Chapter 48

HALSTON

"ALMOST READY?" Mason knocks on my hotel room door. I rise from the vanity and let him in, saying nothing as he takes a seat on the edge of my bed. Facing the mirror, I slick a coat of ruby red stain across my lips. I've found that if you want someone to listen to you, to pay attention to what you say and find you irresistible, you draw attention to your mouth.

It also makes you look fearless, brazen.

People respect you more when you're not afraid to stand out.

Bright red lips say, "I have something important to say, and I'm making damn sure you're going to hear me."

When I'm finished, I dab perfume behind my ears—one with notes of peach, lilac, and geranium—and across each wrist, before giving myself a final glance in the mirror, tugging my sea spray peplum blouse into place and ensuring my linen shorts aren't too revealing for a family gathering. I've never attended a clam bake, but it's almost ninety degrees out and we're going to be by the shore, so I wanted to dress light.

"You look amazing. Car's waiting. Let's go." Mason watches me with an owning smirk on his mouth, clapping his hands and rubbing them together. I can almost see the wheels spinning in his head as he fantasizes about wearing me on his arm, showing me off to his family.

If Mason were an intelligent man, he'd realize he only wants me because he can't have me, but he's too fixated, too obsessed with wanting the one thing he can't have that he neglects to see that.

This world is full of beautiful women who would suck his dick for a ride in his McLaren, women who would give their firstborn child for a chance to spend a luxurious evening with a Silicon Valley billionaire.

I'm not one of them.

Slipping my bag over my shoulder, I follow Mason to the elevator. When the doors part, we step inside, squeezing in with a handful of other hotel guests. His hand finds mine, his fingers interlacing.

I follow the path of the light as it moves from the five to the four to the three and eventually to the ground level. Harboring a breath, I brace myself for the moment the doors open.

Kerouac is staying at this hotel. He could be anywhere.

But he isn't in the lobby.

Exhaling, I follow Mason to the porte cochere and climb into the back of a chauffeured Mercedes.

"How long until we're there?" I ask Mason once we merge onto the highway.

"About thirty minutes," he says. "Shouldn't be long."

I face away, smiling, keeping the reason to myself.

Thirty minutes is nothing, especially when I've been waiting five years for this moment.

A few years back, I hired a private investigator to try and find him when my own feeble Internet attempts got me nowhere. The man said there was a paper trail from Rosefield to New York, but then it was as if Kerouac had completely disappeared without a trace. Off the grid. Nowhere to be found. I worried something unspeakable had happened, but the investigator said he was likely overseas. He offered to keep looking, but it wasn't going to be cheap and I was running out of funds so he gave me everything he'd collected on Ford Hawthorne up to that point, including his father's obituary, which mentioned his stepbrother, Mason Foster.

Some basic Internet research on Mason placed him in Silicon Valley, which ironically was already on my radar since Lila and I were starting up a PR firm and planning to cater specifically to the tech industry. The summer after our college graduation, we moved west, set up shop, and pitched our services to any tech giant CEO who would give us five minutes of their time.

One of those CEOs happened to be Mason, who hired us on the spot.

He saw. He wanted. He took.

I now know that's Mason Foster's obnoxious modus operandi.

"You're going to meet my mother today." He reaches out, placing his hand over mine. "She's dying to meet you."

"Please tell me you didn't give her the impression that we're together? I don't want it to be awkward when I have to set the record straight."

Mason chuckles. "What she doesn't know won't hurt her."

Exhaling, I keep my gaze focused on the passing cars between miniature moments of freaking out on the inside.

The fact that I'm going to see Ford again feels surreal and monumental, like I've been waiting for this moment all my life.

Though five years might as well have been a lifetime without him.

"She just wants to see me settled and happy," he says, finally removing his hand from mine. "I just want to see her smile."

It's a sweet sentiment coming from a man who tends to drop names, hog spotlights, steal credit for other people's hard work, and generally only do things that benefit himself.

"Huh. So, you *do* think of others once in a while." I bite a smirk.

His body shifts toward mine. "What's that supposed to mean?"

"I'm teasing," I say. Not really.

"I'm *always* thinking of everyone else." His brows furrow, his lips thin and tight. If he were Kerouac, he'd have met me with a quick one-liner and a half-smirk.

"Okay." I exhale, letting it go and melting into the buttery leather seat before checking the time on my phone.

Twenty-five minutes.

Chapter 49

FORD

"FORDIE! We were wondering if you were coming or not."
My overly excitable cousin, Bristol, leaps at me, bouncing
on her toes and flinging her arms around my neck. "I'm so
glad you could make it. I didn't see you last night, were you
at the mixer?"

"I was. You were busy making rounds." I give her a
peck on the cheek. "Congratulations."

"Thank you." She places her hand on her heart, brows
raised. "I saw your sister and Arlo. He is getting *so* big!"

I nod, pretending I don't fucking hate small talk.

"Okay, come on," she says, pulling me by the hand
toward the dining room. "Everyone's in here. And you
haven't met Devin yet. You're going to love him."

I follow her down a hallway filled with family portraits
and down a couple of steps toward a sunken dining room
with twelve foot ceilings, a view of the ocean, and a table
that seats twenty-five. Only when we arrive, it isn't the orig-

inal Renoirs and Picassos that capture my attention, it's the red-lipped beauty with the wild jade gaze seated at the far end.

She smiles when she sees me, a coy, hesitant, half-turned smile.

I look away.

Bristol introduces me to her fiancé, and I pretend to pay attention to the generic conversational bullshit coming out of his mouth. Nicolette watches me from where she sits, Arlo to her right. I went for a jog this morning, only meaning to do about three miles so I could clear my head enough to function today, but once I started, I couldn't stop.

I kept going, running harder and faster, pushing myself until I had no choice but to stop and breathe. Really breathe.

The table is packed with family, some of which I hardly recognize. Others I haven't seen since my father's funeral ten years ago.

"Looks like there's an open seat down there, Ford." Bristol points to the spot across from Halston. "Have you met Mason's girlfriend? She's super sweet."

Catherine and Mason flank her sides.

Jaw flexing, I take a sharp breath and make my way to the seat across from the woman who singlehandedly altered the entire trajectory of my career.

"Ford," Catherine says, peering up at me through mascara-caked lashes. Her hand rests beneath her chin, and she still wears the diamond engagement ring my father purchased for her shortly after my mother died.

I suspect she's only wearing it for show.

"Catherine." I'm unable to hide the contempt in my tone, but I don't fucking care. She should know by now that she disgusts me.

"Hi, Ford, I'm Halston," she says, a glint in her emerald irises as she squares her shoulders. "Nice to meet you."

Jaw slanted, I squint in her direction before relaxing enough to compose myself.

Fine. I'll play along.

I'll gladly pretend we're strangers.

I hardly recognize her after all.

"Halston was just telling us she's an avid reader," Catherine says, grinning and twirling the diamond cross around her neck. "I told her I'll have to show her your father's old library. So many first editions."

"Yes," I say. "It's a shame they've been just sitting there. Untouched. All these years."

Catherine's smile fades for a moment. "Those books meant so much to George. I can't quite bring myself to part with them yet."

They were supposed to be mine. My father had always promised them to me.

Must have slipped his mind to put that in the will before he died.

"I'm sure they'll be worth a small fortune by the time you're ready to sell them." I sit back in my chair, eyes locked on Halston's.

"Do you read, Ford?" Halston asks, lashes batting slow.

My chin juts forward as I contemplate my response.

"I'll bet you're a Kerouac kind of guy," she says, propping her head on top of her hand, her full lips drawing upward.

"I had a Kerouac phase once," I say. "Many years ago. Glad to say I finally came to my senses."

Halston's smile disappears. She sits a little straighter. "*On the Road* isn't necessarily one of my favorite books, but it's still an iconic classic in American literary history. It still has a place on my bookshelf, I'll say that much. I revisit it from time to time, when I'm feeling … nostalgic."

"Sounds like a perfectly good waste of time," I snuff, glancing down the table.

"It's not a waste of time at all. I enjoy it. I like thinking about Kerouac, his words and what they meant," she says.

Our eyes hold.

"You know, some people say that Kerouac was just a regular guy, stuck between the life he was expected to live and the life he wanted to live," Halston says. "An ordinary man placed in an extraordinary situation."

From my periphery, I see Catherine and Mason exchanging looks.

"Okay, everyone, we're going to head out to the beach." Aunt Cecily stands at the head of the table. "Roger just got back with the Quahog clams. We're going to dig our hole and get going! There'll be games for the kids and drinks for the grown-ups!"

Chairs scoot, screeching against the wood floors, and everyone files out the sliding doors to the deck that leads to the sandy beach path. I stay back, letting everyone else go on ahead.

"Hey, you doing okay?" Nicolette taps my shoulder. I'd completely forgotten she was here.

Frowning, I say, "Of course I am."

"Sorry you got stuck sitting with the evil queen." She pouts.

"I survived."

"I know you did. I'm proud of you for not causing a scene." Nic pulls me by the arm toward the crashing waves. "God, they're assholes. Did you see she still wears her engagement ring?"

I manage a curt chuckle. "I saw."

"And how the hell did Mason land such a bombshell

girlfriend?" she asks. "He's so phony and awkward and a social idiot and she's so refined and elegant. It's got to be the money. That's the only thing I can think of."

"Does it matter?"

Nic laughs. "No. I suppose it doesn't. I'm just being catty."

By the time we make it to the shoreline, two of my uncles are digging a hole in the sand while the other one is prepping the rocks and seaweed. My aunt hands us each sweaty bottles of beer before chasing after two little kids who are running toward the lapping water.

"I wish Dad was here," Nic says, uncapping her beer. "Seeing everyone … just makes me miss him. He'd be all about the clam bake right now. That was always his thing."

Focused on the sea, I think about the man who made me who I am today, for better or worse.

"You need to forgive him." My sister nudges me. "It's been over ten years. What good is it doing for you to still be angry with him?"

"I'm not."

"*Yes, you are.*"

"He was our father. He was supposed to love us and take care of us." My body tenses, the breeze blowing soft across my skin. "He just abandoned us. He wrote us off. Literally. He wrote us out of his will. Not even so much as a goddamned book to remember him by."

"He was brainwashed by the evil queen. You know it. I know it. The people of the United States of America know it."

Once again, my sister's flippant disregard for a situation so tragic gets under my skin, though I suppose we each have our own ways of dealing with uncomfortable situations.

I build walls.

She makes jokes.

"Seriously though, you have to let it go." Nicolette's hand glides through the air. "Life is too damn short to spend it angry and pissed off, Ford."

Arlo runs past, giggling and chasing after a few of the other kids. The last time I felt that free, that alive, I had just started my new job, and I was spending my nights chatting with a woman who put a genuine fucking smile on my face for the first time in years.

Glancing toward the rest of the group, I find Halston. The wind blows her dark hair, the strands undulating as she brushes them from her absinthe eyes, and she looks my way.

Half of me wants to swallow my pride, ask her how she's been and if she's thought about me as much as I've thought about her.

The other half of me wants to rut around in this anger, my fists still clenched and not yet ready to let it go. It takes a big person to forgive someone for destroying their career and shattering their heart. I always prided myself on doing the right thing, taking the high road, but that was then, when I was Kerouac.

And I haven't been him in a long time.

```
┌─────────────────────────────────┐
│                                 │
│                                 │
│           Chapter 50            │
│                                 │
│                                 │
└─────────────────────────────────┘
```

HALSTON

THIS HAS GOT to be some kind of joke.

I'm wandering the halls of Cecily and Roger Hawthorne's Sag Harbor estate completely lost and disoriented. All I did was come inside to use the restroom five minutes ago, and now I'm in the west wing of the beast's castle. I'm pretty sure the candelabra is going to start singing to me if I don't get the hell out of here soon.

A wall of family portraits seems vaguely familiar ... maybe we passed that on the way to the dining room earlier?

Stopping, I linger in front of them, studying the black and white photos displayed in museum quality arrangements. A large photo on the end catches my eye after a minute. A man who looks exactly like Ford with his dark hair, square, chiseled jaw, and hooded eyes stands in front of an old car, his arms crossed and the ocean in the background.

"That was my father."

His voice startles me, and I take a step back.

"Ford." I release a breath, my palm resting over my frenzied heart. "Hi."

He moves toward me but keeps a safe distance, studying me, taking me in like it's the first time all over again.

"It's good to see you again," I say. "You look ... amazing."

And he does. The tanned skin, the longer hair, the look in his eyes like he wants to devour me ... it's working quite nicely for him.

My attention falls to his hands, which are hooked at his sides. I can't help but to wonder how they'd feel in my hair, under my clothes, tracing my mouth, sliding inside me.

He glances past my shoulder before tightening his mouth into a hard line, and then he pushes past me.

"Wait, so you're just going to walk away?" I ask.

Ford stops, releasing a hard breath before turning to me. "Yeah. I am."

I wince, refusing to accept that I've come this far only to be disregarded by the only man I've ever loved.

"I'm really glad you were able to move on so easily," I say. "Really glad life just went on for you."

Lines spread across his forehead. "Yeah, looks like we both moved on just fine. Good job landing my stepbrother. Real winner you got there."

"You're jealous." I smirk.

"More like disappointed. Thought you had better standards than that. Guess people change."

"I'm not *with* him, Ford." I step closer, taking my time and approaching him like a handler would approach a stray dog in an alley. "We work together. I do his PR. He asked me to come as his wedding date."

Ford doesn't flinch. "That's not what he's telling everyone."

"I know. And we've had that talk. Many, many times." I shake my head. "He has a hard time taking 'no' for an answer, and he's having an even harder time accepting the fact that nice houses and fast cars don't really do it for me. He likes me, Ford. But I don't like him. Unfortunately, I'm still hung up on somebody that I used to know."

"That ship's sailed, Halston." His words sting, but I refuse to take them at face value. There's something else going on here, something I've yet to pinpoint.

"Are you still working in education?" I ask.

He scoffs. "Seriously?"

"I'll take that as a no …"

His hand drags through his hair, his head tilting back as he groans.

"What are you doing now?" I ask.

Ford contemplates his answer, or maybe he contemplates whether or not he wants to give me one at all. "I've been traveling. Internationally. Doing contract work."

"Makes sense. I tried to find you a few years ago," I admit. "Trail went cold in New York. Assumed you left the country, but I never really knew for sure."

He nods, his silence indicative of the fact that he doesn't want to be here, having small talk with me.

"I think about you all the time," I tell him before he walks away and I never get the chance again.

He says nothing, just stands there staring at me.

"You're not going to say anything?" I chuckle, half nervous and half hurt.

"What do you want me to say?"

Shrugging, I blink away the threat of tears before it becomes noticeable from where he stands. "I don't know. Say *something*."

His palm rubs his jaw as he peers at the floor.

"I don't understand," I say.

His gaze flicks onto mine. "What don't you understand?"

"We had a connection," I say. "Something I've never had with anybody else, something I'll probably *never* have with anybody else. We couldn't be together then, but now? I'm almost twenty-four. I'm no longer your student. All the barriers have been removed, and you won't even give me the time of day without acting like I disgust you."

"Yeah, well, pretending like nothing happened has never been my strong suit."

"I'm not asking you to pretend like nothing happened. I'm asking you to treat me like a goddamned human being. One, might I remind you, that you once claimed to love." I step closer, invading his space, my finger pressed against his chest, which at this point is nothing more than a hollow cavity, heartless. "Oh my god. I get it. I get it now. You only wanted me when you couldn't have me. Wow."

"That's not true."

"Yes, it is. You're just like the rest of them." I step back, jaw slack. "How the hell did I not see that?"

"That couldn't be further from the truth." He moves toward me this time. "Wanting you had nothing to do with whether or not I could or couldn't have you."

"Then why don't you want me now? Now that you *can* have me?" I ask.

He pauses, his presence imposing and daunting, yet I can't leave. Not until I get my answer.

"I waited for you," I say, voice breaking. "You asked me to wait for you. You said you loved me. So, I waited. I waited *five* fucking *years*."

I try to say more, but the words get stuck. My eyes

burn, but I won't cry. I won't give him the satisfaction of knowing he hurt me because clearly that's what he wants.

"Halston."

Placing my hand up, I pull in a ragged breath, gather myself, and walk away.

Lila was right.

I was an idiot for waiting.

Chapter 51

FORD

"WHAT ARE YOU DOING OUT HERE?" I ask. The low Atlantic tide is painted in moonlight and there's a slight chill in the summer air. Everyone's long gone inside. I hadn't seen Halston in hours, not since our little confrontation in the hall. "I thought you left."

She's seated on a rocky slope beside the boathouse, her knees drawn to her chest and her arms wrapped around them. The wind ruffles her dark hair, which I'm still not used to on her. The Absinthe I remember had wild blonde waves that matched her wild spirit.

This Absinthe is more controlled, more refined. She's elegant and poised, polished. There's a quiet strength about her that was always there before, but now it's showing itself in a whole new way.

"Just wanted to be alone," she says, not looking at me.

Fair enough.

"You know, I've thought about you every single day for

the last five years," she says, tucking a strand of dark, wind-blown hair behind one ear. "There hasn't been a day when I haven't wondered where you are or if you're thinking about me or if you've moved on or if you're happy or if you're missing me as much as I'm missing you. There hasn't been one day when I haven't wished I was with you, experiencing everything by your side." Halston rests her cheek on top of her knee, glancing up at me, her green eyes shining in the dark. "I know this sounds absolutely ridiculous and I'm going to sound like a schoolgirl with a crush, but I always thought that if things would've worked out differently, you and I would be together now, spending our days reading amazing books and drinking good wine and screwing like crazy."

"You're living in fantasyland," I say, not that I haven't imagined the same things myself.

She presses her lips flat. "I know that. *Now*."

"I'm sorry it didn't work out between us," I say. "And I mean that, Halston."

"Yeah. Same." Dabbing her eyes with the backs of her hands, she chuffs. "You know what's really fucked up?"

"What's that?" It pains me to see one of the strongest women I've ever known so vulnerable, so raw. I wouldn't be surprised if I'm the only person who's ever seen this side of her.

"I'd still let you fuck me. If you wanted," she says. "You don't deserve it, but I'd let you. And only because *I* want it. It'd be for me, not you." Halston shakes her head, half chuckling, half crying. "You've turned into a coldhearted asshole, and clearly you have some hatred toward me that you can't seem to let go of. So maybe … maybe we should?" She rises, drying her cheeks and staring me straight on, shoulders pulled back. "Maybe one night together is all we need? You get closure. I get you out of my system. We're both free to move on after that."

I begin to speak, but she cuts me off.

"All I ever wanted was to be yours," she says. "I've waited and waited—just like you asked me to. And I think … one night with you would be better than never being with you at all."

"I don't understand how you think this would make you feel better?"

"You don't need to understand," she says, speaking quickly, cutting me off. "This is just something I want. For me. It has nothing to do with you."

Before I say another word, her fingers begin to work the buttons of her top until it falls down her shoulders, landing in the sand at her feet. Sliding her shorts down her long legs, she steps toward me, reaching her hand toward my face.

I tense, willing myself not to enjoy this.

I'm going to fuck her.

And just like she has her reasons, I have mine too.

She's the one thing I've always wanted, the one thing I've never had. Maybe one time is all we need so we can both finally move on.

Her fingertips trace my jaw as she presses her half-naked body against mine. Rising on her toes, she hooks her arms around my shoulders, angling her mouth just below mine, an offering of sorts.

Skimming my hands down her hips, I grip her tight ass, lifting her up until her thighs hook around me, and then I carry her inside the boathouse, locking the door behind us.

"You sure you want this?" I ask, my cock beginning to strain against my shorts.

Halston nods, breathing me in with a lungful of damp, salty air, her hair whipping across her pretty face.

Her body slides down mine until her feet hit the floor. Cupping her jaw in my hand, I angle her lips once more, holding them hostage, drawing this moment out a while longer if only to tease her, to punish her.

This woman betrayed me—*ruined* me—when all I wanted to do was love her.

Halston's hands tug at the hem of my shirt, pulling it over my shoulders and tossing it aside. Turning, she peels the tarp off my uncle's speedboat and climbs inside. I follow, unzipping my fly as the boat rocks gently on the water.

Taking a seat in the front of the boat, she shimmies out of her black panties and unclasps her lace bra, throwing them behind me.

I almost lose my breath at the sight of her creamy soft skin and delicate, feminine curves. She places a hand on her hip as we lock eyes, the perfect mix of confidence and vulnerability, and as much as a small part of me wishes I could make love to her tonight, that I could go easy on her and make up for all those years we lost …

… it's not like that.

This woman destroyed me.

She stormed into my life and left a devastating wreckage in her path.

And now she wants to act like it never happened, like we could just pick up where we left off and live happily ever after.

She's lost her goddamned mind.

"Turn around," I say.

"What?"

"Turn around," I repeat myself, my instructions clearer this time, stroking my cock in my hands.

Halston turns, bracing herself on the front of the boat, body slightly angled. From here, I have the perfect view of the most gorgeous ass I've ever laid eyes on. Tight and toned, begging to be slapped and ridden.

Lowering myself, I drag my tongue along the seam of her wet pussy, my right hand reaching around and circling her clit. Her taste is spun sugar, addictive and exhilarating, and her breathy sighs only serve to make me hard as a fucking rock.

Rising, I place my hands above the curve of her hips, spinning her to face me. With one finger, I lift her chin, positioning her mouth near mine. Slipping a finger between her thighs, I drag it along her slit before slowly plunging inside her.

Good God, I've never felt anything so tight, so wet.

Sliding it out, I bring it to her mouth. "Taste yourself, Halston. Taste what I can do to you."

Her mouth accepts my finger, and her velvet tongue grazes my flesh.

Those lips.

Those fuckable, juicy lips.

"The first time I saw that mouth, it was wrapped around a sucker," I say, taking her hand and placing it on my cock. She strokes the length, pumping it in her hand as our eyes hold. I'm going to fuck that pretty little mouth of hers the way I've fantasized about a thousand times before. "On your knees."

Halston lowers herself, her palm gripped around the base of my cock as she strokes the tip with her warm tongue.

"Oh, god." I exhale, tossing my head back as she takes the length of me in her mouth, going deeper and deeper still. Each swirl of her tongue, each pump of her hand, is pure fucking ecstasy … and I almost forget … "Get up."

She pulls my throbbing dick from between her swollen

lips and rises. Tracing her nipples with my fingers, I pinch her rosy buds before taking one in my mouth.

"Your body is fucking perfection." I release a lungful of air before inhaling her sweet arousal all over again, preparing to own her the way I've always wanted to, if only for the smallest sliver of a single night. "And tonight, it belongs to me."

There's a flicker in her eyes, a hint of a spark, as if my words breathed a fading part of her back to life. Her body surrenders to mine, melting with each touch, becoming pliant and malleable. She's breathless, her fingers stroking my face, touching my hair, her mouth waiting for mine. She's dreamed about this moment just as much as I have, only tonight I can't promise it's going to be the magical experience she always hoped it would be.

"This is just sex, Halston," I remind her.

"I know." She presses her mouth against mine, pressing her body against me.

We stumble backwards until I take a seat in one of the captain's chairs and she straddles me. Grinding against my cock, she presses her tits against me and buries her face in my neck.

"No, no, no," I stop her after a minute. "This isn't how this is going to go down tonight."

She sits up, eyes searching mine, and I guide her off of me.

"I want you on your hands and knees," I say, pointing to a bench seat in the back of the boat. She once told me she hated "doggy style," that her favorite position was missionary because it made her feel safe and it was romantic. Unfortunately nothing about this night is romantic, and if she wants to be fucked by me tonight, she's going to get fucked by me tonight.

Halston doesn't protest.

She does what I tell her to do.

Approaching her from behind, I trace my fingertips along her inner thighs before spreading them wider. I want to see everything. I want her body on a silver fucking platter.

Halston sighs, her body quivering, overcome with anticipation as I retrieve a gold foil packet from my wallet. Tearing it between my teeth, I sheathe my cock and stroke the shaft before teasing the tip along her slick seam.

I watch her hands grip the seat cushions in front of her so hard her knuckles turn white, and when she least expects it, I enter her fully, completely, so deep she's gasping for air.

"Oh, god," she whispers, as if she's finally been gifted the relief she's been so desperately seeking all of these years. "Don't stop, Ford. Please. Keep going."

I feed my length harder, faster, my hands gripping her hips, controlling them with each piston and thrust. Her pussy is tight, slick with desire, and she clenches around my cock, the friction building as my thumb circles her clit.

My palm slides up her smooth, soft belly, traveling between her breasts before cupping her jaw. Her moans quicken, her hips convulsing as if she's right there on the edge, and I guide her up until our bodies are melded.

"Come on, baby," I moan into her ear. "Cum on that cock. You've waited a long time for this."

Fucking her harder, with everything I have, her body begins to shudder and tremble, quick sighs leaving her full lips as her hips buck against me. My release is sudden, hot streams jetting as her beautiful body bounces against mine, greedily accepting my cock until I have nothing more to give.

Panting and drained in the literal sense, I pull out of

her and collapse beside her, trying to catch my breath for a moment.

For the first time in years, I taste vindication.

But when I glance her way, she's not wearing the smile of a satisfied woman, a woman content to move forward from this point on and leave the past in the past.

"What?" I ask, brows furrowed as I sit forward.

She shakes her head, not speaking as she gathers her bra and panties, slipping them on like she needs to get the fuck out of here.

"Halston," I say.

Her back is to me now.

"Are you ... *crying*?" I ask.

Without answering, she climbs over the side of the boat toward the door, messing with the lock.

"Fuck. Let me help." I pull my clothes on and get to the door, but first I spin her to face me. Fat tears drip down her cheeks. Two, maybe three. Her expression is tough, determined, but her eyes tell a different story. "You *wanted* this. You *asked* for this."

"I know," she finally speaks.

"Why are you crying? I thought you enjoyed it?" I sure as hell did.

"It's nothing," she says, forcing a smile as two more tears streak down her flushed cheeks.

"It's not *nothing*," I scoff.

"It's complicated. Now will you please unlock the fucking door?"

I get the latch and step back as she rushes outside, searching for her clothes in the dark, sea-scented evening. Waiting in the boathouse, I give her time to get dressed and space to breathe.

But when I come out, she's gone.

Chapter 52

HALSTON

"CAN I say I told you so?" Lila asks from the other end.

I lie on my hotel bed Friday morning, my body damp from the shower and my hair wrapped in a towel. I don't have the energy—or the motivation—to move. It took all the strength I had to take a damn shower this morning.

"You were right." I exhale, rolling to my side and pressing my cheek against a cool spot on the pillow.

"Men are dumb. Literally," she says. "We're smarter than them in every way. The only thing they have on us is physical strength and the ability to get an erection on demand."

I laugh, which is a nice change of pace from last night.

Crying after Kerouac fucked me wasn't part of the plan, and I'm not sure who was more shocked: him or me. I don't cry. Ever.

He knew.

He knew I hated that position, being on my knees and

being fucked like an animal, but he did it anyway. He did it on purpose. It wasn't the way he described it once upon a Karma conversation—the very fantasy I'd played in my mind hundreds of times before. It was nothing like that.

Kerouac was cold, emotionless.

Like I was any other girl and he was any other guy.

"I thought I could fuck him out of my system," I say.

Lila laughs. "That's not a thing."

"All these years, I wanted that from him. I wanted that physical closeness. That intimacy on a level we never had a chance to have," I say. "I guess I was hoping one time together would change things. Would maybe make him feel differently, reconsider things? God, I'm an idiot."

"Did you tell him that?"

"Psh. No. It was just sex to him," I say. "He made that clear."

To be fair, he made it clear five years ago, when he said he'd only fuck the shit out of me and break my heart. Guess he was telling the truth.

"Okay, then fuck him," Lila says. "Not literally but, you know, like … screw that shit. Time to move on. Close that chapter. Meet new and better people. Can't promise you won't get your heart broken again because that's kind of an unavoidable fact of life, but I can promise there are men out there who are worthier of your tears."

My mouth curves. "You're sweet to say that."

"Not trying to be sweet. Just being honest."

"What if I never have that kind of chemistry with anyone else?" I ask.

"You will."

"What if I don't? What if I have to settle for someone who prefers ESPN over Hemingway and has zero sense of humor?

"What if you find someone better?" she asks.

"Don't know if that's possible."

"Anything's possible," Lila says. "So, what's the plan today?"

"Not sure." I check the time on my phone. "The rehearsal dinner is tonight, but we're not in the wedding party, so Mason said something about doing our own thing today. Anyway, he's probably going to be knocking at my door any minute now, so I should probably dry my hair or whatever."

She chuckles. "All right, sweets. Hang in there."

Hanging up, I peel myself out of bed, change into some real clothes, and put myself together. When I'm finished, the hotel phone rings.

"Hello?" I answer.

"Meet me downstairs in ten minutes." It's Mason. "I have a surprise for you today."

Jerking my head back, I'm confused, but all I can manage is a stuttered, "Wh-what?"

"Ten minutes. Surprise. Lobby," he says, words rushed.

"I still have to dry my hair." I yank the damp towel off my head. "I need more than ten minutes."

"Just try to hurry."

"Are we trying to catch a plane or something?" I lift a brow, completely getting my hopes up. I can't deny the fact that I want to go home.

Mason chuckles. "No. I'm taking you somewhere. You'll love it."

Spending the day with Mason holds zero appeal to me, especially after last night and especially with my mind so consumed with … other things. But I came here with him. For him. I have no excuses not to go. There's no getting out of this one.

"Okay. Give me fifteen," I say.

Throwing my bag together, I step into a pair of flats

and make my way downstairs, hoping I don't run into Kerouac on the way down. I know I'm going to run into him tomorrow, at the wedding—that's a given—but today I need some distance.

It would hurt too much to see him so soon.

Floating down to the main floor, the elevator deposits me in the lobby, and I spot Mason standing outside next to a black Escalade. He smiles when he sees me, waving me closer.

"Where are you taking me?" I ask when I climb in.

"My family's estate in Mattituck." He slides in beside me, slipping a pair of shiny sunglasses over his nose.

"Why?"

"You'll see when we get there." Pulling out his phone, he checks his email. I'm dying to know what this is, what he's up to, but I'm sure I'll find out soon enough.

An hour later, the driver pulls up to an iron gate, swiping a security card Mason hands him. Pulling in, we coast around a circle drive, past rows of shade trees and a bubbling fountain with a bronzed eagle in the center.

The home is gargantuan, covered with cedar shingles and white framed windows and nestled on a few acres of land overlooking the sea.

The driver gets my door, and Mason meets me at the back of the SUV.

"Ready?" he asks.

Head cocked and still unsure, I nod before following him inside.

Taking my hand, he leads me through a sweeping foyer, down a hallway, and toward a set of double doors.

"Cover your eyes," he says. I place my hands over them, listening for the click of the door latch. With his hand on the small of my back, he guides me forward. "You can look now."

"Oh my god."

"You like?" Mason grins.

"Is this real life?" I laugh, moving toward a bookcase on my left. This entire room is walls upon walls of bookcases, floor to ceiling, filled to the hilt. Hardcovers. Leather-bounds. First editions. All of them literary classics.

"I know you like books," he says.

"Understatement, but yes."

"I wanted to thank you for coming with me," he says. "I know it's not easy working with me, and I've been a pain in the ass the last couple of days."

"Another understatement." I flash him a smirk, then return to the beautiful book babies before me, sliding a copy of *Anna Karenina* from its proper place.

"As a token of my appreciation, I wanted to bring you here," he says. "And let you pick out a couple of books. Yours to keep."

"What?" I close the classic Tolstoy tome and lift my brows. "Are you serious?"

Mason's lips tug up at one side. "Yeah. Whatever you want."

I don't know how I'm going to choose, but I know we don't have all day, so I'll try to hurry. Scanning the spines, I realize everything is alphabetized, which should at least make things a bit easier. Within minutes, I find a pristine, first-edition copy of The Great Gatsby, sliding it off the shelf and clutching it against my chest.

Making my way to the other side of the room, I maneuver around an oversized desk centered in the space, pausing when I spot a book lying on top of a ten-year-old calendar that seems to be stuck on the month of March.

Setting Gatsby aside, I inspect the other book, my breath hitching when I realize it's a first edition of Jack Kerouac's *On the Road*.

"Oh, that was my stepfather's favorite book," Mason says, his hands in his pockets as he watches me. He hasn't so much as checked out a single book since we've been in here, and I imagine he has no idea how priceless some of these relics are. "He read it all the time. Guess the author used to live on his street or something when he was a kid?"

And now it makes sense, Ford's love of Kerouac.

Flipping the cover open, my fingers trace the messy, faded ink inscription.

"To Bobby Hawthorne,
All of life is a foreign country.
Jack Kerouac."

"Can I have this one?" I ask.

Mason nods. "Have whatever you want."

"Thank you." I grab *Gatsby* and hold both books close to my heart. I'm going to give the second one to Ford. He may have hurt me, but this book belonged to his father, and he should have it.

Mason gives me a tour of the place, I suppose for a lack of something better to do or maybe one last attempt to try and impress me. When we're finished, he orders lunch from a local café and sends the driver out while we wait on the back patio, watching the waves lap onto the shore.

Making myself comfortable on a lounger, I page through my original *Great Gatsby*, dragging my palms along the creamy paper and inhaling its deliciously musty scent, my gaze landing on a line I've always loved: *"He looked at her the way all women want to be looked at by a man."*

Exhaling, I feel a bittersweet smile curl across my lips as I think about Ford. He used to look at me like I was the only person in the room, the only thing that mattered. For a brief sliver of my short life, that man wanted me. And for the last five years, all I've wanted was to recapture that … to have that one more time.

Closing the book, I resolve to accept my fate: Kerouac doesn't want me anymore.

It's time to move on.

Chapter 53

FORD

ALL EYES ARE on the bride and groom ... except mine.

I can't take mine off of *her*. My Absinthe. My intoxicating addiction.

It was only supposed to be sex, but here I am two days later, craving her. Missing her. She's in every face I see, every thought that occupies my one-track mind, her breathy sighs playing like a loop in my ear.

I so badly wanted to fuel the fire, keep the raging torch burning just as bright as it had been all those years. It was easy to resent her from afar than to accept how empty the last five years have been without her in them.

After the boathouse Thursday night, she left Aunt Cecily's and went back to the hotel. I didn't see her once yesterday, and I thought maybe she'd left Sag Harbor altogether. But then Mason walked into the church fifteen minutes before the wedding earlier today, my beautiful Halston draped on his arm in a pale pink dress that hugged her curves, her dark hair swept into a sophisticated bun at her crown.

Almost immediately she saw me.

And just as fast as it happened, she looked away.

I wasn't able to usher her to her seat; the groom's second cousin got to her first, but I intend to find her at the reception, to steal her away and find a quiet place to go so we can sort this out, make sense of what remains.

Bristol and Devin kiss, the priest introducing them as "Mr. and Mrs. Hotchkiss" as music begins to play from the organ pipes up front. The two of them dash down the white satin aisle, and I rise, heading to the front to begin dismissing rows.

When I get to Halston's, she still refuses to meet my penetrating stare, so when she passes, I brush my fingers against her hand.

Our eyes meet for a single unbroken moment before Mason takes her hand and pulls her away. She disappears into the crowd a moment later, and I lose her all over again.

But I'm getting her back tonight.

━━

"HAVE YOU SEEN MASON'S DATE?" I ask Nicolette a couple of hours later. The reception venue is packed, most people either seated at their assigned tables or mingling at the bar. All I've done since we arrived is search for the girl in the pink dress with the sad green eyes.

But she's not here.

"That's a weird question." Nic wrinkles her nose.

I don't have time to explain.

"I wanted to ask her a question," I say. It's the truth. I want to ask her a lot of questions.

"About what?"

I exhale. "I need to find her. I'll be back."

She rests her cheek against her fist, studying me. "You've been acting so freaking weird ever since we got here."

Waving her off, I grab my tumbler of Scotch, take a healthy drink, and leave the table.

Circling the room, I check all forty-two tables, the span of the open bar, the backstage area where the wedding band preps, as well as the hall by the restrooms.

She's nowhere to be found.

The air in the reception hall is thick and stale, a mix of perfumes and colognes and kitchen fumes. Heading outside so I can fucking breathe, I spot Mason walking toward the building, his chauffeured Escalade driving off.

"What's that about?" I keep my cool, pointing to the SUV as it grows smaller in the distance. "You lose your date?"

Mason's hands are in his pockets and he shrugs as if he doesn't care. "Said she didn't feel well. Wanted to go back to the hotel. Couldn't even stay past cocktail hour. Fucking women, right?"

Dragging my palm across my mouth, I suck in a deep breath and let it go. So she doesn't want to talk to me tonight. That's fine. I'll give her space. But tomorrow at brunch, all bets are off. I'll corner her—I'll throw her over my shoulder caveman style if that's what it's going to take, but I *will* talk to her.

Chapter 54

HALSTON

DEAR KEROUAC,

When I was a little girl, I didn't have much. Often times we went without basic necessities like heat and food, running water, or shoes that fit. My parents' addictions were priority one. I never really knew where I fell in the lineup after that, but it was somewhere toward the bottom.

Growing up, things like love and trust and healthy, functional relationships were foreign concepts to me. My parents never once told me they loved me. I didn't have friends because, let's face it, no kids wanted to hang out with the girl with greasy hair and smelly clothes that fit funny. We weren't close with extended family. So I mostly kept to myself. Being alone was all I knew. I was all I had, really.

That and books.

Losing myself for hours in worlds that only existed in the confines of a paper jacket was my only escape from a life I wouldn't wish upon my worst enemy. Shunning contemporary stories in favor of classics, I always felt like I was the only one, but I wasn't interested in reading books that felt like a present-day reality when I wanted nothing to do with my own.

Anyway, my point is, I never knew what true happiness and fulfillment felt like until you. We had a connection that I know in my heart I'm never going to have with anyone else. You made me laugh. You made me smile. You made me cry (much as I hate to admit). You showed me I was still capable of giving love despite the fact that I'd never learned what it meant to accept it.

Our time together may have been brief and tragically fleeting, but it left a lasting mark on my heart. I'm the woman I am today because of you, Kerouac. And for that reason alone, I'll always hold you dear, and I'll forever regret that it never worked out for us.

Thank you for everything. I wish you all good things.

Love,

Absinthe

PS – I think you should know that I never stopped loving you, not once. For whatever it's worth, I just wanted you to know that you were loved.

I FOLD the letter into thirds, slipping it inside the front cover of *On the Road*, and then I carry it to the hotel lobby Sunday morning, lugging my suitcase behind me.

"Hi. Checking out of four-twenty-seven," I say to the clerk. It's eight in the morning, and my flight leaves in three hours. Originally Mason and I were going to fly out tonight on a redeye, but I wanted to get home, lose myself in my work, and try to forget that I wasted the last five years loving a man who, turns out, spent those same five years hating me for reasons I've yet to understand.

"How was your stay, Ms. Kessler?" he asks, sliding the folio toward me. "Initial here and date the bottom, please. The top copy is yours."

I scribble my name on the line. "You have a beautiful hotel. My stay was lovely, thank you."

"Glad to hear it." He smiles.

"Would you mind doing me a favor?" I ask.

The young man nods. "Not at all."

I slide Ford's book across the counter. "Could you please make sure Ford Hawthorne receives this book before he leaves? I'm not sure which room he's in, but I know he's staying here."

He studies the cover. It may not be shiny or new or pretty or modern, and I imagine he's thinking it looks like garage sale junk, but he's polite enough to smile and tuck the book beneath the counter, scribbling a sticky note and placing it on top.

"Thank you so much," I say, slipping my folio into my purse and wheeling my bag outside. My ride should be here any minute.

It's time to go.

It's time to move on.

Chapter 55

FORD

"YES, Mr. Hawthorne, how may we help you?" The man at the front desk answers my call.

"Patch me through to Halston Kessler."

"Sure. One moment—oh." He pauses. "Right. I'm sorry. She just checked out a few minutes ago."

Taking a seat on the edge of my hotel bed, I slide my hand along my jaw and breathe out. I have no way of reaching her, no way of telling her to turn around and come back so we can figure out what the hell is going on.

"She did leave something for you though, sir," he says. "Would you like someone to deliver it to your room later today?"

"No. I'll be right down." Slamming the receiver, I shove my keys, phone, and wallet in my pocket and head downstairs.

The man at the front desk smiles when he sees me. "You must be Mr. Hawthorne?"

"Yes." I watch as he reaches beneath the counter and retrieves a book.

But it's not just any book.

It's *On the Road*.

And when I flip open the dust jacket and see the inscription, I know it's not just any *On the Road* ... it's my father's.

A folded piece of hotel monogrammed paper slides out of the book, and I catch it before it lands on the floor.

I read. And time stands still. There are no sounds around me, no hustle and chatter of guests in the lobby, no dinging of elevators or whooshing of sliding doors.

It's just her words on paper.

My heart sinks as I soak in a portrait of the most beautiful, resilient soul I've ever known. Her love for me is sweet and understated yet undeniable present until the very last word on the page.

And that may be the saddest part of all—she still loves me.

And she gave up on me.

Because I let her go.

With the book gripped beneath my arm, I scan the room in time to spy Mason heading toward the café for breakfast. Within seconds, I'm striding across the lobby, a man on a mission, and he freezes when he sees me.

"I need to talk to Halston," I say. "You have her number. Give it to me."

Mason's face morphs from shock to amusement and a Cheshire smirk begins to form. "How about, 'May I have her number, please?'"

Rolling my eyes, I'm seconds from slamming him against the wall. He's lucky he's not worth the hassle.

"I need to speak to her," I say.

"Why would I give you her number?" he asks, huffing. "You don't even know her. She was my date. She works with me. Trust me when I say you're not her type, and no offense."

If he had any fucking idea …

"Mason, where's that girlfriend of yours?" My father's cousin, Sherry, ambles our way, wearing a clueless smile and placing her hands on both our shoulders. "Good morning, Ford. Mason, I was hoping to speak to her before she left? I wanted to hire her to do a little PR for my design firm."

"I'm sorry, Sherry, she had to head back early today," Mason says.

"Well, that's all right. She gave me her card. I'll just have to give her a call in the next couple of days. Not a problem." Sherry shrugs, letting her hands fall.

"You have her card?" I ask, ensuring I heard her correctly the first time.

"I do." She glances down at her quilted Chanel bag, unsnapping the flap and digging until she finds a little white rectangle.

"Mind if I see that for a minute?" I ask.

Mason shoots daggers in my direction.

I take a photo of the card with my phone before handing it back. "Thanks, Sherry. Appreciate it."

She seems confused, but gracious, and she gives us each a wave before heading into the café.

From my periphery, I see Mason trying to say something to me, but I'm already across the lobby, intending to claim the parked Yellow Cab in the circle drive before someone else takes it.

A minute later, I'm en route to the airport. I'm not sure how long ago Halston left, but according to her business card, she's based out of San Francisco, and the next flight leaving for San Francisco International doesn't leave for at least two more hours.

"Can you speed this thing up?" I exhale from the back-seat, fishing a twenty from my wallet and passing it over. The driver snatches the bill from my hand, checks his rearview, and veers into the passing lane before gunning it.

Each mile is endless and excruciating, but the second we arrive, there's only one thing on my mind. I hand him a fifty and tell him to keep the change before bolting out of the backseat and maneuvering through groups of aimless travelers with entirely too much luggage.

Once inside, I pass lines upon lines of fliers waiting to check in, but Halston isn't one of them.

Heading toward the security line, I dodge between a traveling family of ten and sidestep a woman who feels the need to hold up the flow of pedestrian traffic with her little white dog and incessant need to gawk at every poster, sign, and departure schedule we pass.

Up ahead a small group of passengers wait their turn for the escalator, and a sign reads, "Only Ticketed Guests Beyond This Point."

"Halston!" I yell her name when I spot a woman in a t-shirt and jeans, a mess of dark hair piled on top of her head, begin to step on the moving stairs.

Several people turn, gawking. I couldn't care less if I'm making a scene. I need to get to her.

"Halston!" I yell again, only this time she hears me.

Turning, her eyes scan the airport until they land on me.

"What are you doing?" she yells back, turning and shoving past annoyed travelers as she runs the wrong way down the escalator. I wait. And she returns to me, her eyes wild, her forehead covered in lines. "How did you …? Why are you …? What is this?"

"Thank you for the book," I say.

Her arms fold as she lifts a single brow. "You chased me down like some cheesy scene from a romance novel just to thank me for a book?"

Chuckling, I reach for her, unclasping her arms because she doesn't need to be so defensive.

"I read your letter," I say.

"Okay …"

"You still love me."

"You act like you didn't already know that," she says. "Pretty sure I made that abundantly clear the last several days."

"You never stopped," I add.

"And your point is what?" She checks her watch, but it's pointless because I'm not letting her get on that plane. Not until I have my answer.

"I just need to know," I say, "if you loved me that much, if you loved me so much you waited for me for five years … why did you betray me?"

Her expression jerks, and she takes a step back. "*Betray* you? What the hell are you talking about?"

"The night of the dance," I say. "You called me from the hotel. You were drunk. We had a fight because you wanted to be with me, and I refused. You were upset with me, and you hung up. The next day, your uncle barged into my house. He knew everything. He knew everything we'd ever talked about."

Her full mouth is shaped in an 'o', her eyes squinting. "I … didn't tell him *anything*, Ford."

Hooking my hands on my hips, I tuck my chin. "This makes no sense."

"Why would you think I ..." Her words trail. "All these years, you thought it was *me*?"

Her hand trembles as it stretches across her heart.

"I told you I would never ... I gave you my word," she says. "The night of the dance, I didn't come home. The next morning, Uncle Victor flipped out, taking away my phone and my computer, telling me to pack my bags. Bree went through my phone. She saw your email, the last one you sent. Then she went through the Karma app. Long story short, she showed my uncle and told him she suspected it was you, and the next day, I was sitting on a plane, flying to New Hampshire for boarding school. I never knew what happened to you. I never knew he confronted you."

"Confronted is a bit of an understatement." I release a heated breath, my jaw tensing. "I didn't know his proof was nothing more than a teenage girl's assumption. He made it sound like he knew, like he had damning evidence."

"Sounds like Victor." She rolls her eyes. "What did he say?"

"He demanded my resignation, told me he'd personally make sure I never set foot in a school again."

Her hand raises to her mouth. "Everything you worked for, just ... gone."

My lips press together.

"No wonder you've spent the last five years hating me," she says. "I'd have hated me too."

Halston steps into my space, her hand reaching toward my cheek, brushing her fingers tenderly against my skin as her electric eyes soften on mine.

"I'm so sorry, Ford," she says. "You didn't deserve that. You were nothing but professional. I was the one who kept pushing, begging for more."

"What's done is done." I inhale the faded scent of her sweet perfume, my gaze focused on her rosebud lips.

"It's all the same, though. It's still my fault you lost your job—your *career*."

"I could have kept you at a distance, but I didn't," I say. "You may have pushed the line, but I was the one giving you slack. Neither of us are completely at fault here. Neither of us are innocent."

"I hate that you thought it was me who told him. Breaks my heart," she says. We linger here, the buzz of a busy airport filling the silence. "So what now? Where do we go from here?"

"I say we take it one day at a time." Cupping her sweet face in my hand, I angle her mouth toward mine, grazing my lips across hers before claiming them as my own. "What are you doing tomorrow?" I kiss her again, my thumb pressed beneath her jaw and my fingers threaded along the nape of her neck. "And the day after that?" My lips dance with hers, our tongues skating, her minty taste invading my senses. "And how about the day after that?"

Her kiss turns into a smile, and she slinks her arms over my shoulders, rising on her toes.

"You want to go somewhere?" she asks. "Catch up on the last five years?"

"I'd fucking love that." I slip my hand around hers as I take her carry-on and lead her to the nearest exit. We find a cab and ask the driver to drop us off at a little park by the water, just outside Sag Harbor.

"So, tell me about your travels," she says as we walk along a little path lined with nothing but blue hydrangeas. She stops to pick one, lifting it to her nose. "Where did you go? What did you do?"

"Everywhere," I say. "And everything."

Halston elbows me. "Specifics. I want to know everything I missed. Except … you know, girlfriends and stuff. I don't need to know if you fell in love with someone else."

Clearing my throat, I squeeze her hand. "There was no one."

"Yeah, right. I find that extremely hard to believe. You're fucking gorgeous. I'm sure you were dripping in international beauty queens everywhere you went."

"Was kind of hard to focus on other women when I couldn't get the last one out of my head," I say, glancing down at her. She looks up through her long, dark lashes. "I never wanted to admit it, but I was still hung up on you. Being with anyone else just didn't appeal to me."

Halston cups her hand over her eyes to block the sun, smirking. "Same here."

"Really? You went to college—I presume—"

"I did," she says.

"And you never hooked up with anyone? Dated anyone?" I ask.

She shakes her head. "No one. I kept looking for someone exactly like you, thinking if I couldn't have the original, I'd settle for an imitation. Turns out you're the only damn one, Ford."

"That's probably a good thing. I don't think the world could handle two of me." I laugh. "How was boarding school? I had no idea they sent you away. Honestly had no idea what became of you after I left Rosefield."

"It wasn't as bad as I thought it was going to be," she says. "I mean, they made us wear these awful uniforms and we had these ridiculously militant schedules and they made us take etiquette classes that were probably better suited for a housewife in the 1950s, but I secretly kind of liked it."

"No shit?"

"Yeah. There was no Internet. The house was at least a

hundred years old. It was like traveling back in time," she says. "And for the first time, I felt like I had a place that was mine. It was just a room that I shared with a roommate, but it wasn't a foster home. It wasn't my aunt and uncle's guest room. I had heat and running water and warm meals. Honestly, the hardest part about it was not being able to pick up my phone and message you. I had some major withdrawals those first few weeks."

I chuff. "Same. I was pissed at you. But every night, I'd dream about you, and I'd find myself reaching for my phone in the dark, wanting to hear your voice one more time."

"I can't even count how many dreams I had about you." She presses her cheek against my shoulder for a moment, like she can't go more than a few minutes without touching me, checking to see if I'm real, if this moment is real.

"How's your family? You still keep in touch with anyone?"

Halston smirks. "Well, Bree flunked out of Northwestern her sophomore year. Turns out when you raise your daughter like a Puritan, it doesn't exactly prepare her for the real world. She got one taste of freedom that first semester, and it brought out the wild child in her."

"Bree?!"

She laughs. "Yes, Bree. She was partying pretty hardcore, from what I heard. Also heard she slept with half of the Delta Omega Psi frat her freshman year. Had a baby too. The dad's not in the picture as far as I know. Uncle Vic cut her off financially. She's waiting tables now and taking night classes."

"Jesus. Didn't see that coming."

"But, yeah, I hear from Vic and Tab from time to time.

They always invite me over for Thanksgiving dinner each year. I think they feel bad about sending me away like that, but honestly, it was harder on them than it was on me. And it all worked out in the end. I can set a fancy table like no one's business, my posture is amazing, and I know how to make an entrance."

"I noticed." I kiss the top of her head, her hair silky soft and smelling of honey and almonds.

"My mom passed away a few years ago," she says.

My smile wanes. "I'm sorry to hear that."

"It was an overdose. And it was only a matter of time. Dad took it pretty hard though. He's been getting treatment," she says. "He wants to reconnect, but I'm not really there yet. Maybe with time? But he did some … pretty terrible things."

"I read your case file," I confess. "Back at Rosefield. I was curious about you."

She glances up at me. "I kind of figured you did."

"Why'd you figure that?"

"Because one day you were looking at me like you wanted to devour me, and the next day you were acting like I was some fragile china dove, afraid to touch me," she says. "People catch wind of all the shit I've been through and they start treating me like I'm made of tissue paper."

"You're the strongest woman I've ever known."

"I don't know about that."

"It's true," I say. "And it takes a strong woman to put up with me."

"Okay, *that* I believe." She nudges my arm. "You're kind of a pain in the ass, but you're worth it."

Halston pulls me toward a park bench up ahead, and we watch a fleet of sailboats racing across the open waters.

"So where are you going after this?" she asks.

"Prague," I say. "I leave Friday."

"Can I come?"

Glancing down at her, I cup her face in my hand and press my mouth against hers. "Like you have a choice."

She smiles, her mouth still pressed against mine.

"I love you, Halston," I whisper. "I've loved you since the very beginning. And I'll love you until the very end."

Chapter 56

HALSTON

I TRACE my fingers against his biceps, my thighs wrapped around his hips as his cock thrusts, quelling the throbbing ache between my legs.

We may be in Prague, physically, but I'm also in heaven.

Studying his face, he brings his mouth onto mine every few seconds, whispering the occasional "I love you" here and there, and fucking me harder when he hears my soft moan in his ear and his name on my lips.

"Missionary's not so bad, is it?" I tease, lifting my fingers to his chiseled, beautiful face. Someone should make a statue out of him, immortalize this gorgeous man so the rest of the world can enjoy a piece of him.

His full lips turn at the corners, and he fucks me harder.

"You can try all you want to make missionary sex erotic, but it's still romantic," I tease, bucking my hips against his and relishing in the weight of his body pinning me down, anchoring me to the bed we haven't left since we got here on Friday.

I can't get enough of him, finding excuses to touch him and kiss him and make love to him every chance I get. For a while, I worried he was getting annoyed by it, sure that sooner or later he's going to want space, and then he woke me up in the middle of the night because he missed me. He missed *this*.

But to be fair, we've got five years to make up for.

We're only getting started.

Ford fills me with his cock, pushing himself deeper inside me, his hips bucking faster as we inch closer to the brink. My body relaxes, surrendering to him as I ride the wave and he fills me with his hot seed.

When we're finished, he collapses on the bed and pulls me into his arms, running his fingers through my hair as we wait for our breaths to steady.

"So what's with you ditching the blonde hair?" he asks a moment later.

"That's random."

"Don't get me wrong. You're sexy as hell as a brunette, and this whole classy charm school thing you have going on is top notch. But I miss my wild girl. The one with the wavy blonde hair, the one who was a little less restrained, a little more undone."

"I'm still that girl," I say, rolling to my side and resting my chin on his shoulder as I look up at him. Visually tracing his perfect profile, I rest my hand over his beating heart. I smirk. "That said, I have nothing against bringing the blonde back for old times' sake. Maybe we can even do a little roleplaying? You can be the big, bad principal, and I can be the naughty school girl, and you can call me into your office and punish me."

Ford almost chokes on his spit. "Oh, god."

"What?" I play dumb. "You know it'd be really fucking hot."

He's speechless.

"Too soon?" I ask. "Too close to home? What?"

Ford sits up against a propped pillow, pulling me over top of him and resting his hands at the small of my back.

"It was never about the student-teacher dynamic," he says. "It was only ever about you. All I ever wanted was the smart-mouthed girl who quoted *Great Gatsby* in a world where everyone else quoted Nickelback."

I laugh. "Can I at least call you Principal Hawthorne next time?"

"*No.*"

"What if it accidentally slips out?" I fight a giggle. "Are you going to punish me? Put me in detention? Oh! You could spank me with a ruler. That'd be kind of hot."

Ford tries not to laugh. "All right, smart ass. Meet me in the shower in two minutes. I'm showing you the sights today. Thought we'd see the Kafka Museum first."

"A man after my own heart." I kiss him, my hand sliding up his muscled neck and stopping at his chiseled jaw. I'd let him take me all over again if he asked.

Ford climbs out of our bed, and I keep my gaze shamelessly trained on his exquisite derrière which officially belongs to me, a fact I'm content to bask in for the rest of my existence.

Chapter 57

FORD

"SO THIS IS HIM?" Halston's roommate, Lila, leans against the kitchen island in the San Francisco apartment they share, her pale blue eyes studying me from head to toe.

"Yep. This is Ford," Halston says, squeezing my hand. "Or as you knew of him ... Kerouac."

Lila ambles toward us. "I mean, I guess he does all right in the looks department."

Halston chuckles, resting her cheek against my arm.

"Just don't fuck this up." Her roommate points at me. "Halston might do second chances, but I don't."

"Lila." Halston chuckles. "I don't think you intimidate him in the least bit, but good try."

Lila's hardened expression morphs into a giggle. "You knew I was messing with you, right?"

I nod. "The whole time."

"Damn it." Lila lifts her fist in the air. "This is why I

could never be an actress. Anyway, come on in. It's good to finally meet you. Halston's always spoken fondly of you."

Moving toward a wine fridge, Lila chooses a bottle of Riesling and retrieves three pieces of stemware from a cabinet. "Figured you guys might want a drink after a day of intercontinental travel. How was Prague?"

"Beautiful," Halston says. "Bridges everywhere, cobblestone streets ... the architecture, the food ... it was all incredible." She turns my way. "Best. Trip. Ever."

I'd have to agree.

"How'd it go with Mason?" Halston asks.

She mentioned before we left the States that she was going to sever her professional relationship with him after Sag Harbor, and apparently Lila offered to do the honors because she never could stand him.

"He was a pompous douche, as always," Lila says. "He said our services were pointless and he was planning on cancelling our contract next month anyway."

"Liar," Halston chuckles.

"Oh, I know." Lila takes a sip of wine. "He's totally butt hurt."

I chuckle.

"And he kept asking about you," Lila adds. "So fucking pathetic."

"What'd you tell him?" Halston asks.

"The truth. That you ran off to Prague with his stepbrother." Lila shrugs, taking another drink. "Oh, god. I wish you could've seen his face ..."

Me too.

I smirk, shaking my head. I like this Lila. She reminds me a lot of Halston, and it's clear to see how they became fast friends.

"But get this," Lila says, topping off her wine glass. "So I heard through the grapevine that Mason invested almost all of his money in some company that just went public last year. It was supposed to be the next hot thing. Anyway, I don't know the details, but that company's stock plummeted. He lost a shit ton of money. I mean, he's still rich as hell, but just not as rich."

"Serves him right," I say.

"Mason built his empire with Ford's inheritance," Halston says, mouth twisted at the side.

"I knew I didn't like that guy." Lila exhales. "Some people you meet, and you know they're hardworking and innovative and they've worked their ass off to get to where they are. Then there are pricks like Mason who get a free ride and take all the credit."

"Anyway." I take my wine glass off the counter. "Enough about him."

Halston lifts her glass. "Should we toast to something?"

"Yes!" Lila raises hers. "Let's toast to the fact that the wait is finally over. You found each other. And now you're going to get married, have a ton of beautiful babies, and live happily ever after. The end."

I clink my glass against theirs. "I'll drink to that."

Chapter 58

HALSTON

6 MONTHS LATER...

"HI, welcome to *Absinthe Rare and Used*!" The greeter we've hired for the grand opening of Ford's new bookshop welcomes a couple of hipster types who wandered in from the street. "Help yourself to a complimentary absinthe cocktail at the bar, and feel free to take a look around."

The sensation of warm hands on my sides and soft lips against my cheek bring a smile to my face.

"Hey, babe." I turn to face Ford, cupping his cheek in my hand. Tonight's his big night, the culmination of a brainchild we dreamed up one lust-and-booze-fueled night in Belfast several months ago. "How are you doing? You doing okay?"

He chuckles through his nose. "I'm on fucking cloud nine."

"Perfect." I run my fingers through his soft, dark hair, loving that he kept it on the longer side. It suits him better, I think. He's so buttoned up and in control in every other aspect of his life, so the casual hair is a sexy contrast. "Your sister took Arlo back to the apartment since it was getting so late."

"I saw them on their way out," he says. "Did you try one of those cocktails? With the sugar cube and the flame?"

Lifting my martini glass, I nod. "Delicious. Want to try?"

"Ford Hawthorne?" A silver-haired man in jeans and a blazer interrupts us.

"Yes," he says.

"Jake Fairweather." He extends his hand. "I work for the San Francisco Register. Not sure if you're aware, but we're the biggest newspaper in the area. Anyway, we have a section devoted to local businesses, and we'd love to feature you."

"That would be amazing," Ford says, offering his hand. "We'd love that."

"Very impressed with this place," he says, peering around the room and soaking in the scene. "I'll have my assistant give you a call next week."

When we first started planning, we wanted it to feel more like a cozy study or library than a bookstore. From the hand-scraped, reclaimed floors to the vintage-inspired custom bookcases and leather seating arrangements to the cedar and mahogany scent we pipe through the air system and the golden age jazz music piping through an old phonograph, everything is intentional and planned out with excruciating attention to detail. Our goal was to make Absinthe Rare and Used feel otherworldly, like taking a step back in time, to an era before Stephen King and

Danielle Steele, before Jack Reacher and Game of Thrones.

"Oh, one of my clients just got here. I should go say hello." I lift on my toes, kissing Ford's cheek before scampering away.

Ford is a gracious host, and throughout the night I watch him from across the room. For a man who hates small talk, he certainly knows how to make it seem tranquil and effortless. Moving around the room, he ensures there's a drink in every hand as he welcomes his visitors personally, and I smirk when I overhear him recommending *Rebecca* to a couple of elderly ladies who are "looking for a good edge-of-your-seat thriller."

When the last of the visitors leave, we send the hired hostess home and turn out the vintage green lighted sign out front.

The store is dark, save for a few Tiffany lamps.

"We did it," I say, strutting toward him and placing my empty martini glass on a nearby table. Tomorrow we'll get this place back in order. Tonight I don't have the energy.

"Yes, we did." He reaches for me, bringing me into his arms, his nose grazing mine before he claims my lips with an impatient kiss. "I've been wanting to do that all night."

"I've been wanting you to do that to me all night," I say. "I'm not used to having to keep my hands off you for such a long period of time."

"How do you think it went?" he asks.

"Compared to several of my other grand openings?" I think back to the last handful of events Lila and I have organized. "Exactly as planned. If not better."

My feet ache from dashing around in heels all evening and my eyes feel like paperweights. All I want to do is go home with my boyfriend, curl into bed, and close my eyes for a hundred-year nap, but when he gives me that look … the one with the wicked glint and hungry smile, I find myself curiously awake all of a sudden.

Ford runs his greedy hands down my sides, curving around to my ass before scooping me up and depositing me on the glass counter near the register. Spreading my knees apart, he slides a hand up my skirt, and I bury my smile in his neck, waiting for his reaction.

A moment later, he moans. "Where are your panties, Halston?"

"I ditched them a little bit ago."

His other hand cradles my chin, pulling my mouth to his once more. "You dirty, dirty girl."

"One step ahead of you, Hawthorne," I say as his fingers separate my folds and plunge inside me. "I know this isn't technically a library, and there's no librarian to catch us, but I think we could still make use of that F-K section over there, don't you think?"

Ford's mouth curls against mine before taking my bottom lip between his teeth. "I like the way you think, Absinthe."

Helping me down, he leads me to a dark corner of the shop, away from the store front, somewhere between Fitzgerald and Kafka, and he places my hands on a shelf, spreading my legs apart before gathering the hem of my skirt in his hands.

Tugging the fabric higher, his hand squeezes my ass before sliding lower, teasing my clit.

"God, you're so fucking wet," he says, exhaling and pressing the outline of his engorged cock against the back of my thigh as his fingers explore my depths.

A moment later, a metallic zip is followed by the sensation of smooth, warm flesh pressing against my seam. My legs tremble, weak with anticipation, and the second he slides his length inside me, as deep as it can go, my body is his all over again.

"I love you, baby," I breathe, placing one hand over his. He kisses the back of my neck before nipping the sensitive spot between his teeth.

"I love you more."

Ford's hands control my hips, bringing my body against his with each thrust as we christen Absinthe Rare and Used.

This store is ours.

This life is ours.

This love is ours.

Epilogue

HALSTON

FIVE YEARS LATER ...

I PEEK through the doorway to the room our three-year-old twins share, watching as Truman and Harper are cuddled up to their father under the dim glow of a bedside lamp. Ford reads to them from their favorite book, a collection of bedtime fairytales, and they fight their hardest to stay awake until the very last page, but just like every other night, it's a losing battle.

Placing my hand on my growing belly, I think about what it's going to be like transitioning from a family of four to a family of five in a few months. Our life is beautifully chaotic already, so I suppose adding one more to the mix won't make that huge of a difference.

Besides, we make really freaking adorable babies.

Truman has my pale hair and creamy complexion, but

his father's striking, dark eyes and long lashes. Sweet Harper has Ford's cocoa-colored locks and a face that matches mine down to the tiniest dimple at the tip of her nose.

He's so amazing with them, better than I ever could have imagined he would be. Growing up, I never really had an example of what a proper father was like. There were the ones in books and the ones on TV, and then there were the ones that everyone else had; the ones I'd catch glimpses of from time to time, like little snippets that never truly showed the whole picture.

Watching Ford with them is one of my favorite things in the world. From the moment those two were born, he hit the ground running, waking in the middle of the night to change diapers and fix bottles, documenting their every milestone, archiving and preserving every photograph, every video.

I may be biased, but I'm pretty sure any other dad would pale in comparison to Ford Hawthorne.

Almost six years ago, this beautiful man came back into my life.

Almost five years ago, he whisked me away to Key West, arranging for a private tour of Ernest Hemingway's house, where he proceeded to pop the question outside next to the famed fresh water swimming pool.

I'll never forget what he said as he took a knee and held my hand in his: "I spent so many years thinking we were the broken ones, but it was never us. It was always everyone else. We were the good ones. We have good hearts and good souls and we deserve to be happy. We deserve each other."

He presented me with a beautiful brilliant cut diamond on a classic gold band with the words: "Absinthe + Kerouac Always" engraved on the inside.

Six months later, we returned to that same site, exchanging our vows and hosting our reception under a string of party lights and a moonlit sky, laughing and dancing as our guests gathered around a sparkling, well-lit pool and a home rich with significance.

Ford finishes the book despite the fact that the twins are well past asleep now. I chuckle at the notion that he was too into *Hansel and Gretel*, too busy doing the voices and bringing the story to life to even notice the drool dripping down Truman's chin or the faint snore escaping Harper's heart-shaped lips.

Sneaking away, I return to our room, climbing beneath the covers and flicking on a bedside lamp to catch up on a little reading before calling it a day. If I'm lucky, this new little one will let me get some sleep tonight. Lately she's been kicking up a storm around two AM like clockwork. Ford calls it her "witching hour," and last night he proceeded to crawl out of bed in the pitch darkness, locate his noise canceling earphones and an old iPod, and when he returned, he insisted I wear the headset on my belly because he read an article about how classical music in the womb creates genius babies, but if the baby's anything like him, it'll just make her pass out.

"Either way, it's win-win," he said that night. "She'll either be a baby genius or you'll be able to get some sleep."

We're naming her Scout. Ford's idea. I think it's cute, and I can't wait to meet her someday soon.

Ford shuffles into bed, mussing his dark hair with his fingers as he yawns and slides in beside me. Even with tired dad eyes and constantly covered in the scent of play dough and dried mac and cheese, I still find him wildly sexy, addictive in each and every way.

"Hey, baby," I say when he pulls me close to him. I nuzzle against the crook of his neck. He smells like the kids with a touch of his cologne, and my heart feels so full I think it might explode.

"Get some rest," he whispers. "She's going to be waking you up in about four hours."

I smile, turning to a bookmarked page in Virginia Woolf's *Selected Letters*.

"Read to me, Halston," Ford requests, his eyelids heavy and closing as he draws in his last deep breath of the evening.

Clearing my throat, I turn the page and begin to read Virginia's words to my husband. *"In case you ever foolishly forget, I am never not thinking of you."*

1. I'm deaf in my left ear, and my parents had no idea until I was three.
2. If I couldn't be a writer, I'd probably pursue a career in interior design or makeup art. I live to create!
3. I'm a Leo, though I feel more like a Cancer most of the time. (Proud homebody!)
4. My favorite band is The Weepies, followed closely by Iron and Wine.
5. Thunderstorms are my favorite kind of weather.
6. I've watched SNL religiously for the last 20 years.
7. I'm a total introvert. I could go weeks without human interaction and not even notice.
8. I've been obsessed with names since I was 13. Imagine my dismay when my husband refused to give me free reign when it came to naming our three children.
9. I'm related to T-boz from TLC by marriage. I

met her once at a family reunion. She's the sweetest!

10. A psychic medium claimed my deceased grandfather told her I was going to be having twins ... two weeks before I even knew I was pregnant ... with twins.

11. I literally cannot go to sleep at night until I've perused Ask Reddit. My favorites threads are the creepy/scary/freaky questions and the glitch-in-the-matrix posts.

12. I love discussing a good conspiracy theory.

13. My favorite movies are: My Best Friend's Wedding, Interstellar, This Is 40, Lawless, The Others, and Magnolia.

14. I'm a first-born, so I'm bossy, responsible, and ambitious.

15. Organizing relaxes me. The Container Store is life.

16. I could eat Mexican food 24/7/365.

17. My celebrity crushes are Tom Hardy and Joseph Gordon Levitt.

18. I'm a pineapple-on-pizza kind of girl.

19. I've known my best friend since first grade. We are complete opposites when it comes to most things, but I wouldn't trade her for the world.

20. I'm terrible at small talk, sewing, and cooking most kinds of meat.

21. I'll never say no to a round of mini golf. And I almost always win. ;-p

22. I love, love, love classic board games! Monopoly, Sorry, Life, Clue, etc. And old school NES!

23. My favorite adult beverages are margaritas and sangrias.

24. I changed my major several times in college:

Fashion Design and Apparel Merchandising, Psychology, Human Development and Family Studies, and finally Liberal Studies so I could graduate! My electives were mostly writing classes.

25. If I could have any super power, it would be time travel. I'd give anything to be able to experience life from other perspectives and to live through certain major historic moments.

Acknowledgements for Absinthe

This book would not have been possible if it weren't for the help of these amazing individuals. In no particular order ...

Louisa, not only is this cover H-O-T-T hot, it captured the feel of the book with the utmost perfection. Working with you is a joy, as always. Thank you!

Wong, thank you for an amazing photo!! And thank you for being so quick with everything.

Ashley, thank you for beta'ing as always. I couldn't do this without you, and I love your brutal honesty to the moon and back.

K, C, and M—hoes for life!

Wendy, thank you for being so flexible! You're a dream to work with.

Neda, Rachel, and Liz, thank you for ALL the behind-the-scenes stuff you do. Your service is invaluable and you are a joy to work with!

Last, but not least, thank you to all the readers and book bloggers, whether you're a longtime loyalist or reading me for the first time. It's because of you that I get to live my dream, and I'm forever grateful for that.

About the Author

Wall Street Journal and #1 Amazon bestselling author Winter Renshaw is a bona fide daydream believer. She lives somewhere in the middle of the USA and can rarely be seen without her trusty Mead notebook and ultra-portable laptop. When she's not writing, she's living the American Dream with her husband, three kids, the laziest puggle this side of the Mississippi, and her ankle biting pug pup.

Like Winter on Facebook.

Join the private mailing list.

Join Winter's Facebook reader group/discussion group/street team, CAMP WINTER.

Made in the USA
Middletown, DE
30 July 2020

14037318R10184